The
SEASIDE
MURDERS

BOOKS BY HELENA DIXON

The
SEASIDE
MURDERS

HELENA DIXON

Bookouture

Published by Bookouture in 2025

An imprint of Storyfire Ltd.
Carmelite House
50 Victoria Embankment
London EC4Y 0DZ

www.bookouture.com

The authorised representative in the EEA is Hachette Ireland
8 Castlecourt Centre
Dublin 15 D15 XTP3
Ireland
(email: info@hbgi.ie)

ISBN: 978-1-83618-137-8
eBook ISBN: 978-1-83618-135-4

For all those who gave their todays for our tomorrows.

If you wake at midnight, and hear a horse's feet,
Don't go drawing back the blind, or looking in the street,
Them that ask no questions isn't told a lie.
Watch the wall, my darling, while the Gentlemen go by!

Five and twenty ponies,
Trotting through the dark –
Brandy for the Parson, 'Baccy for the Clerk.
Laces for a lady; letters for a spy,
And watch the wall, my darling, while the Gentlemen go by!

A Smuggler's Song – Rudyard Kipling

CHAPTER ONE

OCTOBER 1941

Jane Treen seated herself on the wooden chair in front of Brigadier Remmington-Blythe's desk in the heart of Whitehall and waited. She smoothed the tweed material of her fitted skirt over her knees and resisted the urge to pat her dark-brown hair to check it was neat and tidy.

The building was quiet as most of the office workers had already left, having finished for the day. Her employer slid a folded copy of the evening newspaper towards her, with one small article circled in red ink.

'What do you make of that?' he asked.

Jane raised one immaculately pencilled eyebrow as she collected the flimsy paper and read the article aloud.

'The body of a man in his late twenties was discovered by two boys today at Farthingale Beach near the village of Ashbourne in Kent. The man had no clothing or possessions. The only identifying mark is an unusual tattoo on the victim's left arm, comprising a rose surrounded by seven blue dots. The police are investigating and invite anyone who may know the man's identity to come forward.'

'I believe you are familiar with that particular part of Kent?' The brigadier, an older man in his late sixties, looked at her.

Jane swallowed the lump which had crept unexpectedly into her throat at his question. She knew full well that he already knew the answer. She paused for a moment to collect herself before replying. 'Yes, sir, I lived very near there for many years. My father's house is situated in Ashbourne. I know it well.'

'And do you still have connections there?' The brigadier had been pacing behind his desk, hands behind his back, while Jane studied the short paragraph. Something he had a habit of doing when thinking deeply on a matter.

'I do, sir, yes. My father's house has been shut up since last year. He left it to me when...' Jane couldn't quite bring herself to mention her beloved father's unexpected death which had rocked her world. She gave herself a mental shake, there was no room for sentimentality in her line of work.

'I see. Then I want you and Arthur to go there, stay for a short time and look into this matter.' The brigadier halted in his pacing to look at her. 'I know this is asking a lot of you, Jane,' he said in a softer tone.

'This is in connection with the death of this mysterious man?' she asked. Composed once more she waited for her employer to fill in the blanks for her. There had to be a reason beyond this sparse paragraph in a local Kentish paper which had led to the brigadier urgently summoning her from her office to make this request.

The mention of Arthur Cilento's name also indicated that this was a special project. One which fell outside the usual boundaries of her role within the war office managing various agents and espionage projects.

A few months earlier she and Arthur, along with his manservant Benson, had solved several tricky murders. These had centred around an attempt by enemy agents within

England to sabotage various military targets and undermine the war effort.

In the aftermath of their success, the brigadier had recruited the three of them into a secret agency within the department. Since then, they had undertaken a couple more such projects. Now it seemed that the death of this particular individual was something which merited the three of them working together again.

'Yes, amongst other things. There have been a number of troubling reports around that area of the country about looting, theft and black marketeering.' The brigadier stroked his silvery moustache with a thoughtful air. Jane waited impatiently. There had to be more to this than the brigadier had told her so far.

Arthur Cilento was unfit medically to enlist. He had suffered from severe asthma since childhood, something which his manservant Benson helped him to manage. He was, however, gifted academically and used his keen intellect to work on complicated mathematical puzzles and codes for the ministry. Clearly, her employer felt there was something here that required Arthur's particular skillset.

'Mr Wood, the government inspector responsible for that area, has encountered a wall of silence everywhere he's gone. Normally, someone somewhere would have let something slip. Now there is this.' He poked the offending newspaper article with his forefinger. 'Is your father's house habitable?' he asked.

Jane's pulse speeded up. 'Yes, sir.'

'And you said you have a key? Permission to use it?' he continued.

Jane nodded reluctantly. 'Yes, sir, as I said it was willed to me. I own it. My parents were separated for many years, so my father wanted me to have the house.' Jane's mouth dried and she ran her tongue over her lips to try to moisten them. She wanted to tell the brigadier that she hadn't been able to face returning there since the day she had closed it up after her father's funeral. The explanation thankfully remained stuck in her throat, and she hoped her expression had remained impassive.

'Very good. I shall let Arthur know that his and Benson's services are required, and I'd like the three of you to go there as soon as possible. I think you may be more accepted locally than a complete outsider since you already know the people.'

Jane looked at the brigadier. 'Do *you* know who this man in the newspaper is, sir?' she asked.

'Not who he is, but I wager I know where he is from, and I expect that will be confirmed very shortly. If I'm right, then questions will be asked at the highest level. I shall brief you again before you leave.' He looked keenly at her.

'Of course, sir.' Jane was relieved to be dismissed. She wanted to seclude herself back in the safety of her own office to have a cigarette and hopefully even try to obtain a cup of coffee from somewhere. She needed a moment to collect herself and return to her usual efficient, unemotional self.

Once back inside the safety of her neat and tidy office, she took a seat behind her desk. Her mind raced over everything she would need to prepare before heading for Kent. Sorting out her work, packing up her things. Her hand shook slightly as she took out her cigarettes.

Back to Kent, to the slightly run-down Georgian house not far from the sea where she had spent most of her childhood and teenage years. The one stable, safe space she had known, thanks to her father.

She took a pull on her cigarette, allowing the flow of nicotine to calm the anxieties flooding through her. It was all quite ridiculous really. She wasn't a person who was normally anxious about anything. Living with her mother's chaotic whirl had trained that out of her.

Her mother and father had been such completely different people it always amazed her that they had ever met, married and produced a child. It was no surprise that the marriage had been unsuccessful, leading to a separation and her mother vanishing from her life for long periods.

It also didn't help that her father had been an older academic, lover of ancient texts and classical music. Her mother was a vivacious American actress some fifteen years his junior and now a star of stage, screen and radio in England.

Even worse, once Jane had passed the adorable baby stage, she had become an impediment to her mother's career. Increasingly, Jane was left at home with her father while her mother, when reminded of her existence, would make her out to be much younger than her real age. Then once Jane was in her teens, she would introduce her as her younger sister rather than her daughter. Even now not everyone knew the truth.

At the outbreak of war, her mother had decided to remain in England rather than return to America. She currently worked and resided in London and was hugely popular as a singer and actress. Every now and again she would recall she had a daughter and would attempt to coerce Jane into taking tea, going to lunch, or to running numerous trivial errands on her behalf.

Jane sighed and stubbed out her cigarette in the overflowing tin ashtray on her desk. If her mother discovered she had returned to live at Ashbourne House, even temporarily, then she was highly likely to simply turn up with her luggage expecting to stay. The possibility sent a shudder down her spine.

* * *

Benson took the brigadier's telephone call while Arthur Cilento was dressing for dinner. Having understood the brigadier's instructions, he replaced the receiver on the handset in the study and went upstairs to break the news to his master.

'I say, Benson, was that the telephone?' Arthur had finished battling with his collar studs and attempted to restore some order to his hair with a brush.

'Yes, sir, Brigadier Remmington-Blythe.' Benson retrieved Arthur's brush and set about tidying and flattening Arthur's unruly curls.

'Oh?' Arthur didn't like the sound of this. Usually any work he was commissioned to perform for the war office came via written instructions. He had recently been involved with secret operations at Bletchley Park, a challenge he had relished.

'We are to make ourselves ready to depart for a stay in Kent tomorrow, sir.' Benson's gaze met Arthur's in the large silver-backed mirror above the dressing table.

'Is this one of the brigadier's special missions?' Arthur's sense of unease increased.

'I believe so, sir.'

'With Miss Treen?' Arthur wasn't sure if he was fully recovered from the last few times he and Benson had worked with Jane Treen. Or, indeed, her wretched one-eyed, ginger cat, Marmaduke.

'Yes, sir. Shall I commence packing after dinner?' Benson asked, finishing his ministrations with the brush.

'I don't suppose we have a choice.' Arthur turned around on the dressing-table stool and looked for his shoes.

'No, sir.'

Arthur located his footwear and looked at his manservant. 'Did the brigadier say what this case is about?'

Benson was already preparing to leave the room to return downstairs. 'Something about a body in the dunes at Farthingale Beach. He said Miss Treen would brief us fully on our arrival in Ashbourne.' The manservant excused himself to return to his duties, leaving Arthur to finish glumly preparing to dine on some indifferent pork chops with the local bank manager.

* * *

Jane had packed for the journey into Kent on her return to her small, serviced apartment that evening. All that was needed the next day was to go into the office, obtain her final instructions from the brigadier and hand some of her workload over to Stephen, his secretary.

'Off on your jollies again, Jane?' Stephen remarked as she placed a large bundle of manila folders on his desk. 'It's all right for some.' He smirked into his pencil moustache.

'Some of us have important work to do outside this office.'

There was no love lost between herself and Stephen. Handsome and debonair, he had pursued her relentlessly for quite some time. He had at least now finally given up trying to ask her out to dinner or to dance at one of the few venues that remained open. He was also one of the few people at her office, or indeed in her life, who knew who her mother was.

Much to Jane's horror, it had transpired that Stephen and her mother moved in the same social circles when he was not at work. This was something he constantly appeared to enjoy needling her about. Even worse, her mother appeared to approve of Stephen as a potential suitor for Jane.

Jane left Stephen to read through the meticulous notes she had attached to the front of each file and tapped on the brigadier's door.

'Jane, my dear, are you all set to leave for Kent?' the brigadier asked.

He was seated behind his desk studying a sheet of paper.

'Yes, sir. I take it you have briefed Arthur?' she asked.

'Indeed. He and his manservant will meet you at your house. A car will collect them from the station. I take it you were successful in contacting the woman with the key to prepare everything for your arrival?' The brigadier raised one questioning, silvery, bushy eyebrow.

Jane nodded. 'Yes, everything should be prepared for us.'

She hoped this was the case. She had packed her own meagre food supply to add to whatever Arthur and Benson would be bringing with them. Mrs Dawes, the lady who held her key, would also look after them whilst they were in residence.

'Jolly good. The identity of the man in the dunes appears to have been confirmed.' He looked at Jane.

'Who was he?' she asked, feeling sure that the man's identity held the key to why they were being dispatched to Kent with such haste.

'Antonio Russo, Italian, from the prisoner of war camp some two miles inland from the coast.'

'An escapee looking to try and get back across the channel?' Jane asked. It would account for the lack of clothing if he had hidden his uniform somewhere and had managed to steal or obtain some civilian clothing. But if that were the case then why had he been found naked?

'I don't know. That is one of the things I want you and Arthur to find out.' The brigadier looked at her. 'This is quite sensitive, Jane. The influx of Italian prisoners is fairly recent, and the granting of permission to use prisoners for agricultural labour is still controversial in some circles. This is something of a trial. The man would have been approved by a local panel. We need more labour on the farms and it's important the public accept the situation and feel secure. An incident like this could upset the apple cart. The high-ups are very twitchy about this.'

'I understand, sir. We will be careful. And the other things? You mentioned black marketeering?' Jane asked.

'Exactly. The inspector responsible for shutting this kind of thing down is very worried about the whole business and the policing resources are stretched thin. I have asked him to contact you when you get into Kent, along with the police inspector in charge of the case. Keep your eyes and ears open and see what you can discover. I don't know if this death is connected, but it may be.'

'Very good, sir.' Jane rose, ready to depart.

'There is something that feels decidedly odd going on there. Keep me informed,' the brigadier instructed.

CHAPTER TWO

'Where are we staying?' Arthur asked Benson as their luggage was loaded into the boot of the black departmental car that had arrived to collect them from the station in Kent. There was, as yet, no sign of Miss Treen.

'The brigadier said it was a property formerly belonging to Miss Treen's late father, sir.' Benson took his place inside the car and the chauffeur set off through the town towards the open countryside beyond.

'Do we have any more information about why we are here?' Arthur was aware that he sounded rather peevish. He considered though that he had a right to be a little put out. Ordered from his home at short notice to work under Jane Treen at some unknown spot on the Kentish coast. He had been hoping for more work along similar lines to his recent tasks at Bletchley Park.

'Not really, sir. The brigadier said Miss Treen would brief us more fully on arrival.' Benson was preoccupied with looking out of the windows as if keen to note any landmarks.

Outside the car the sun was shining, and the fields were bright with yellow stubble. The driver took a few more turns and after speeding along the country lanes they found themselves passing through a small Kentish village strung out along a narrow high street. They turned again at the stone-built church and up ahead they could see a fine, if slightly run-down, Georgian country house.

White, with a small wooden portico above the front door, it looked as if at one time it may have been the rectory for the church. The car pulled to a stop near the black-painted front gate and Arthur saw 'Ashbourne House', written in fine black italic script along the edge of the portico. It seemed that this was to be their destination.

He followed his manservant out of the car and waited on the stone doorstep. Benson pressed the brass bell push beside the wide, dark-blue front door.

Jane Treen opened the door. 'Welcome to Ashbourne House.'

She stood aside to allow them entry and for the driver to bring their bags into the long hallway, which seemed to run from the front towards the rear of the house.

'Thank you, miss,' Benson answered as he supervised Arthur's medical paraphernalia as it was placed on the broad elm planks of the hall floor. Once the luggage was safely inside, the driver touched his cap to Jane and took his leave.

'Do come through. I'm afraid the house is a little chilly at the moment despite the sun. It's been closed up for a while, but I've got the fire going so it should soon warm up.' Jane led the way into a large square drawing room.

True to her word, a fire was crackling merrily in the grate of a handsome marble fireplace and the room was filled with bright, autumnal sunshine. Marmaduke, Jane's cat, was snoozing peacefully near the hearth. A vase of orange dahlias added a cheery note. Arthur took a seat on one of the shabby chintz-covered armchairs beside the fire. He gave Marmaduke a sideways glance and waited for Jane to explain why they were there.

'It's been something of a scramble to arrange things at short notice.' Jane looked at Arthur and then at Benson, who stood patiently waiting near the door of the room.

She gave a succinct explanation of their mission, the concerns about the black marketeering and the discovery of the man found on the dunes.

'His identity has been confirmed as that of an Italian prisoner of war, Antonio Russo.' Jane picked up a folder from the side table and passed it to Arthur.

The contents were slim. A press cutting from the previous day which outlined the circumstances in which the man had been found. A report from the local inspector responsible for monitoring and preventing black market activities in the local area. A hand-drawn map showing where the camp was sited in relation to where the body was found and the proximity to the village. There was also a sketch of the dead man's distinctive tattoo.

Arthur looked through the contents of the folder and passed it over to Benson. The manservant also perused the items inside.

'I assume from the inclusion of the inspector's report that the brigadier somehow suspects these two things are linked in some way?' Arthur asked. He could see no other reason why they would both be in the file, but could also see no obvious reason to connect them.

The dead man could have been making an ill-judged bid for freedom to try and return back over the channel. The black market activities could be organised locally or even by gangs operating out of London. He wasn't sure if they were to work on two separate cases or if the brigadier had felt they were linked. Perhaps this was why he had been asked to work with Jane again.

'He doesn't know. That is why we're here. To determine what happened to Antonio Russo and also to see what we can learn about these black marketeers. There may or may not be a link.' Jane had taken out her cigarettes.

Arthur sighed. 'Surely the police are better placed to sort out the black marketeers?'

'They have very few resources and they have received no assistance from the local people. As for the dead man, don't you think the circumstances in which he was found were rather odd?' Jane asked, blowing out a thin stream of smoke after she spoke.

'His lack of clothing? Could have been freak currents, it doesn't say how damaged the body was,' Arthur countered.

'There were no signs of a boat or wreckage reported. And there is that tattoo on his arm.' Jane looked at Arthur. 'It sounds unusual, that has to mean something, don't you think?'

Arthur rubbed his face with his hands, trying to clear his thoughts. 'In other words, we are here because the brigadier has a hunch that there is something going on to link the two events?'

It seemed his suspicions were correct.

Jane knocked some ash from the end of her cigarette into a pressed-glass ashtray. 'Questions will be asked about national security and the advisability of utilising the labour of prisoners of war. Although we did the same thing in the last war, I gather this is something new, so it has been kept on the down-low. There is also the scale of the activities the government inspector has reported. The brigadier is a shrewd man, as you know, and he has to answer the concerns put to him by the cabinet. If there is a link, then we need to find it.'

Benson coughed politely and passed the file back to Arthur. 'I expect we shall discover more tomorrow.'

Jane locked the file away inside a small walnut bureau which stood in the window. 'Yes, I expect so. Now, I'll show you to your rooms so you can unpack and get settled. I'm afraid I have very little domestic help here. Mrs Dawes from the village has agreed to come and cook and clean for us. She used to assist my father, and her husband has been managing the garden.' A shadow appeared to cross Jane's expressive features as she led them out of the drawing room and up the staircase to the first floor.

'My room is this end. The bathroom is in the centre, and I've given you rooms that are linked at the end of the corridor.' She took them down to two white-painted panelled doors at the far end of the landing.

Arthur could see there were two more doors on the other side of the landing which he assumed may have been her father's room. He knew Jane's family circumstances were a little complicated. He and Benson had previously met her mother briefly at Paddington station at the end of their first case together.

It had been quite a surprise to discover Jane's mother was the famous American singer and actress, Elsa Macintyre. The meeting had appeared awkward, and it was clear the relationship between the two women was somewhat fraught.

Jane left them to sort out their luggage and vanished back downstairs. Benson immediately followed in order to carry their bags upstairs. Arthur wandered over to the sash window to look out. The room was a large, square one, simply but tastefully furnished. A fire was laid, but unlit in the grate and the air in the room was cool.

He closed the window where it had been left open a crack, no doubt to air the room. From his vantage point he could see over the small front garden and down the length of the main street of the village.

A couple of horse-drawn carts were plodding their way along the road and a few women, baskets over their arms, were going in and out of the shops. Beyond the village, through the trees, he saw something sparkling in the distance and realised they were very close to the coast.

Benson was busy hanging suits and tutting over creases in his shirts while Arthur continued to study his surroundings. His manservant's smaller room was linked to his through an adjoining door. His view was much as Arthur's except he could see something of the side garden where a small brook bubbled noisily along near the vegetable beds.

The dunes where the Italian's body had been found could not be that far away, perhaps a quarter of a mile or a half mile at most. No wonder the brigadier had thought Miss Treen's family home would make a good base for their investigations. The business of the dead man's tattoo puzzled him. He could have sworn there was something about the design that he had seen or read about somewhere before.

Normally he had excellent recall, and had he been at his home at Half Moon Manor in Devon he could have delved into his library of notebooks and found the answer immediately. Here in Kent, however, he had none of his usual resources and would have to wait for his memory to supply him with the answer.

Benson finished his arrangements. 'Ahem, Miss Treen said she only had this Mrs Dawes to assist domestically in the house. I think it may be a good idea if I go to the kitchen to make this lady's acquaintance.'

'What? Oh yes, good thinking, Benson.' Arthur had dismissed Jane's domestic arrangements without a second thought, but he supposed his manservant was right. It had sounded as if this Mrs Dawes person could use some assistance. She might also have some useful inside knowledge about what had happened at the dunes.

Arthur followed Benson downstairs. His manservant headed for the kitchen, disappearing behind the green-baize door at the far end of the hallway. Arthur wandered back into the drawing room, following the sound of a baby grand piano being played quite skilfully.

He was a little surprised to discover Jane seated on the piano stool.

'I didn't know you played,' he said as he approached her.

'Ever since I was a child. My mother insisted that I took lessons. I think at one point she thought I might go with her on tours as her accompanist. Then she realised she would have to admit I was her daughter, instead of trying to pass me off as her younger sister.' Jane finished playing with a crash of her fingers on the keys.

'Ah.' Arthur wasn't sure what to say to this revelation so settled for a sympathetic sound.

'I think we should start our investigations tomorrow by trying to get to the dunes. They are barricaded off to prevent access to the beach with rolls of barbed wire, but it would give us an idea of where this man was discovered.' Jane swivelled around on the piano bench so she could look him in the eye.

'Very true. I presume you know both this area and the people in the village well?' Arthur asked.

'I moved away to London about five years ago, but I still visited frequently. I was here last year for a few months when my father became ill.' She pressed one of the ivory piano keys and it responded with a soft plink of sound.

'I hadn't realised your loss was so recent. I'm sorry,' Arthur said.

'His illness was quite sudden and unexpected, he seemed to be recovering. We thought he'd turned a corner, then I went to take him his morning tea and he was gone.' Jane swallowed, and he could see the loss was still deeply affecting her.

'Were you here alone at the time?' he asked.

She gave a slight shrug. 'Just me, Marmaduke and Mrs Dawes. She had just arrived to start work that morning when I found him. She was an absolute brick afterwards helping me to deal with everything.' Jane pulled out her cigarettes and took one from the packet ready to light it.

'And your mother?' Arthur phrased the question delicately. He knew there were issues between Jane and her glamorous and famous mother.

'She came for the funeral. My parents were separated. They had been for a long time, but for some reason they never divorced.' Jane lit her cigarette and inhaled, before releasing a long stream of smoke.

Arthur coughed and moved away nearer the fireplace. The mention of Marmaduke made him wonder where the cat had gone. At least it had moved from the drawing room before his asthma could be triggered.

'I think she thought she would get Ashbourne. The house was Father's though. He owned it before they married, and he left it to me in his will. She got some money and that was it. Everything else was mine. She went back to London to work as soon as the wake was over.' Jane flicked the ash from the end of her cigarette into a glass ashtray on top of the piano.

Arthur wasn't certain what he was supposed to say to that so settled for another sympathetic-sounding, non-committal noise.

'The house has been shut up ever since then.' Jane finished her cigarette.

'Until the brigadier asked us to investigate this man and his death,' Arthur said.

'And whatever is going on with this black market racket to see if there is a link somewhere,' Jane added.

* * *

Jane was quietly pleased that Arthur had taken the time to dress for dinner. It wasn't as if she expected him to wear formal black tie or anything since there were only the two of them to dine. It was nice that he had combed his hair and was wearing a dinner jacket, however. There might be a war on, but the niceties of life should still be observed in her opinion.

She herself had changed into a plain dark-blue silk dress. She had owned it for more years than she cared to recall but it always made her feel better whenever she wore it. Thankfully, her father had kept a good wine cellar so for once they had been able to enjoy a good sherry before eating and a nice crisp white wine to accompany the rather bland fish pie.

Mrs Dawes returned home to her cottage after clearing away the dinner things, assisted by Benson. He had seen her off along the high street to her cottage before coming back to the house. The evening was still light, and it would be at least another hour until the blackout, unless of course the sirens should sound.

Jane had already shown them the shelter her father had constructed near the rear of the house. It was quite a large affair buried half into the ground with turf laid over a sturdy corrugated iron roof. He had kitted it out with a hurricane lantern, a slightly rickety kitchen table and chairs, cushions and blankets and a stash of sweets in an old biscuit tin. A spirit stove and supplies for tea had also been installed.

Her father had even managed to find a square of an old rug for the floor. As shelters went, it was quite luxurious. Benson had already acquainted himself with the layout of the kitchen and Mrs Dawes had shared her knowledge of how to fire up the slightly unreliable gas-fired range. Marmaduke, her cat, was happily prowling about the garden stalking something in the long grass near the compost heap.

With everything and everyone seemingly settled in the house she started to relax a little. The door to her father's former bedroom remained closed and locked. She knew Mrs Dawes had emptied it of all his clothes, but she couldn't face opening it back up yet. Perhaps once she had been home for a little while she might be able to.

Arthur had seemed impressed by the small library of books within her father's study and happily browsed the selection on the shelves to choose something to read. Jane turned on the wireless and found a play to listen to. Tomorrow would see them setting out to discover what had befallen the murdered man and whether it was linked to the black marketeers. For now though, she was content to simply settle back into her former home.

CHAPTER THREE

The following morning dawned bright and clear. Jane came downstairs early to the delicious smell of bacon, a rare treat these days. Mrs Dawes was already busy in the kitchen and Benson was laying the table in the dining room.

'Good morning, Benson.' Jane popped her head into the dining room. 'I trust you slept well?'

'Like a top, thank you, Miss Jane.' He favoured her with one of his rare smiles.

Jane hummed happily to herself as she wandered back into the drawing room and over to her beloved piano. She ran her hand over the keys and smiled. She had forgotten how much she loved to play. Despite her misgivings at having accepted this assignment initially, she was starting to enjoy herself.

Arthur appeared a short while later and came to join her just after she had sat down at the breakfast table.

'I presume you would like to set off for the beach straight after we've eaten?' he asked, spreading his linen napkin across his lap.

'I think so. The weather is good so we should make the most of it. One can never tell at this time of year when it might break,' Jane said. The weather had been unusually warm for the last few days. September had been wet and miserable, delaying the harvest.

'Is it far to walk?' he asked, helping himself to his half of the meagre portion of bacon.

'Don't worry, I'm certain it's within your capabilities,' she remarked somewhat drily.

On their case in January, Arthur had gone everywhere swathed in layers of wool and had constantly grumbled and complained about the cold. In addition to being England's slowest diner, he was also a slow walker. Jane had often been forced to curb her speed so as not to leave him behind.

He raised an eyebrow at her comment and applied himself to his breakfast without saying anything further.

They arranged for Benson to go into the village and visit the various shops to see what he could learn about the body in the dunes. Jane also asked him to listen out for any talk of contraband goods that might be on sale.

True to form, despite the warm autumnal day, Arthur emerged from the house wearing a winter overcoat with a knitted scarf around his throat. Jane rolled her eyes but refrained from commenting as they set off together along the village high street.

They had not gone far when a familiar voice hailed her from the other side of the street.

'Jane, is that you? Good heavens, when did you arrive home?' A sprightly, older man dressed in a smart grey jacket waved to her.

'Doctor Denning, how are you?' Jane paused to greet her father's former doctor warmly as he crossed the road towards them.

'I'm fine, my dear. How are you?' the doctor asked, scrutinising her face keenly as if looking for signs of ill health.

'I'm very well. I'm just down for a brief holiday with a

friend of mine. Arthur Cilento, Doctor Denning. Arthur suffers from asthma and his own doctor recommended he come to the coast for a short time.' Jane crossed her fingers behind her back and hoped the lie sounded medically plausible.

'That sounds like a sensible suggestion. Fresh sea air is very beneficial for the lungs,' the doctor agreed as he shook hands with Arthur. 'By the way, have you heard of our little excitement lately?'

'Oh, you mean that poor man they found on the beach?' Jane asked. 'I think I saw something in the newspaper. I could hardly believe it.'

'Quite, my dear, it's absolutely shocking. Seems the fella was one of those Italian chappies from the POW camp. Quite how he ended up dead on the beach no one knows.' Doctor Denning frowned.

'Were you called when the boys discovered him? I think the papers said some local children had found him?' Jane asked.

'Yes, there was nothing to be done for him by that point though, I'm afraid. The boys who spotted him were Mrs Kerrigan's lads. You must remember the Kerrigans, Jane? Large family living on Mill Street.'

'Oh yes, the mother takes in washing.' Jane knew the family he meant. There were about seven children in the family, and it took all their parents' time to keep their brood out of trouble.

'That's the family. The two eldest boys had decided to sneak onto the beach to go for a swim. It was an unusually hot day. They had found a breach in the barbed wire, or so they claimed. Anyway, they found him and came haring back to fetch Constable Martin,' Doctor Denning said.

'And then you were called?' Jane asked. 'It sounded strange in the report as it said he was naked and referred to a peculiar tattoo?'

'Yes, both very peculiar things. There is a theory that he was heading for France, had arranged his escape and planned to change clothes. He reportedly spoke English well,' Doctor Denning agreed.

'Which part of the beach was he on?' Jane asked.

'The boys discovered him not too far from the old gateway, you know the one near the bench. He was just visible from the path on the dunes,' the doctor said.

'How very odd. I presume he drowned?' Arthur asked.

'Well, I suppose he must have, although he was some distance from the sea, but by then the constable had come so whether he had been moved I'm really not certain. He may have been there for a little while, poor fellow,' Doctor Denning said.

'Arthur and I were just walking to the sea now as he's never visited this part of the world before.' Jane looked along the street in the direction of the coast.

'Not much to see there now, sadly. The barbed wire is in place to keep everyone off the sands. Still, the air should be of benefit. Let's hope there are no more bodies, eh?' Doctor Denning gave a small chuckle.

'I hope not. You must call in for drinks one evening,' Jane invited the genial doctor. She knew her father would have expected her to extend an invitation to his friend and she and Arthur needed to demonstrate that they were on holiday.

'That sounds most delightful, my dear. I shall look forward to your invitation.' The doctor raised his hat politely and they continued on their way towards the sea.

'That was a useful meeting,' Arthur said as he strolled slowly along beside her.

Jane, forced to slow her usual brisk pace to allow Arthur to keep up with her, agreed. 'Doctor Denning has been the local doctor here now for a number of years. He was good friends with my father. I thought he would have been called to attend to the body in the dunes. He does a lot of work with the police.'

'We know who the children were now too who found the body,' Arthur observed.

'The Kerrigan boys. The family run their poor mother ragged, seven children and I think the oldest is probably eleven. Her husband spends all of his time in the public house. At least he used to. I suppose he may be more active now the war is on.' Jane doubted that Mr Kerrigan would have been found fit to enlist and he couldn't be in a reserved occupation since, to her knowledge, he had never held down any occupation for long. Reserved or otherwise.

They were approaching the end of the high street at the point where it curved out to follow the line of the coast. The cottages were more spread out and there was a salt tang in the air. The sounds of the waves crashing onto the shore was louder and the gulls screamed overhead as they circled on the breeze.

As they rounded the corner by the last cottage, they saw the dunes ahead of them. The hillocks of pale sand and tufts of grass were behind a wooden post and rail fence. Rolls of razor wire had been placed across and signs telling everyone that entrance was forbidden were on every other post.

'Is this the spot where he was found?' Arthur asked as they crossed the road to get closer to the dunes.

Jane indicated a narrow informal path running alongside the fence that led away from the road towards the cliff in the distance. 'I suspect the boys would have gone along here from what Doctor Denning said.'

She led the way with Arthur following behind her. The path led through the sand with tufts of coarse dune grass growing on either side. The fence barring them from the sea, complete with the menacing rolls of wire, continued on their left.

Before long the village houses were behind them and all that was visible was the dunes. In between the heaps of sand

and fading clumps of pink sea thrift the sea sparkled a blue and silver invitation.

Presently Jane halted. The path broadened out at this point and once there had been a wooden bench which had provided a welcome rest stop for picnickers and hikers. Now it was in poor condition with the back rail hanging down to the ground at one end.

Old cigarette butts littered the ground, and it was still clearly a favourite place for people to halt, look at the sea and light a cigarette. The post and rail fencing had an opening opposite the bench which must have once had a gate. The rusted hinges which would have supported it were still attached to the bleached wooden posts.

Now the way to the sea was barred with what looked to Jane like fresh rolls of barbed wire. The metal tips of the spikes were still sharp and shiny, having not yet been dulled by the sand and the wind that could spring up from the sea. A path led down on the other side towards the beach and the sand was heavily imprinted with a mixture of footprints.

'This looks like the place.' Arthur had bent to look at the footprints and he indicated a couple that bore the distinct large boot marks that were likely to be made by the police.

Jane nodded and took out her own cigarettes to have a smoke while she looked over the scene. Arthur frowned at her and moved further away when she lit her cigarette. The tide had washed the beach clean of any possible identifying marks. Even if there had been anything, the police would have trampled the scene anyway.

The newspaper had said he had been found on the beach, implying he had been carried in on the tide and deposited there. Yet Doctor Denning had said he had been at the top of the beach. Jane inhaled her cigarette and tried to recall how the tides worked on that part of the coast. Just because the man had been discovered there didn't mean he had to have entered the water there, or did it?

She glanced around. Behind her on the dunes was a ramshackle cottage. It was an old fisherman's house that had been empty and decaying for years. She had always recalled it as being unoccupied when she had been younger. Now, however, it had a newish rail fence around the perimeter and a fresh coat of whitewash on the walls. She wondered who lived there and if they might have noticed anything.

Arthur seemed to be consulting a booklet he had pulled from his pocket. Jane recognised it as being one her father had kept in his study, which provided a guide to the tide times as a way of calculating high and low water. She also recognised the thoughtful expression on her companion's face as he squinted at the leaflet and then at the sea.

She finished her cigarette and dropped it on the sand by the bench ready to stub it out with the highly polished toe of her shoe. Many of the cigarette butts were old, the ends discoloured and frayed from exposure to the elements. There were some newer ones, however.

They could have been dropped by the police or sightseers from the village come to gawp at the scene where the body had been found but a few of the butts caught her attention. They were fresh and marked with lipstick in a very distinct dark red, almost plum colour.

She filed it away in her memory. It might mean nothing. A courting couple, perhaps, who used the spot regularly, or maybe it might lead somewhere. Arthur appeared satisfied with his mental arithmetic and had returned the leaflet to his pocket.

'I suppose we shall have to wait until the children are out of school before we can talk to the Kerrigan boys?' Arthur said.

'That's if the boys have gone to school.' Jane knew the Kerrigans' school attendance was patchy at best. Mrs Dawes told her much of the village gossip in the short letters she sent to Jane every few weeks when Jane had checked that all was well with the house.

'Where shall we go to next?' Arthur asked, digging his hands into the pockets of his coat as if still cold despite the warmth of the morning sun.

'I think we need to speak to Mr Wood, the government inspector responsible for discovering and dealing with black marketeering activities in the area. He was obviously concerned enough about the scale of things that he brought it to the department's attention. We might find out why the brigadier thinks there is possibly a link between that and this dead man.' Jane turned, ready to walk back to the village.

Arthur started back alongside her. 'Benson may have unearthed something useful in the village,' he said.

'He is quite adept at getting people to talk to him,' Jane agreed.

'The dead man was released daily to do farm labour?' Arthur asked.

'Yes, several of the prisoners help out locally at various farms. It's a new thing. He was classed as low risk, not interested in the Nazi cause, simply a conscript by all accounts from what the brigadier had discovered.' Jane glanced at Arthur who was panting slightly as he tried to keep up with her now they were at the end of the rabbit path and back at the start of the road.

'We also need to speak to the police inspector in charge of the investigation,' Arthur said.

'The brigadier was going to contact him. He said he would say the department was concerned since the victim was a foreign national.' Jane had discussed the matter with the brigadier before leaving for Kent.

'Then let us hope we hear from him soon too.' Arthur started to lag behind her as they reached the part of the high street where the shops started.

Jane was forced to slow her pace so that he could keep up with her. She saw a few people she knew who greeted her with surprise and pleasure at her return to the village. A few people asked after her mother, saying they had heard her recently on the radio.

She pasted a smile on her face and made polite small talk. Introducing Arthur as a friend who was staying to recover his health earned her a few knowing looks. She pretended not to notice the implications in their smiles. Fortunately, Arthur appeared blissfully unaware that some of the villagers thought they were romantically involved.

By the time they were back at the house, Jane was ready for a cup of coffee and was tired of making small talk. After living in London for a while where everyone minded their own business, she had forgotten how socially demanding village life could be.

Benson opened the front door to them on their return.

'A Mr Wood has telephoned, Miss Jane. He wishes to call this afternoon at around two thirty. He is the government inspector in charge of the investigations into the black market activities locally.' Benson dropped his voice slightly when he imparted the last piece of information.

'Splendid, we need to speak to him. I don't suppose the police have telephoned as well?' she asked as Benson assisted Arthur in removing his scarf and coat.

'Not as yet, Miss Jane.'

'Could you ask Mrs Dawes to prepare some coffee, please? Then I think we should all have a brief catch-up in the drawing room,' Jane suggested.

'Very good, miss.' Benson disappeared off along the hall towards the kitchen.

Arthur followed her into the large drawing room and took a seat next to the fire, only to jump back up again when

Marmaduke appeared from under the carved wooden legs of the fireside chair.

'I swear that cat of yours will give me a heart attack.'

Jane scooped her beloved pet into her arms and cooed as she stroked the animal's thick orange fur. 'There, there, Marmaduke, naughty Uncle Arthur didn't mean to startle you.'

Arthur gave her a look. 'For the last time, Jane, I will not be uncle to a cat. Please can you put that beastly creature down and away from me.'

Jane laughed and carried her pet out of the room, shooing him towards the kitchen where she knew Mrs Dawes would happily receive him.

'Better now?' Jane asked as she re-entered the drawing room to find that Arthur had reinstated himself beside the small fire. 'You are in his chair, you know, so you can't be too surprised if he objects to you sitting there.'

Benson appeared carrying a brass-rimmed mahogany tray replete with chrome coffee pot and milk jug, along with an elegant set of china cups. He placed the tray down on the rosewood occasional table and served them both a cup of coffee.

'How did you fare in the village?' Jane asked, tucking her stocking-clad feet up under herself as she took the seat opposite Arthur.

Benson had refrained from sitting down or pouring himself a drink. Instead, he stood behind the sofa, hands loosely clasped behind his back as if about to present evidence in a law court.

'In accordance with your instructions I visited several establishments on the high street. I made some small purchases of goods not covered by rationing and engaged in conversations as much as possible.'

'What did you find out?' Arthur asked.

Benson cleared his throat. 'The deceased gentleman was being held at Finehaven, a small local camp. All the prisoners there are low risk, mainly Italian conscripts as the brigadier ascertained. Antonio Russo and another prisoner, Matteo Gambini, went daily from the camp to work on the farm of Mr Lloyd Briggs. He is also the local magistrate, according to the lady in the greengrocers.'

'They had no escort with them from the camp?' Jane asked.

'It seems not. They had been working there for a few months ever since arriving in Kent. They were not considered a risk and assistance from the Home Guard to provide an escort was not forthcoming,' Benson confirmed.

Jane thought she vaguely remembered Mr Briggs. He was not someone who had called regularly at the house, but she had a feeling he had attended her father's funeral.

'Did you learn anything else?' Arthur looked at his manservant.

'Only a rumour that the man found on the beach was thought to have been over friendly with a Miss Katie Hargreaves, the school mistress,' Benson said. 'She had been volunteering to teach English at the camp. Another new initiative apparently.'

From the tone of Benson's voice, Jane guessed that this too had met with considerable disquiet in the village.

CHAPTER FOUR

Lunch consisted of late green salad stuffs from the garden grown under an ingenious cold frame devised many years earlier by Jane's father. Mr Dawes had been tending to the growing in Jane's absence in return for the crops. It was accompanied by quiche and leftover cold potatoes.

Once the matter of food was out of the way, Arthur busied himself with making notes about all they had learned so far. He also drew a small map for himself of the village and cross-referenced it with information from Jane about the route to the camp and the location of Mr Briggs's farm.

'And you say you don't know this school teacher, Katie Hargreaves?' Arthur asked, looking at Jane as she stood smoking next to the study window. She turned to face him.

'No, she's a fairly new arrival to the village. I think she came here just after Father died. Mrs Dawes mentioned in her letters to me that Miss Pilver, the previous teacher, had retired. She was very old and had been quite ill. I think they thought they were fortunate to secure a replacement who was actually experienced given the difficulties in recruitment.' Jane stubbed her cigarette out in the glass ashtray on the corner of the desk.

'What do you know of Mr Briggs?' Arthur asked as he made more notes in his book. Jane's inside knowledge of various members of the community at least gave them some extra information.

'Not very much, I'm afraid. He attended Father's funeral. I think mainly because he knew my father from various committees that they both served on, rather than a personal connection. I don't ever remember him coming here for dinner or drinks.' Jane's brow furrowed. He guessed she was attempting to recollect what she knew about the man. 'He does own a large farm on the edge of the village, not too far from the camp.'

'Hmm, and he is the local magistrate, so I expect he holds some sway in the village,' Arthur observed. 'I presume that's why the camp had stopped sending a guard with the men working on his farm. If they had proven themselves trustworthy and if he was collecting or taking them back. Benson said the Home Guard hadn't been involved.'

Arthur was aware from what the brigadier had told Jane that being allowed out for work was something of a privilege as it relieved boredom for the prisoners and gave them a taste of freedom.

'Yes, it didn't sound as if they had an escort,' Jane agreed.

'We shall have to try and find out for certain when we eventually get to talk to the police, or Mr Briggs.' Arthur rubbed his chin distractedly.

'Did you notice when we were at the beach there is a cottage set back above the dunes? It used to be empty, but it looked as if someone might be occupying it now. Whoever is living there may have seen something that afternoon,' Jane suggested.

'I did notice a house, yes. I assumed it must be a fisherman's cottage or an old holiday place. I expect whoever lives there will have been spoken to by the police, but it's worth double-checking,' Arthur agreed.

There was the sound of a car drawing up outside the house and Jane turned to peek through the window. 'This must be the man from the ministry, Mr Wood, the chap who is in charge of monitoring black market activities.'

They heard the murmur of voices in the hall outside the study and Arthur assumed that Benson was showing their guest into the drawing room.

Benson opened the study door and looked in. 'Mr Wood is here for you, sir, miss. I have seated him in the drawing room.'

'Thank you.' Arthur picked up his notebook to take it with him. He was keen to hear about the other part of the task they had been set. The growing concerns about the level of black market activities in the area.

'Shall I ask Mrs Dawes to prepare a tea tray?' Benson asked as Jane prepared to lead the way to the drawing room.

'Please, if you would be so good,' she agreed.

Mr Wood proved to be a small, peevish-looking man in his mid-fifties with thinning hair, wire-framed spectacles and a Scottish accent. He leapt to his feet as they entered the room and shook hands with them both, before returning to his seat next to the fireplace.

'I am so pleased the department has finally taken some notice of my reports. I have telephoned, sent letters and nothing. All the while the problems in the area seem to be worsening.' He peered over the top of his spectacles, first at Jane and then at Arthur.

'I'm so sorry to hear that, Mr Wood. Perhaps you could enlighten us about the main causes of concern,' Jane said as she took her seat opposite him.

Arthur had perched himself on one end of the sofa and had his notebook open to take down anything of interest. Mr Wood immediately directed his attention towards him.

'When I took over the inspector's post last November there was the usual amount of sporadic, isolated incidents of looting, petty theft, et cetera. Regrettable, but nothing untoward. Then by the end of June things began to escalate.' Mr Wood's voice took on a peevish note.

'In what way?' Jane asked.

Mr Wood continued to direct his responses to Arthur. 'I keep a very precise log of all reported incidents. Most of them follow bombing raids that have affected commercial premises in the local towns. That is, the coastal towns and inland such as Ashford. I began to become aware of people arriving on the scene shortly after the all-clear. Sometimes even before the all-clear, usually dressed as ARP wardens. They always had a commercial vehicle of some kind and told the shopkeepers they would take the stock to a secure warehouse until the premises were able to be repaired or relocated. The shopkeepers signed falsified documents that looked as if they were official.'

'I presume this then didn't happen and the shopkeepers lost their goods?' Jane said.

'Indeed, within days I was informed that items matching those stolen were being offered on the black market from various outlets. I am one man, Mr Cilento, I cannot be everywhere trying to stamp this out and the police have other problems to deal with. Not to mention that when we have conducted raids on premises, we have been too late. This gang are one step ahead of us it seems.' Mr Wood was quite pink in the face with indignation.

Benson arrived and placed a tray of tea on the table before discreetly withdrawing. This provided an opportune moment for Mr Wood to collect himself and calm down a little while Jane poured their drinks.

'You feel these black market activities are being coordinated across a wide area? And you are sure the people involved are the same?' Jane asked as she handed the man his teacup.

'The coastal towns have suffered heavy damage so are most affected, but the operation does extend inland. There were lulls when we had fewer raids. There have been statements from the witnesses saying some of those involved have a cockney accent. The descriptions of the miscreants are the same in each case,' Mr Wood said. 'But they must be being coordinated from somewhere near at hand to arrive on the scene so swiftly after the bombs are dropped.'

'I presume too that you have not been able to determine where they are storing the items they are stealing?' Arthur remarked mildly, while making notes in his book.

'My assumption is there must be a warehouse or couple of units where the things are held before being redistributed through a network of suppliers. We raided a couple of premises but found nothing. I've said this several times in my reports to the department.' Mr Wood got quite agitated as he spoke, spilling some of his tea into his saucer.

Jane raised her neatly arched eyebrows and looked at Arthur. 'What kind of goods are being stolen?' she asked.

'Tinned and bottled goods, alcohol, cigarettes and clothing mainly. Luxury items such as sweets and chocolate. Last week, they stole vast quantities of lavatory paper.' Mr Wood's eyes bulged, and Arthur thought the little man was about to have a stroke such was his level of indignation at this event.

'You said this seemed to happen after every bombing run that caused damage in one of the major Kentish towns?' Jane asked.

'Yes. They seem to arrive so quickly it's plain that they must track the aircraft as they come through from the coast and then follow where the bombs are likely to fall. A lot of them have fallen short of their targets recently and there has been an increase in the number of incendiary devices used. Smoke and fire damage is another reason they give the shopkeepers for removing the goods.'

Jane frowned. 'What do you mean?'

Mr Wood gave her an impatient glance. 'They tell the

proprietors that the goods are damaged and unfit for sale so they are to be removed and compensation will be paid. I enclosed a copy of the documents they were giving out with my last three reports. Have you not seen them?'

'I'm afraid we haven't—' Jane started to explain but was cut off by Mr Wood.

'Well, really, I knew London was not taking my reports seriously. Mr Cilento, I did think that you and your assistant had been sent from the department to work with me on this matter,' he huffed.

Arthur bit down hard on the inside of his cheek to prevent himself from laughing out loud at the expression on Jane's face when she realised that Mr Wood had assumed that Arthur was in charge.

'My colleague and I have been dispatched to assist you, Mr Wood, hence our questions.' The look on Jane's face and her icy tone was enough to fell a much braver man than Mr Wood.

The government inspector suddenly seemed to realise he may have committed a faux pas. 'Well, all I can say is that it's about time. The country is descending into lawlessness. Trying to get information from people is like trying to get blood from a stone. You'd think people would want to assist and to behave properly, but no, they would rather have a tin of ham or a roll of lavatory paper under the counter instead.'

'So do you have any clues at all about where this gang are likely to be based?' Arthur asked. He assumed it must be somewhere central within the county, or possibly not far from Ashbourne itself since Mr Wood seemed to think the gang followed the flight path of the bombers.

'No one is talking. I'm one man covering a large area. I have some informants but by the time I get the information it's after the event and these people are long gone.' Mr Wood paused to take a sip of his rapidly cooling cup of tea. 'I often don't get contacted until the next day when it dawns on the shopkeepers that they've been had. The papers and receipts are bogus and everything they own has disappeared on the back of a truck.'

Arthur could see that this must be difficult for the inspector. The storekeepers would be angry and upset, trying to salvage their livelihoods and discovering they had been robbed as well as bombed must be heartbreaking.

'You said you have descriptions of the men involved? Do you have registration plates for the vehicles?' Jane asked.

'It's usually night-time, no lights, people are running here, there and everywhere trying to put out fires, rescuing people. The lorry is blue but no idea as to the plate. The description of one man is of a quite large individual, he seems to stay silent loading the lorry. The other man does the talking. He has been described as late fifties, early sixties and either cockney or south London. That's it.' Mr Wood finished the rest of his tea and set his cup and saucer back on the tray.

Arthur finished his notes and tapped the end of the pen thoughtfully against his chin. 'Do you have a list of premises and places where this gang has struck? It may be helpful if Miss Treen and I can plot them out on a map.'

'I have put all of this information—' Mr Wood started to say in a huffy tone. Jane cut him off.

'—in your reports. Yes, I'm sure that you have, Mr Wood, but if you could indulge us and provide us with a list of, say, the ones targeted in the last month or so? It would be enormously helpful.' She bestowed an icy smile at the government inspector.

'I suppose I could get that to you in a day or so,' Mr Wood conceded.

'Thank you.' Jane inclined her head graciously towards him. 'I think that will be all we shall require for now. If you discover more information, please pass it on to us straight away. We expect to be based here for a little while whilst we investigate the matter.'

'Right, very well.' Mr Wood didn't sound terribly pleased by Jane's instruction.

Arthur wondered what the man had been expecting. No doubt he had been convinced that Miss Treen could whip up the police or bring in some of the army to try to root out the matter. It was obvious he had expected some sort of immediate action.

Unfortunately, Arthur suspected it would take them a little while to work out who might be behind the black market operation and where they might be based.

'We shall, of course, be speaking to the police about this matter as well,' Jane said.

'Then I hope you have more luck and co-operation than I have experienced,' Mr Wood said somewhat stiffly.

Arthur hoped that would be the case on both strands of their task, the murder of the Italian prisoner of war and the black market activities.

* * *

Jane relaxed back in her seat after the government inspector had finally made his farewell after another litany of complaints.

'Dear me, I suppose I should ask the brigadier to send us the copies of Mr Wood's reports.' She looked at Arthur.

'I think that might be worthwhile.' Arthur sounded as unenthusiastic about her suggestion as Jane felt on the subject.

She had no doubt that Mr Wood had a legitimate concern and that something serious was happening in this part of Kent. However, she suspected the reports he had submitted would be somewhat reflective of the inspector's personality and would not make light reading.

'What did you think of the information he gave us?' Jane was interested to hear what Arthur's thoughts were, and if they matched her own.

'There is very little to go on. The descriptions of those involved lack detail. We have no idea of what kind of vehicle they are using other than it being described as a small blue lorry. We really need that list of where the gang have struck to try and possibly triangulate an area where they may be based.' Arthur flicked back through his notes as he spoke.

'In other words, we are hunting the proverbial needle in a haystack.' Jane lit one of her cigarettes, ignoring Arthur's disapproving frown.

'I fear that unless we receive more information from somewhere, our chances of success in finding this gang will be slim,' Arthur agreed, wafting his hand in front of his face as a trace of cigarette smoke reached him.

'The scale of the operation does sound concerning, if Mr Wood is to be believed. It sounds like a well-organised gang,' Jane said.

'Yes, I can see why he is so anxious that London does something to assist him. I'm just not certain that our small team will prove sufficient,' Arthur said, closing his notes.

Jane knew what he meant. This gang sounded efficient and with a highly effective network. There were only three of them, including Benson. They could hardly cover the whole county between them.

CHAPTER FIVE

Mr Wood had scarcely departed the house when there was another ring on the front doorbell. A moment later Benson opened the drawing-room door.

'Inspector Topping from the Kent constabulary to see you, Miss Treen, Mr Cilento.' The manservant stood aside and ushered in a heavyset man in his late forties.

Arthur stood to shake hands with the inspector and Jane followed suit.

'Please, take a seat, Inspector Topping.' She was keen to find out as much as she could about both the death of the prisoner and the black market activities.

The inspector sat on the sofa and produced his own police notebook.

'I was asked to call regarding the discovery of the dead man on the beach just down the road from here. I understand there have been some concerns raised in Whitehall.' The inspector looked at them from beneath his bushy grey-streaked eyebrows. He had a slow, deliberate way of speaking and moving that reminded Jane of an amiable tortoise.

'That's correct, Inspector,' Jane said. 'We were sent into

Kent for two purposes. One, this man who was discovered dead on the beach is an Italian national. There are obviously questions about a potential risk to national security. This pertains to how he came to be on the beach and how he may have died. Our other mission is to work with Mr Wood, the government inspector in charge of monitoring black market activity. His recent reports have caused grave concern in London.'

Jane waited to see what the inspector might have to say in response to both of these items. The policeman blinked slowly and painstakingly thumbed his way through his notebook until he reached the page he was looking for.

'We were called to the beach after some local children said they had seen a man's body on the sand. Constable Martin, the local man, attended. As I'm sure you know, the man was unclothed and his only identification was an unusual tattoo on his arm. A rose surrounded by several dots. Doctor Denning was sent for to confirm the death. We then received a message from the POW camp at Finehaven that one of their prisoners had failed to return from day release. The description fitted the man discovered on the sands near the dunes,' the inspector said.

'I understand that the prisoners at Finehaven are categorised as low risk. Two of them, one of them being the dead man, had been approved to work on land belonging to Mr Briggs, a local farmer. I believe he is also the local magistrate?' Jane said, looking at the inspector who had not raised his gaze from his notebook.

'That's all correct, miss, yes,' Inspector Topping agreed.

Arthur looked at Jane. It seemed the inspector was not exactly inclined to be forthcoming with information about the dead man. She couldn't help wondering why that would be so.

'Who raised the alert? Was it the camp or was it this Antonio Russo's work partner? When did he go missing?' Jane's tone became crisper as she waited for the inspector to reply.

'Russo's work partner, a Matteo Gambini, alerted the camp

when he returned from his day release. He claims that he and Russo had been working separately on different tasks and he waited for Russo at the farm gate to join him to walk back to Finehaven Camp. Russo failed to show. He waited for a while but when he didn't appear, he decided to head back by himself. He raised the alarm when he reached the camp.' The inspector's tone was relaxed as if this story made perfect sense.

'Why did he not look for Russo at the farm? Or ask the other workers? I presume Mr Briggs would be there or some other labourers? Why walk all the way back to Finehaven before alerting someone?' Arthur asked.

The inspector made a show of consulting his notebook once more. 'Gambini said he waited and looked around the farmyard. No one else was around and he didn't want to be penalised himself by arriving back late to camp. He said he thought Russo might have mistaken the time and already set off, so he went to the camp expecting to find him there.'

'And where were the other farm employees?' Jane asked. Frankly, she was incredulous that no matter how low risk the prisoners of war were deemed to be, there surely should have been someone supervising them. One did not expect to have enemy agents roaming unsupervised about the countryside. They had only been in the country for a few months.

The inspector's nose crinkled, and Jane suspected her question had annoyed him.

'Mr Briggs had gone into the farmhouse to prepare for an evening engagement. He had thought the Italians had already left for the day. Two of the land girls were busy in the dairy. The other two had gone to see to the pigs. They also assumed that the prisoners had gone since it was after their time to leave,' the inspector said.

'This all sounds very lax,' Arthur commented. 'No wonder London is concerned that something this serious has occurred so early in this trial of use of enemy labour.'

Jane noticed the inspector's already ruddy cheeks turn a shade darker at Arthur's remark.

'Russo and Gambini were trusted prisoners. They had been assigned to work at Mr Briggs's farm since they arrived at Finehaven.' The inspector sounded a little put out.

'That's as maybe, but it still begs the question about why Russo was discovered naked and dead on the beach.' Jane wasn't prepared to put up with any nonsense in the matter. 'Had he said anything to the other man, Gambini, about possibly wishing to escape?'

'Gambini said that his friend was a good swimmer, and he had said nothing about wanting to return to Italy. On the contrary, he was under the impression that Russo liked England and wished to remain here once the war had ended.' Inspector Topping once again referred to his notebook.

'There was no sign that either man was converted to the Nazi cause?' Arthur asked.

'Not according to the people in charge of the camp. It was an unusually hot day so it may well be that Russo fancied a swim to cool off before going back to the camp and got caught out by the currents.' Inspector Topping shrugged his wide shoulders.

Jane stared at him incredulously. 'Are you a local man, Inspector?' she asked.

The policeman bridled at her tone. 'Not exactly, Miss Treen, but I've lived near the coast for a good while.'

'Then you would know that you have to swim a long way out before encountering any currents here. Russo was found on the beach not long after he was reported missing. I don't believe he could have arrived there alone. You said he was near the dunes, that would be above the high-water mark. Surely it points to someone having placed him there. Were there any signs on the sands of him being dragged or any injuries that could have occurred prior to him drowning? I assume he did definitely drown?' Jane was aware her tone was sharp.

The inspector eyed her with disfavour. 'We have no reason to believe he didn't simply drown and was fetched up by a wave.'

'Then he will have a post-mortem to prove drowning? The sea would have been like a millpond that day,' Jane asked. 'Doctor Denning said he had merely confirmed the man was dead. He was not asked for a cause of death, and I believe did no more than make a very cursory examination. I presume you have your own police doctor who will have examined Russo more closely?' She strongly suspected the inspector had been intending to do none of these things. He was content to write Russo's demise off as drowning, but Jane was far from satisfied by this. It simply didn't fit the facts.

'Are you requesting a post-mortem?' the inspector asked. His expression and tone suggested that he thought Jane had lost her mind for making so much fuss over a prisoner.

'Yes, we are. My department wishes this matter to be fully investigated. I would be surprised if the coroner were not of the same mind since Russo was under the protection of the government at the time of his death.' Jane fixed the inspector with a steely gaze.

'Very good, Miss Treen. I expect it will only confirm what we already know but if London wants a post-mortem...' the inspector muttered unhappily.

'London does,' Jane said firmly. 'We shall also need to speak to this Matteo Gambini and to Mr Briggs and the land girls. I expect you can make arrangements for this?'

Out of the corner of her eye she saw Arthur give a small nod of approval at her demands.

'I'll pass the message on, Miss Treen. Will there be anything else?' Inspector Topping had closed his notebook. It seemed to Jane that he was preparing to leave.

'There is the second matter that my department is very concerned about. Mr Wood's reports indicate a very high level of black market activity in the area by what seems to be a well-organised gang. What can you tell us about the matter?' Jane asked.

'Mr Wood is somewhat prone to exaggeration in my opinion, Miss Treen,' Inspector Topping said with an air of disdain. 'He is a most excitable gentleman. And he is Scottish.'

'So, there have not been several incidents where people have impersonated ARP wardens to steal shop loads of goods for resale on the black market, defrauding the shopkeepers?' Arthur asked.

'Well, obviously there have been a few reports, but I doubt the incidents roundabouts are much higher here than elsewhere.' Inspector Topping looked most uncomfortable. He was teetering now on the edge of his seat clearly eager to get away from their awkward questions.

'Have you had reports of these events following bombing raids by the enemy?' Jane pressed the matter.

'Like I said, Miss Treen, I'll admit that there have been a few but nothing more than in other places I don't suppose. It's a side effect of the conflict. Criminals will always find a way to turn a situation to their advantage.' Inspector Topping glared at her as if trying to provoke her into disagreeing with him.

'Whitehall does not take the same lenient view of the matter that you do, Inspector. They are extremely concerned at the level of lawlessness being reported by Mr Wood,' Arthur said.

'I don't have much manpower, Mr Cilento. These reports are happening in the aftermath of a raid. My men are out saving lives, not worrying about a few tins of corned beef or rolls of lavatory paper going astray. I have to prioritise.' Inspector Topping puffed out his chest in indignation at the inference that his area was not being policed adequately.

'But are your men on the alert for the distributors of these stolen goods? Or searching for where they may be being stored? Not to mention any descriptions of the miscreants and their vehicle or vehicles,' Jane said.

She was quite irritated by Inspector Topping. His laissez-faire approach to the seriousness of the incidents Mr Wood had reported was concerning.

'We are doing all we can, Miss Treen. My resources are extremely limited.' The inspector was clearly most unhappy that she was pressing him in this way. 'Now, if there is nothing more that I can assist you with, I need to return to my duties.'

The inspector rose and Arthur showed him out of the house. Jane thought there seemed little point in detaining him any further since he clearly had very little information to give them.

'I fear Inspector Topping will prove to be of little use to us,' Arthur remarked as he re-entered the drawing room and retook his seat.

'I think you're right,' Jane agreed. 'I can see now why Mr Wood was so frustrated.'

Arthur regarded her with a thoughtful air. 'I couldn't decide if the inspector was genuinely not particularly competent or if he was being deliberately obstructive in his responses to our questions.'

Jane could see he had the same impression of the inspector that she had. 'He appeared set on doing the bare minimum, didn't he? It will be interesting to learn what a post-mortem reveals on the chap from the prisoner of war camp.'

'Yes. I hope he arranges the interviews you requested in a timely manner too.' Arthur's tone indicated that he felt this was unlikely.

'If he drags his feet then I shall have to light a fire under him.' Jane had no intention of being messed about by Inspector

Topping. They were there to do a job and the sooner it was completed the happier she would be.

She drew out her silver cigarette case, ignoring the frown on Arthur's face. 'We could try and find the Kerrigan children. They will be out of school by now. That is, assuming that they went into school in the first place. There is a piece of common land not far from their cottage where all the children usually go. I expect they may be there.' She looked at her companion who appeared to be trying to avoid the thin plume of smoke drifting in his direction.

Arthur didn't look as if he wanted to venture outside again, but he obviously decided it might be better to get it over with and agreed to accompany her.

Half an hour later, Arthur was ensconced again inside his winter overcoat and woollen scarf ignoring the warmth of the late afternoon sunshine as he followed Jane onto the high street. He really wished she would temper her walking pace. Hurrying always made him short of breath and Jane had a habit of marching everywhere as if she were late to catch a train.

They had not gone very far when Jane took a turn beside the church and led him along a narrow lane past a few cottages to a small field surrounded by a wooden picket-style fence. In the centre of the space there were a few straggly bushes and a lone tree. The tree appeared to have some kind of home-made rope swing attached to a branch.

He could hear the sound of children's voices mingled with excited woofs, presumably from an accompanying dog. Jane took hold of one of the fence posts and tested it to ensure it was secure. Once satisfied, she hitched up her tweed skirt and clambered over the fence into the field.

The ease with which Jane shinned over the fence led

Arthur to suspect that this was something she had done many times before in her past. He followed after her, somewhat more clumsily since it had been several years since he had been forced to scramble over a fence. Berlin, before the war, if his memory served him correctly.

Jane led the way along a narrow rabbit path in a sea of tall grasses which led towards the tree and surrounding scrubby bushes. Arthur's nose twitched as he detected smoke, as if a small fire was burning somewhere up ahead.

'Halt! Who goes there?' A dirty-faced little girl with what appeared to be the remnants of a tin bucket on her head had appeared on the path barring their way. Arthur guessed she was probably aged about five or six and was brandishing a large branch almost as big as her.

'I'm looking for the boys who found the body on the beach,' Jane said.

The girl frowned as she looked Jane up and down before turning her attention to Arthur. 'What about him?' she asked.

'He's with me,' Jane assured her.

The girl squinted at him as if assessing if he was allowed to venture further into the field. As she did so a boy, who seemed a little older, with grass stains on his shorts and his shirt untucked, appeared.

'What you doing, Cynthia?' He looked at the girl, before looking at Jane and Arthur. 'Did you ask if they were friend or foe?' he hissed in the girl's ear.

'No, Joe, I forgot. The lady says she was looking for Patrick and Davey.' The little girl's face crumpled as if she was about to cry.

'Are you from the papers? Mum said as we wasn't to talk to anyone from the papers.' The boy glared accusingly at Jane.

'No, we're not from the newspapers. We are from the government,' Jane said.

This statement drew a look of consternation from the lad while the girl continued to regard them with a stern gaze.

'Wait there.' The boy disappeared as quickly as he had appeared, leaving them with the little girl.

A tall, skinny youth of about eleven or twelve arrived, accompanied by the boy who had obviously gone to fetch him.

'Patrick Kerrigan?' Jane asked. 'I'm Jane Treen. Doctor Denning told us that you and your brother found the man on the beach and alerted the police.'

The lad looked first at Jane and then at Arthur. His clothes were cleaner but well-worn and mended and he showed signs of obviously growing out of them.

'Are you the lady that owns the big house near the church?' he asked.

'Yes. We work for the government in London and have been sent to check the security arrangements regarding the prisoners who are allowed out on day release. Part of our work means we need to ask you and your brother what you found when you noticed the body on the sands,' Jane said.

The older lad licked his lips nervously. 'I know the name Treen. There was an older man used to live in the house. He used to give us apples from his trees.'

'That was my father,' Jane said.

The boy appeared to accept this and nodded to the little girl who stepped aside.

'You may pass,' she said, her bucket hat slipping down over one eye.

CHAPTER SIX

Jane and Arthur followed the older boy along the path towards the trees. The ground rose up then fell away again as they passed through a gap between the bushes. Arthur could see the children had made a den beside a small stream. A fire burned inside a ring of stones and a group of children of varying ages watched them warily as they approached.

He guessed that few adults made their way there and the village children used this space for themselves. A makeshift den built of old packing crates topped with a sheet of rusting corrugated iron for the roof was near the tree where the rope swing was suspended.

A couple of fallen logs serving as seats were placed near the campsite. Another boy, the oldest there, stood up as they approached. Arthur guessed he must be the older of the Kerrigan boys as he bore a distinct resemblance to the lad who had brought them to the camp.

'Davey Kerrigan?' Jane extended her hand to the boy. 'I'm Jane Treen and this is my colleague, Arthur Cilento. You may remember my father, Mr Treen, he owned Ashbourne House near the church.'

The boy wiped his hand on the leg of his shorts before shaking hands with Jane and then with Arthur.

'They want to know about that Italian we found on the beach,' Patrick said.

'We've been sent by the government to look at the security of the prisoner of war camp. Any help you can give us would be much appreciated,' Jane said.

Arthur noticed that the other children had stopped paddling in the stream and had stepped out onto the grass, watching and listening.

Davey Kerrigan nodded and indicated the logs for them to take a seat. 'What do you want to know?' he asked as they sat down.

'We understand that you and your brother discovered the body just below the dunes,' Jane said.

'That's right, he was at the top, above the high-water mark.' Patrick had also perched himself on the logs.

Arthur shuffled uncomfortably on the tree trunk. 'You are certain the man was lying above the high-water mark?' he asked.

Davey nodded his head. 'Yes, sir. The sand was all trampled and the wet sand was lower down. I thought he had been dragged clear so we, Patrick and me, thought someone must have already found him.'

Jane exchanged a glance with Arthur. 'And this man had no clothes?' she asked.

Dull colour crept onto Patrick's cheeks. 'No, miss. He was lying face down on the sand. He hadn't any clothes at all. There was just a tattoo mark on his arm.'

'What time was this?' Arthur asked.

Davey scrunched up his face in thought. 'It must have been about half past four because Constable Martin complained he would be late for his tea when Patrick fetched him.'

'There was nothing else near the man? No cigarette ends or clear footprints?' Jane asked.

Arthur had noticed her looking at the floor around the bench when they had been on the path by the beach. She had clearly seen something then that was leading her to ask her questions.

Both boys shook their heads. 'Nothing, miss. The sand was soft and churned up, you know how it is. There was some marks on the damp smooth sand but they were just dents, nothing clear. We saw he was just lying there dead, and Patrick went to fetch the constable,' Davey said.

'We were worried we might get in bother for trying to get on the beach.' Patrick turned anxiously to Arthur. 'That artist woman who lives in the old cottage is always spying out of her windows to see who's down by the dunes.'

'It's quite all right. You aren't in any trouble over that,' Arthur confirmed. He saw the boys' shoulders relax a little at his reassurance. He assumed the artist woman must be the occupant of the run-down cottage he and Jane had noticed.

'What happened next?' Jane asked.

Davey frowned and scratched his tousled brown hair. 'The constable came. He was cross at first. I think he thought we were pulling his leg. When he saw the body, he sent our Patrick back again to his house to get a telephone message to the police station in the town.'

'I had to get Doctor Denning as well. Although we knew that wasn't going to do no good as the bloke was definitely dead,' Patrick said.

'I assume that the police inspector came then to investigate?' Arthur asked.

'Inspector Topping, yeah, he was the one that came,' Davey said.

'He asked us questions like you asked and then told us to clear off,' Patrick added.

'Did anyone have any idea who the man was at this time?' Jane asked.

'Me and Davey said we thought as he was from the camp. We'd seen him in the village. Him and the other one walking backwards and forwards to work at Chafford House Farm.' Patrick glanced at his brother and Arthur sensed the boy was seeking unspoken approval from the older boy to continue talking.

'This would be Mr Briggs's farm?' Arthur asked.

Patrick nodded vigorously. 'That's right.'

'We usually saw them. They used to stop by the school sometimes. The one we found on the beach, he would bring flowers for Miss Hargreaves. He used to pick them in the hedgerows,' Davey said.

Arthur saw Jane's brows rise slightly at this new piece of information.

'He liked Miss Hargreaves, he used to call her *bella*.' Cynthia, the little girl they had encountered on their way in had crept closer to the group.

'Cyn, what are you doing back here? You're supposed to be guarding the path.' Patrick rounded on the girl.

'No, wait, I would like to hear what she has to say.' Jane turned to the child who stuck her tongue out defiantly at Patrick.

'Don't pay her any attention, miss. She's probably making stuff up.' Patrick glowered at Cynthia as he spoke.

'Am not.' Cynthia folded her arms and stamped one foot down hard on the ground. 'I saw them.' The girl's lower lip wobbled.

'Please tell us what you saw and heard, Cynthia,' Arthur said.

'The Italians used to come past the school on their way to Mr Briggs's farm and the taller one used to smile and wave to Miss Hargreaves when he thought nobody was taking much notice. Then on their way home, his friend would go on ahead while the other one would give Miss Hargreaves a posy or stop to talk to her for a minute. Then he would run and catch the other one up. I was there the one day in the classroom because I'd forgotten my book, and I knew Mum would be cross, so I'd gone back inside to get them. Miss Hargreaves was talking to the man, and he kissed her and called her *bella*.'

Arthur thought Cynthia's words had a ring of truth. There was certainly no reason for the child to have invented the story. Davey had also mentioned the flowers.

'I see. Thank you, Cynthia. I think we shall have to talk to Miss Hargreaves,' Jane said.

'She won't get in trouble, will she?' Davey asked. The boy's thin face looked anxious.

'No, I'm sure it will be fine. It's just our job. We have to examine the safety of prisoners working in the community,' Arthur said. He attempted to sound calm and reassuring as he could see concerned looks on the faces of the other children. Miss Hargreaves was clearly a popular teacher.

'Thank you, you've all been very helpful,' Jane said. 'By the way, do any of you know the name of the lady who lives in the cottage overlooking the dunes?'

Several of the children shook their heads. One little lad holding a net on a pole, who had remained paddling in the stream spoke up. 'Miss Carstairs. My mum says she's an artist. Though, we know as she's really a witch.' The other children nodded in agreement.

'She has a black cat and everything,' Cynthia said.

'Thank you.' Jane rose from the log and brushed down the back of her skirt with her hand to remove any detritus that might have attached itself to her clothing.

'Is there a reward for helping?' Cynthia suddenly piped up again.

'Shut up, Cyn.' Patrick gave her a small push.

'Well, obviously assisting us is part of your patriotic duty,' Jane said. 'However, I suppose a small reward might be in order in this case.' She opened her handbag and handed a small paper twist of pear drops to Cynthia, before bestowing a few shillings to Patrick and Davey.

Cynthia's grubby face lit up at the sight of sweets and the boys happily tucked their unexpected windfalls into the pockets of their shorts.

'I don't suppose any of you have noticed any unusual activity in or near the village?' Arthur asked as he too stood ready to follow Jane out of the camp.

'What sort of activity?' Davey asked.

'Any lorries or cars that you haven't seen before or anyone using a shed or barn or derelict building to store boxes?' Arthur asked. It was something of a long shot. He knew though that children could be very observant and there was no harm in seeing if they knew anything of the black market activities.

The children looked at one another and a couple of the smaller ones shrugged their shoulders.

'Mum said there's been a few lorries going through the village at night. She thought it was probably military traffic. She heard them when she was up with the baby,' Patrick said, looking at Davey for confirmation.

'That's right. She looked out of the window but because of the blackout she couldn't see what was going on,' Davey said. 'She said as they should be more considerate of people trying to sleep.'

'Thank you. If you do hear or see something like that which you feel is unusual, come and let Miss Treen or myself know,' Arthur said.

'Will there be another reward?' Cynthia asked, her cheek bulging with a pear drop.

'Mr Cilento here will be more than happy to provide a reward for useful information.' Jane gave Arthur a sharp look as she emphasised the word useful.

Arthur raised his eyebrows at the expectation that he was

being made responsible for the distribution of rewards. Unlike Jane, he didn't make a habit of carrying sweets around. They were not that easy to obtain and the ration was not generous.

They said goodbye to the children and made their way back the way they had come. Once at the fence, Jane scrambled over it with ease. Arthur, weighed down with his heavy coat, had more of a struggle and was forced to accept assistance from Jane.

'That was a useful exercise,' Jane said once he was safely back on the path on the other side of the fence.

'Very interesting,' Arthur agreed as he brushed bits of lichen from his coat.

'It seems we have two new people we need to speak to. This Miss Carstairs who has the tenancy of the cottage closest to the dunes and, of course, Miss Hargreaves, the children's teacher.' Jane sounded thoughtful as she walked alongside Arthur on their way back to the house.

'Yes, it sounded as if there was some kind of relationship between the schoolteacher and our murdered man,' Arthur said.

He knew there was some talk about the effects of the handsome young Italian men on the women left behind while their menfolk were off fighting. In some places the prisoners were avoided and any talk of fraternisation discouraged. Here though, it seemed that this was not the case and the arrangements for the prisoners to have day release for labouring had been going well.

They were soon back at the house and Benson opened the front door as they approached.

'A gentleman telephoned, Miss Jane, while you were out. A Captain Prudhoe, he is in charge of the prisoner of war camp. He said he had received instructions from London and his commanding officer that he was to contact you,' Benson said as he took Arthur's hat and coat to hang in the cloakroom.

'Thank you, Benson. Did you take his details?' Jane asked.

'I've placed them on the desk in the study, miss,' Benson assured her.

She murmured her thanks and went off presumably to return the camp commander's telephone call.

'Was your afternoon productive, sir?' Benson enquired discreetly.

Arthur provided his manservant with a precis of the information the children had given them. He also made sure Benson was aware of everything Inspector Topping and Mr Wood had said that might be relevant to the enquiries they had been tasked with.

'Most useful then, sir. I shall endeavour to find out more in the village tomorrow about Miss Carstairs and Miss Hargreaves.'

'Thank you, Benson, that would be very helpful. I know Jane has lived in the village and knows some of the people, but both those ladies I think have moved here recently so we don't know much about their backgrounds,' Arthur said. 'Oh, and if you could procure some sweets, I would be much obliged. Jane seems to feel they are useful when extracting information from the local children.'

'Very good, sir.' Benson bowed his head in agreement without any expression of surprise at the request and glided off towards the kitchen to prepare a tray of coffee.

* * *

Jane picked up the telephone and connected to the exchange before requesting the camp number. After a moment she heard a tinny voice inform her she was connected before the call was answered by Captain Prudhoe.

'Jane Treen, sir, returning your call. I believe Brigadier Remmington-Blythe has asked you to contact me regarding the regrettable death of one of your prisoners.' Jane automatically assumed the clipped, efficient tone she kept for dealing with anyone from the military.

'That's correct, Miss Treen. He said your department had some questions and that you had been asked to inspect the camp.' Captain Prudhoe sounded unhappy at this direction from Whitehall.

'Yes, sir. It's just a formality really. You know what the top brass are like. They get the wind-up over all sorts of things. May we call on you tomorrow morning? It will be myself and Mr Cilento, who also works for the department.' Jane hoped it was clear that her question was more of an instruction.

'Yes, I suppose so. Ten o'clock suit you both?' Captain Prudhoe seemed resigned.

'Marvellous, we don't want to be in your hair for too long,' Jane agreed and with the arrangements made she put down the receiver but not before she was sure she had heard another faint click on the line.

Someone at the exchange had been listening in to the conversation. This was not unusual these days and was why she was always careful when speaking on the telephone. It was all too easy for someone to listen in to the call.

She made her way back to the drawing room to inform Arthur of their plans. Benson had thoughtfully produced a most welcome tray of coffee, much to Jane's relief.

'Captain Prudhoe is expecting us at ten o'clock tomorrow morning,' Jane said as she sank down on the sofa.

'Splendid.' Arthur accepted a cup of coffee from Benson.

'I assume Arthur has informed you of everything we have discovered so far?' Jane asked as the manservant poured another cup and passed it across to her.

'Yes, Miss Jane. It sounded as if your discussion with the children was very productive,' Benson replied.

'Benson has said that he will see what he can discover

tomorrow in the village about Miss Carstairs and Miss Hargreaves,' Arthur said.

'Good idea.' Jane took a sip of coffee. 'I was thinking it might be an idea to organise a small evening party. Perhaps invite Doctor Denning, Mr Briggs, the vicar and his wife, Miss Hargreaves and Miss Carstairs, perhaps, and a few more people. Just sherry and a few nibbles?'

'Very good, Miss Jane. Do you wish me to liaise with Mrs Dawes to organise things?' Benson asked.

'Yes, please. It might be a good way just to chat to people and see what we can find out informally. People tend to be more forthcoming in social situations.' Jane looked at Arthur, who appeared to have drifted off into a world of his own once more.

'What? Oh yes, good thinking.' He seemed to realise that some kind of response was required from him.

'Perhaps tomorrow evening. Seven 'til nine? That shouldn't be too dark for people to find their way home again,' Jane suggested.

'No absolutely,' Arthur agreed.

'Very good, Miss Jane.' Benson bowed his head and disappeared off, presumably to discuss the matter with Mrs Dawes.

'You seem very thoughtful, Arthur.' Jane gave him a sharp look over the brim of her cup.

'I was just thinking about what the children said about the dead man and Miss Hargreaves. His death could have been caused by someone in the village who was jealous of their relationship, perhaps.'

'It's possible but until Inspector Topping pulls his finger out, we won't know for certain how he died. We can assume there were no obvious injuries or Doctor Denning would have said so.' Jane frowned into the remnants of her coffee.

'True, we don't know the exact cause of his death, but he didn't arrive above the high-water mark on his own. Someone presumably dragged him up the beach from the sea,' Arthur said.

'What baffles me too is why was he naked?' Jane set her cup and saucer back down on the tray.

'To delay identification? Or to give the impression that he was attempting to return across the channel?' Arthur suggested.

'It doesn't feel right though, does it?' Jane said. 'And that tattoo on his arm. Have you had any further thoughts on the matter?'

'I have been trying to recall where I have seen those kinds of markings before. The rose itself is of no great note. It's those small blue circles that form the pattern around it that I think have significance,' Arthur said.

'I wonder if any of the other prisoners in the camp have similar tattoos?' Jane asked.

'That may be a question for Captain Prudhoe tomorrow. I'm sure they list such identifying marks in the records when they take the details of the prisoners,' Arthur said.

Jane hoped he was right. It was becoming very clear that Antonio Russo's death was not an accident.

CHAPTER SEVEN

The following morning dawned grey and gloomy with thick cloud and lowering skies. It looked as if they were likely to get a shower of rain later in the day Arthur thought. He took his time as usual cutting up his toast and neatly removing the top from his boiled egg.

He wondered how they were going to get to the POW camp. The map he had consulted had indicated it was at least two miles from the village. He had no desire to accompany Jane on yet another of her route marches through drizzle to interrogate the camp captain and the Italian prisoners.

Jane had not yet come into the dining room, which was most unlike her as she was usually very punctual.

'I say, Benson, have you seen Jane yet this morning?' he asked when his manservant entered the room with a pot of tea.

'I believe Miss Jane is in the study, sir. A telephone call from London,' Benson said as he deposited the chrome-plated teapot in front of Arthur.

'Whitehall?' Arthur asked.

'I think I heard the brigadier, sir.' Benson had a slight smile as he spoke.

The brigadier was well known for his tendency to bellow down the telephone deafening any poor soul on the other end. He expected the brigadier was obtaining an update on their progress. No doubt Jane would pass on anything she had learned when she came to join him at the breakfast table.

Benson withdrew back to the kitchen, presumably to make Jane's coffee. After a moment Jane herself came to join him, taking her place at the table. She peered hopefully at the half-empty chrome toast rack.

'Sorry, I'm late. The brigadier called to see how we were getting on. I've told him everything we've learned so far and our plans for today.' Jane reached for the toast and sighed at the somewhat sad sight of the so-called margarine that now graced the table instead of butter.

Benson returned bearing a tall, slim chrome coffee pot which matched the teapot that was already on the table.

'Oh, thank you, Benson.' Jane's spirits seemed to lift at the sight of the coffee pot.

'How are we to get to the camp this morning?' Arthur was aware there was a slightly querulous note to his voice.

Jane's immaculately arched brows lifted lightly as she poured her beverage. 'I don't suppose you feel up to walking? It is only a mile or so away.' As she spoke a gust of wind spattered rain against the window.

'I rather fear the weather has become somewhat inclement this morning, miss,' Benson interjected.

'Well, I have a couple of bicycles in the garage,' Jane mused. 'They were mine and my father's.'

The corners of her mouth tilted upwards at the appalled look Arthur gave her and he was glad she found his reaction amusing. 'I don't think so, Jane,' he said stiffly.

'Very well, we'll take the car,' she relented with a smile. 'I won't make you suffer.'

'You have a car? Can you drive?' Arthur asked. He wished

he had known she had a car before. It would have saved him the ordeal of the march to the beach.

'It was my father's car, and of course I can drive. I think there should be enough petrol since we are not going far.' Jane sounded rather offended that he seemed to believe her incapable of driving.

After breakfast they left Benson to continue making arrangements with Mrs Dawes for the evening's supper party. Jane had gone out to the large red-brick garage situated further along the lane at the rear of the garden to bring the car around to the front of the house.

Arthur hoped it would start. It had sounded as if, following her father's death, Jane had simply parked his car in the garage and left it. The tyres could be rotted or anything he supposed in that time.

He dressed with his usual caution and waited in the hall for Jane to fetch the car around. A moment or two later he heard the purr of an engine, and a rather splendid dark-grey Rolls Royce stopped at the front of the house. An impatient toot of the horn made him realise that this must be Jane's father's car.

He hurried out and climbed into the passenger seat. 'This is jolly nice,' he remarked appreciatively.

'My father was very fond of his motors. They all had names. This one was called Cilla,' Jane said as she turned the car around and they set off on the road out of the village towards the camp.

'Why Cilla?' Arthur couldn't quite grasp the logic of naming inanimate objects, although he was aware that it was something some people did.

'He said she reminded him of his late aunt,' Jane explained as she changed up a gear and sped along the lane.

Arthur gave up. It was clear he was not going to be able to follow Jane's father's thought process with any success. Plus, he was rather perturbed by Jane's driving abilities.

'Should we be going this quickly?' he asked as she took a corner very fast, causing him to lean towards the window.

Jane just gave him a look and he regretted saying anything if it meant she was taking her attention from the road.

'Here is the camp,' Jane said as they approached a small, white-painted sign buried in the hedge. She took the turn, and Arthur saw the camp spread out on a field before them. A tall wire fence topped with coils of razor wire surrounded a group of six dark-green wooden huts. A gatehouse with a barrier guarded by a uniformed soldier was at the entrance. He noticed a few prisoners in their uniforms walking around the huts despite the drizzle.

Jane pulled her car to a halt near the gatehouse and jumped out to go and speak to the guard. Arthur reluctantly followed her when she beckoned impatiently to him to come and join her.

The guard was speaking to someone via the telephone inside his hut. Apparently satisfied with the response he set the receiver down and a tall man in a captain's uniform emerged from a nearby hut and came over to the barrier to greet them.

'Miss Treen, Mr Cilento? I'm Captain Prudhoe, do come through to my office. The weather has taken a bit of a turn this morning, hasn't it? Still, I believe it's set to improve again this afternoon.' Captain Prudhoe shook their hands before escorting them to a nearby hut. He was probably slightly younger than Arthur and Jane. Late twenties, Arthur thought at a guess.

The hut was dry at least and furnished with a desk, some chairs, several filing cabinets and a tray with tea-making equipment next to a small spirit stove.

Captain Prudhoe urged them to make themselves comfortable while he set about making a pot of tea.

Once they were settled on the wooden chairs and tea had been distributed, the captain seated himself behind his desk. 'Now, how can I assist you both? Miss Treen, you said that obviously the death of one of our prisoners, Antonio Russo, had caused some alarm in Whitehall.' He looked at Jane.

'That's correct. My superior, Brigadier Remmington-Blythe, has taxed us with investigating the circumstances behind this man's death. As you may be aware the use of prisoners to fill the labour gap on farms has not been met with universal approval despite the need. There are always those who are worried that it may be detrimental to our security. This unfortunate incident has caused some consternation in Whitehall,' Jane said.

Captain Prudhoe surveyed her levelly. 'I can understand some of their concerns. The prisoners here, however, are mainly Italian conscripts. We opened at the end of June to receive inmates. They are all classed as being very low risk and do not appear to have bought into Nazi ideology. Most of them were previously farm labourers or manual workers.'

'Antonio Russo and the other prisoner, Matteo Gambini, they had both been approved to work on Mr Briggs's farm by the local panel?' Jane asked.

'Yes, we have several prisoners who have been selected and approved to assist locally on various farms. It's something of a trial at present. We are one of a few locally participating in the scheme and it's been going well. Gambini and Russo had been going to Briggs's farm for three months. Reports were good on their work, and they were trusted to make their own way there and back without incident,' Captain Prudhoe said. 'My manpower is limited, and neither the farms nor the Home Guard have anyone to spare as escorts. We escort them for the first month and if all goes well the prisoners make their own way to and from the farms. Briggs himself is a former soldier. We obviously have tight time frames for them to clock in and out. We are not so lax that they can do exactly as they please. My commanding officer, Lieutenant Colonel Wicke, has approved the arrangements. He is in overall charge of the camps in this area.'

'I am pleased to hear it. So all was going well you said, until this incident,' Arthur commented.

A dark-red flush tinged the youthful captain's cheeks. 'Until this incident, yes,' he agreed.

'When was it noted that Russo was missing?' Jane asked.

Arthur guessed she wanted to confirm the details they had already gleaned from various sources.

'Gambini raised the alarm at the gatehouse when he arrived back at camp and learned his companion had not arrived. He had believed Russo had gone on ahead of him. Gambini was not late back, but because he appeared certain that Russo had set off before him the guard informed me straight away.' Captain Prudhoe looked a little uncomfortable.

'What happened then?' Arthur asked.

'We questioned Gambini and sent a soldier out to the farm to question the land girls and Mr Briggs. It was confirmed that Russo had indeed left the farm before Gambini. Therefore, he was officially declared missing, and a search started,' the captain said. 'I assure you that no time was lost.'

'And in the meantime, the boys had discovered Russo's naked body above the high-water mark on the beach near the dunes,' Jane said.

'I was not made aware of his exact position on the beach.' Captain Prudhoe looked first at Jane and then at Arthur as the implications of her words hit him. 'Are you inferring that Russo didn't drown accidentally?'

'We have asked Inspector Topping to ensure an autopsy is carried out. Certainly, he didn't get above the high-water mark on his own so yes, there are questions to be answered about this prisoner's death. Where did he go and why? Who did he meet and why? Why was he left naked? Where are his clothes?' Jane ticked all the questions off on her slim, elegant fingers as she spoke.

Arthur thought Captain Prudhoe looked rather as if

someone had just pulled the pin from a grenade right in front of him.

'I see, well yes, it seems your report will be quite wide-ranging. I sincerely hope you will not discover any evidence of misdemeanours on the part of the camp.' The captain appeared most uncomfortable.

'I'm sure your paperwork will prove to be exemplary,' Arthur said in a conciliatory tone. 'One thing that I am curious about is the tattoo Russo had on his upper left arm. It seems quite unusual, a rose surrounded by a series of small dots in a specific shape. Do you keep records for your prisoners that make a note of such markings?'

Captain Prudhoe blinked. 'Well, yes, as a matter of fact we do. I feel it is important should a prisoner try to disguise themselves in an attempt to escape. Records of things like birth defects, curious body markings and tattoos could be invaluable in proving identity.'

Arthur was relieved the camp had implemented such a system of record-keeping. 'Excellent, may I look through the prisoner records, including the ones for Russo and Gambini?'

'Certainly.' The captain stood and crossed over to the small green bank of metal filing cabinets. 'They are all here in alphabetical order. Russo's file is separate at the back of the last cabinet where we keep those of deceased prisoners.'

Arthur rose and joined the captain at the filing cabinet where Captain Prudhoe showed him his system.

'Do you know offhand of any other prisoner here having a similar marking on his arm to the one Russo had?' Arthur asked as he began to methodically flick through the files looking for the information he wanted. He started with the file belonging to the dead man.

'I can't be certain, but I believe Gambini has a similar tattoo. They were from the same area of Italy, I believe.' The captain returned to his seat behind his desk.

'I see, thank you.' Arthur wished he could work out the significance of the tattoo. It was niggling at the back of his mind. Something he had encountered before somewhere before the war, a few years ago. Naples, perhaps, or Rome. He knew tattoos were common amongst sailors but this didn't apply to the two Italians.

'How were Russo and Gambini allocated to Mr Briggs's farm?' Jane asked.

Arthur was only listening with half an ear, he was much more interested in what he might discover in the files. He assumed either Jane or the captain or both of them had lit cigarettes since he could smell the smoke in the air.

'Several local landowners had submitted a case for using prisoners as extra labour. A local committee was set up to decide on the matter. You know, if the need was really there, the security and the suitability of available prisoners. Mr Briggs is a local magistrate with a sizeable acreage. He employed several labourers before the war and although he has land girls, there are some jobs that are more difficult physically for them to carry out. He had also recently lost a land girl in June,' Captain Prudhoe explained.

Arthur finished with Russo's file, having committed it to memory, and then looked at Gambini's folder.

'Why those two prisoners? Was it a random allocation?' Jane asked as she continued with the interview.

'I believe so. We had a pool of suitable men. They had to be physically fit, have experience in farm work and have a good grasp of English. They also had to put themselves forward for the task,' the captain said. 'Oh, and we only use men who are well behaved in camp. No history of violence, that kind of thing.'

Arthur read through Gambini's file. The man was from the same town as Russo so he may well have known him before they enlisted. They could even have enlisted at the same time since they were in the same regiment.

This was not unusual. It was the same with many of the English regiments where whole workplaces had joined up at the same time. He looked at Gambini's physical characteristics. Like Russo he had a background in farm work. He had brown eyes and hair, olive complexion and a small scar near his upper lip.

He also had a tattoo on his left upper arm. The hairs in the nape of Arthur's neck prickled. The description sounded the same as that of Russo. A rose surrounded by a group of dots in a pattern. This was not a coincidence. That tattoo had a meaning.

'Russo and Gambini both speak good English?' Jane confirmed.

'Yes, quite good. It was thought necessary since they would have to understand and follow the instructions they received from the farmer and the girls they were working alongside,' Captain Prudhoe explained. 'As I explained, for the first month they were escorted there and back and closely supervised whilst working. It was made clear that they would be recalled and confined to camp should anything untoward be reported to me.'

'I presume there were no issues reported with either man?' Jane asked.

'No, no concerns at all. Like I said, neither I nor the farms have manpower to spare for extended escort duties. We used to drive the men around dropping them off and picking them up at the various farms. I must emphasise, however, that the men at this camp are classed as very low risk, and my staff levels have been reduced.'

Arthur had begun to work through the other files. He paid particular attention to any other prisoners from the same area of Italy and any that might bear similar markings.

'Were Gambini and Russo particular friends, do you know, before they started working together at the farm?' Jane asked.

'I think so. They certainly always appeared to get on well together. Russo was generally well liked amongst the prisoners. There were no reports of any arguments and disagreements,' Captain Prudhoe said.

'And Gambini? Is he also as well liked?' Jane asked.

There was a slight pause. Arthur glanced up from his perusal of the files to see the captain scratching his chin. 'No, I don't think he is as well regarded. There have been a few minor altercations. Nothing serious obviously or his placement on the farm would have been revoked. But there have been several heated arguments.'

'Any recently? Or any between him and Russo?' Jane continued as Arthur returned his attention to the files.

'Not that I'm aware of. There has been nothing reported in the camp logs,' Captain Prudhoe said.

Jane's chair scraped on the brown lino-covered floor as she adjusted her position. 'Do the prisoners have much contact with the villagers? Socially, I mean?' she asked.

Arthur had finished looking through the first drawer and turned his attention to the second cabinet of files.

'We do encourage integration as much as possible. We find it helps to reduce hostility and benefits our prisoners' well-being. The prisoners have been escorted to events such as the harvest festival a few weeks ago. They have also undertaken work to benefit the village as a whole like scything the grass in the churchyard, that kind of thing. All under escort obviously as a small work party.' Captain Prudhoe sounded as if he were quite proud of the programme he had set up.

'Does your set-up include things like English lessons?' Jane asked.

'We have had some English lessons in the camp, yes. Miss Hargreaves, the school mistress, has very generously given up some of her Saturday mornings to spend an hour teaching the prisoners the basics.'

Arthur's ears pricked up at this and he guessed Jane's would have too.

'That's very kind of her.' Jane sounded non-committal in her response. 'Arthur, how are you doing with those files? Do you require my assistance?'

'Almost done,' Arthur assured her. He had no wish for Jane to start poking through the folders. She would upset his method and order. Plus, she wouldn't really know what he had been looking for and Arthur didn't wish to spell that out to the captain.

'Jolly good. Then I think when Arthur has finished we need to speak to Gambini,' Jane said to the captain.

'Yes, of course. He has been confined to camp since the incident. I can arrange to have him brought over here for you to see him when you are ready.' Captain Prudhoe sounded a little relieved that his own period of interrogation seemed to be coming to an end.

Arthur worked his way through the remaining files while Captain Prudhoe used his telephone to request that one of the camp guards bring Gambini in to be questioned. He discovered four more men from the same town as Gambini and Russo, but none of them had any mention of a tattoo in their characteristics.

He closed the files and joined Jane. She had acquired another chair and had repositioned the seats she and Arthur had been using so they faced away from the desk and towards the vacant chair, which he assumed was for Gambini.

CHAPTER EIGHT

Jane squared her narrow shoulders and prepared herself mentally ready to question the Italian prisoner. Arthur had finished with the files and had come to stand beside her. She guessed that he would share anything useful that he had discovered later when they were back at the house.

Outside she heard the rhythmic crunch of boots on gravel before there was a sharp rap on the door of the hut and the captain gave the order for Gambini and his soldier escort to enter. The Italian prisoner was a wiry man, in his late twenties, with dark-brown hair and eyes and a thin scar near his lip.

The escort saluted Captain Prudhoe and stepped back.

'Signore Gambini, please take a seat.' Jane indicated the chair she had placed opposite the ones she had prepared for herself and Arthur. Captain Prudhoe had seated himself behind his desk.

Once Gambini was seated, Jane and Arthur took their own places. The prisoner had a wary, worried look in his brown eyes.

'My name is Jane Treen and this is my colleague, Arthur Cilento. We have been tasked with investigating the death of your comrade, Signore Russo.'

The wary expression was replaced by a spark of curiosity as Gambini looked at them.

'We know that you have already given a statement to the police and have co-operated with Captain Prudhoe in this matter, but we would like you to go through the events of that day once again for us, please.' Jane had taken a small leather-bound notebook from her bag, and a pencil, so she could make notes of anything that she felt stood out.

Gambini looked at the captain and then back to Jane. 'Everything was as usual. We make our way to the farm, and we see the land girls. We have our instructions for the day. I go with one party and Antonio, he go with the others.' His English was heavily accented but clear.

'And was this often how your work was arranged?' Jane asked.

'Si, sometimes we are altogether, other times we are apart. There is much work to do and we help with the heavy lifting or the skilled work. Antonio and me we worked at home on our family farms,' Gambini explained.

'Thank you. Did you see your friend again that day?' Jane asked.

The prisoner nodded. 'Si, we all eat together at the lunchtime. It is a hot day so one of the girls has fetched a jug of cold fruit drink from the farmhouse and we sit in the shade to eat.'

'Your comrade was his usual self at this time? He wasn't anxious or acting unusually?' Arthur asked.

'No, everything was as always.' Gambini relaxed a little in his chair, slouching slightly.

'And after lunch was finished?' Jane asked.

Gambini gave a small shrug. 'We return to our work. I tell Antonio I meet him at the gate to go back later. He say yes and we go our different ways. When we finish, I go to the gate and wait for him. The girls they have all gone back to the farmhouse for a drink before they do the evening work. I see the girls Antonio was with, and they say he has already finished.'

'I see. This was when you first thought something might be wrong?' Jane looked at the prisoner.

He shifted in his chair, shuffling to sit a little more upright. Jane was aware of Captain Prudhoe also moving slightly in his seat.

'I think he is held up, so I wait but he does not come and then I think perhaps he has thought I did not wait for him and has gone on ahead. I don't know what to do so I think I go back to camp. If he is there all is good. If he is not, then maybe he will arrive after me. We have set times to be back, if not we are in trouble,' Gambini explained.

Jane could see how the events of the afternoon had unfolded. 'This was presumably when the alarm was raised, and action taken to search for Russo?' She turned her head to look at Captain Prudhoe for confirmation, although they had already been told this was what had happened.

'Indeed,' the captain said.

'You and Russo are both from the same town in Italy, I believe?' Arthur asked the prisoner.

Jane sat back and watched as Arthur now took the lead questioning the Italian. She assumed his enquiries would be based on whatever he had discovered from the files.

'Si, that is correct.' Gambini's body had stiffened, and his eyes had that wary expression once more.

'You were in the same regiment, as are some of the other men held here. Did you know each other before you enlisted?' Arthur asked.

'Antonio's family are from my village so yes, I knew him.' Gambini attempted to sound offhand.

'Were you friends before joining the army? Or did you have family connections?' Arthur's tone was soft, almost casual.

'Where we are from most of us are related in the past someway. It is a small place, and our roots are deep.' Gambini too seemed to be trying to downplay his response.

Jane could feel there was an odd tension in the air though between the two men. It was almost like two chess players, each trying to work out their opponent's moves in order to avoid defeat.

'And you both have another connection to each other, don't you?' Arthur looked directly at Gambini.

Jane's breath hitched in her throat as she waited for the prisoner's response. Gambini didn't answer. Instead, he stared at Arthur as if intending to intimidate him into backing down and asking another question instead.

'Please answer the question.' There was an unexpected thread of steel in Arthur's usual mild tone.

The corner of Gambini's lip curled up. 'You seem to know the answer already,' he said.

'Yes, I do, and unless you want to be charged with the murder of your comrade, I suggest you start to talk.' Arthur met the Italian's gaze head-on.

The soldier standing behind Gambini's chair shuffled his boots uneasily on the lino.

The two men continued to stare at each other without blinking, until finally Gambini dropped his gaze.

'I'm waiting,' Arthur said.

Jane was aware of Captain Prudhoe moving on his chair, as if about to intervene, and she held up her hand in a gesture to prevent him from speaking.

'Russo and I were both members of the same club,' Gambini said.

'Club is an interesting way to describe the group you were both part of. I've seen the tattoo you and Russo bear before. It has taken me a while to remember where I last saw it. It was some years ago in Rome,' Arthur said.

Gambini was completely still now. He raised his head to look at Arthur once more.

'It was during a trial, a rather notorious murder trial. There were several men in the dock. They all bore markings like the one you and Russo have on your left arms.' Arthur met Gambini's stare once more.

Jane noticed that Gambini's hands were gripping the wooden arms on the side of his chair. The knuckles showing white through the naturally olive tan of his skin.

'I don't know about that.' Gambini's jaw was tight, and he ground the reply out between his teeth.

'The tattoo you and Russo share is the mark of membership of a particular organisation. The rose is the sign of membership and the number and placement of the circles around it signifies your position within the organisation,' Arthur continued.

Jane had to hand it to Arthur, his memory was quite remarkable.

'I have nothing to say. I wish to go back to my hut.' Gambini made as if to stand.

A hand on his shoulder from the armed guard behind him compelled him to remain in his seat.

'You will stay and answer Mr Cilento's questions. You are in no position to demand anything,' Captain Prudhoe said. 'Mr Cilento is correct. You may find yourself facing a noose if you do not tell the truth. If you are a member of such a secret organisation and that membership is a factor in Russo's death, then you are in a very grave situation.'

'Thank you, Captain.' Arthur inclined his head towards the camp commander.

'I have said to you the truth and all that I know. Now you are saying that Antonio was murdered and that I am involved. I was told he had drowned, even though I knew him to swim like a fish.' Words exploded from Gambini.

'You suspected he had been murdered all along though,

didn't you? Right from when he went missing, even before he turned up on the beach?' Jane was certain she was right. She could tell from the prisoner's body language. Was Gambini Antonio's killer? Was his death to do with this crime organisation the men both seemed to belong to?

'I knew when they said he had drowned something bad had happened to him. That is all I knew,' Gambini said.

'And did you think his death might be connected to the mark you both bear?' Arthur asked.

Gambini's lips clamped shut and he gave a slight shake of his head.

Jane couldn't decide if this sudden silence was due to fear, lack of knowledge or something darker. It was clear that there would be little more to obtain on the subject of the tattoos or the murder. She tried a different line.

'Did your friend have any contacts in the village? Anyone he enjoyed speaking to?' she asked.

Gambini wiped the palms of his hands on his thighs as if he were sweating. 'We spoke to many people if they were nice to us. Some of them were not nice. They spit as we go past on our way to work or throw stones.'

'But there was one person Antonio liked to talk to, wasn't there? He had an affection for her?' Jane chose her words carefully.

She could see Captain Prudhoe paying close attention to her question.

Gambini shifted again in his seat, and she sensed his reluctance to respond.

'Miss Hargreaves was helpful in assisting you with improving your English?' she said.

Gambini slumped forward and closed his eyes momentarily. 'Si, Antonio, he liked her. He would take her a flower sometimes to thank her for her kindness. She was kind to him. He wanted to stay in England.'

'Thank you.' Jane looked at Arthur and he gave a tiny shake of his head.

'We have no further questions at this point, Captain. Although we may need to question Mr Gambini again if we uncover more information,' Jane addressed the camp commander.

Captain Prudhoe gave the order, and the escort marched the prisoner back out of the hut.

'I hope that exercise was helpful to you, Miss Treen?' Captain Prudhoe said as Jane gathered her brown leather handbag ready to depart.

'It was very helpful, thank you, Captain. By the bye, I am holding a small soirée at my house this evening if you would care to drop in, and do please bring a companion if you wish. It's just a few drinks and nibbles.' Jane extended the invitation as she wished to keep the youthful captain onside.

'Thank you, that sounds jolly nice.' Captain Prudhoe's face brightened.

Jane gave him her address and the time before he walked her and Arthur back to the gatehouse.

'I shall look forward to seeing you this evening.' She gave him a bright smile as they were allowed to exit through the barrier and got back into the car.

Arthur had been fairly quiet throughout their exit, and he settled into the passenger seat staring out miserably at the still grey, damp morning.

'Are you all right, Arthur?' Jane asked as she started up the engine.

'Perfectly. I am annoyed that I didn't recall where I had seen that tattoo before sooner. It concerns me when that happens.' He sounded sulky.

Jane's nose wrinkled as she crunched her way into gear and pulled away from the gatehouse.

'This tattoo business, do you think it may be significant to our case?' she asked, changing up the box as she spoke. She ignored Arthur's sharp intake of breath as she squeezed the car through a narrow space between a stone wall and an approaching vegetable lorry.

'I don't know. Gambini was not keen to talk about it, was he? Which is not surprising. I believe the gang concerned, like many similar criminal organisations, has a code of silence. Tattoos have been around for years, more common amongst seafaring men but some of these gangs use them as a mark of membership. It may be that Russo's death is down to a falling out between gang members.' Arthur clung on to his seat as they sped along towards the village centre.

'Hmm, it's all rather interesting, isn't it?' Jane said as she swung the car up the side of the house. 'Jump out here, Arthur, and I'll go and put the car away. I expect it's almost time for lunch and we can see how Benson has got on with the arrangements for tonight.' She pulled up the brake, causing the car to jerk to a sudden halt.

Arthur threw her a dark look and exited the car with what she considered to be unseemly haste. Jane put the car in the garage and padlocked the door shut as she left. She had no wish for anyone to siphon off her precious petrol or discover the small stash of fuel her father had kept in the garage.

She opened the back door into the house, passing through the scullery and the kitchen. Mrs Dawes was hard at work and Jane could hear her singing one of the new popular songs as she prepared the lunch.

Marmaduke was safely asleep on an old, crocheted blanket at the side of the range. Jane smiled happily at seeing him so settled as she hurried through to hang her raincoat in the hall. Despite her initial misgivings at returning to the house that meant so much to her, she was now feeling much more positive about being there.

Arthur had hung up his things and was seated in the chair

he had taken a shine to beside the fireplace. Benson had lit a fire there earlier in the morning and the room was pleasantly warm. The recent spell of unusually clement weather belied the late time of year.

Jane took a seat opposite and watched as Arthur diligently made notes in his book.

'Mrs Dawes was straining the potatoes when I came in so I expect lunch will be ready in a tick.' Jane took out her cigarettes and lit one while Arthur completed his writing.

Arthur grunted an acknowledgement.

Benson appeared in the room in his usual silent way. 'Luncheon is ready, Miss Jane,' he announced.

Jane wished he would call her just by her first name, but Arthur assured her that Benson was a stickler for formality. It had been a battle to get him to address her as Miss Jane and not Miss Treen.

'Thank you. Did you manage to issue invitations for tonight?' she asked.

'Yes, miss, all gratefully accepted,' Benson said as she finished her cigarette and stubbed it out in the ashtray, before standing to go to the dining room.

'Jolly good. We have also invited Captain Prudhoe and a companion to attend too,' Jane said as Arthur reluctantly set aside his notes, ready to join her.

'Very good, miss.' Benson stood aside to allow them to pass into the hall. 'By the way, Inspector Topping has telephoned to confirm that he has arranged an autopsy with the coroner for the deceased prisoner.'

Jane gave a small smile of satisfaction as she took her seat at the dining table. Perhaps an autopsy might give them a few more answers.

CHAPTER NINE

Arthur stood near the piano as Jane circulated the room greeting her guests. The earlier rain had died down during the afternoon leaving behind a breezy but dry evening. The curtains were drawn early to comply with the blackout and the green-silk shaded Chinese lamps cast a pleasant glow around the room. Benson, dressed in black tie, offered the guests canapés from a silver platter.

Captain Prudhoe, pink-cheeked with pleasure at inclusion in the evening, had arrived with a charming young lady wearing a blue-spotted frock. Doctor Denning was talking to the vicar and his wife. Jane had decided against inviting Mr Wood and Inspector Topping, fearing it might spoil the social ambience she had wished to create. Arthur had understood her reasoning and agreed. When people were more relaxed, they tended to be more forthcoming.

A pretty, dark-haired young woman in a pale-yellow dress had just entered the room and was shaking Jane's hand. Jane offered the girl a drink and brought her over to make introductions.

'Arthur, may I present Miss Katie Hargreaves, the village

schoolteacher. This is my colleague, Arthur Cilento.' Jane raised one neatly pencilled eyebrow as if to warn him to engage socially. He rather resented the implication behind her gesture.

'It's very nice to meet you. Jane tells me you have only recently come into post at the school.' Arthur shifted his weight from one foot to the other and wished his evening shoes, polished to a nice shine by Benson, would stop pinching.

'Oh, it's not so recent really. I've been here for a while now. I came at the start of the term in January.' Katie shook his hand.

'And how are you finding it here?' Arthur asked as Jane bobbed off to greet another newcomer.

'Well, it was all rather quiet really until we had this terrible event this week. I suppose you heard about what happened at the beach.' Katie's expression changed, and her dark-brown eyes shimmered with unshed tears.

'Yes, most distressing. I believe Captain Prudhoe said you knew the deceased man?' Arthur hoped she wasn't about to cry. He hated women crying. He never knew what he was supposed to do, and when he did do something, it was invariably the wrong thing.

Katie pulled a small white-cotton handkerchief from her belt. 'I used to teach him English, along with some of the other prisoners, of course.' She added the last part hastily as she dabbed delicately at her nose. 'He was a very sweet man.'

'He used to give you flowers, I understand,' Arthur said.

Katie's eyes widened in surprise. 'Why, whoever told you that? Yes, he did. Little posies from the hedgerows. He wanted to thank me for my help in language lessons. He hoped to stay in England after the war.' She smiled sadly.

'Did he ever mention being worried about anything or being afraid of anyone at all?' Arthur asked.

Katie shook her head. 'No, he got on well with everyone, I believe. We only ever had brief conversations though.'

'I see. Did you know his friend at all? Gambini?' Arthur asked, before taking a sip from his sherry glass.

'Only by sight, he was often with Antonio when they went back and forth to the camp. We didn't ever talk much.' She gave Arthur a brief smile before murmuring an excuse and leaving him to go and talk to Captain Prudhoe and his companion.

Arthur had little time to analyse the brief conversation before Jane was back, this time accompanied by a slightly older lady with untidy silver hair.

'Arthur, may I present Miss Alicia Carstairs, she is the artist residing in the cottage near the dunes. Alicia, my colleague, Arthur Cilento.' Jane gave him another warning look before disappearing again to talk to the vicar.

'How nice to meet you. I hope the cottage and its setting are providing good artistic inspiration?' Arthur asked as he dredged his memory to try and find some scraps of information about art that might prove useful.

Alicia was dressed in some kind of flowing chiffon dress in shades of orange and peach. Strands of amber beads were around her neck and long silver and amber earrings sparkled in her ears.

'Oh yes, I find being by the sea terribly soothing. I always lived near the sea as a child, you know. The quiet is so very welcome too.'

'I hope you were not distressed by the unfortunate incident at the beach the other day. It happened quite close to your home, I understand.' Arthur looked around for Jane, but she had disappeared.

'Oh, that poor Italian boy? Yes, it was rather awful. Such an exceptionally hot day for the time of year, one can understand the urge to cool off in the water. Of course, the sea is still frightfully cold, and I'm told one must be wary of the currents.' Alicia accepted a glass of sherry from Benson as he circulated around refreshing people's drinks.

'Do many people try to get onto the beach still? With it being closed off?' Arthur asked.

'Oh yes, courting couples do go into the dunes.' Alicia gave an unexpected wink and nudged him in his ribs with a bony elbow. 'And the children, of course.'

Arthur smiled politely and resisted the urge to rub his chest from where his companion had poked him.

'Had you ever seen any of the prisoners there before?' he asked.

'I think they are kept to quite tight schedules from what I understand,' Alicia said. 'Of course, I had been out that particular day. I had not long returned home when the alarm was raised. I'd been at the hospital. There is this problem I've been having for quite some time with my bunion. After I finally decided to see Doctor Denning, he referred me straight away and the appointment happened to be that day.'

Arthur zoned out at this point, simply nodding and murmuring whenever Alicia Carstairs paused for breath, which was not often.

Jane was back in the room. This time she was escorting a large, well-set man in his late fifties. He was well dressed and had a self-satisfied expression on his ruddy face as he approached.

'I'm so sorry to interrupt, Alicia, but I wanted Arthur to meet Mr Lloyd Briggs. Mr Briggs, this is Arthur Cilento, my colleague, and I presume you already know Miss Alicia Carstairs?' Jane asked as she performed the introductions.

'Yes, we have met before on a couple of occasions,' Alicia assured her.

Arthur surveyed Mr Briggs with interest. This was the landowner who owned Chafford House Farm where the prisoners had been working. He was also the local magistrate.

Benson proffered Mr Briggs a glass of sherry.

'Thank you.' Lloyd Briggs looked around the room with

some satisfaction as Alicia chirped on about being pleased to make his acquaintance again. 'A most charming room, Miss Treen. I have often admired this house when I've driven through the village.'

'Thank you, Mr Briggs. My family are very attached to it.' Arthur thought there was a touch of frost in Jane's reply. Not that Mr Briggs appeared aware of it.

'Are you from around here, Mr Cilento?' Miss Carstairs asked.

'No, my family home is in Devon,' Arthur replied politely.

'Ah Devon, rolling green hills and beautiful coastline. I almost chose Devon, you know, but my muse said Kent so here I am. One must follow one's artistic impulses, mustn't one?' Alicia Carstairs smiled dreamily at Arthur and Mr Briggs, leading Arthur to wonder at the strength of Jane's late father's sherry.

'I wouldn't know about artistic muses, Miss Carstairs. I'm a simple farmer.' Mr Briggs took a large gulp of the sherry in his glass.

'Oh, you are much too modest, Mr Briggs. Doctor Denning told me you were our local magistrate and that you have a fine, large farm just outside the village. Weren't you employing the prisoner who was drowned?' Jane smiled sweetly at him.

Personally, Arthur thought Jane was at her most terrifying when she was being nice to people.

'Yes, he was one of two men helping the land girls with some of the heavier tasks. Great shame, he was a good worker and had a lot of knowledge about the work that needs to be done. Got to feed people, you know, valuable war work.' Mr Briggs beamed avuncularly at them all.

'Quite. Arthur and I have been tasked by Whitehall to gather some information regarding the security of using prisoners of war for such work while we are here. Obviously, we are having a nice evening now, but maybe we could come and see you, look around the farm. Perhaps tomorrow?' Jane said.

'Of course, of course,' Lloyd Briggs agreed.

Arthur thought he appeared a little less smiley than a few minutes earlier.

'That's so kind of you. It's just a formality. You know how the top brass can be when they get a bee in their bonnet.' Jane bestowed another smile on Mr Briggs. 'We were just supposed to be taking a little holiday. Arthur's health, you know, but then they asked if we would mind just gathering a few facts for a report. You know how it is when something is a new scheme.'

'It will be my pleasure to assist you, Miss Treen. Shall we say around eleven?' Mr Briggs appeared resigned to his fate.

'Excellent, we shall look forward to it, won't we, Arthur?' Jane agreed.

'Oh yes, certainly.' Arthur hoped Jane wouldn't insist on marching him around a smelly, muddy farmyard. Especially after today's rain. Benson would not be pleased if he covered himself with mud.

'The land girls are doing such a splendid job. If I had been younger, you know, I think I should have enjoyed having a bash at it myself,' Miss Carstairs said.

'I'm sure you are making your own contribution to the war effort,' Arthur responded gallantly.

Miss Carstairs beamed. 'Oh well, one tries. I design some of the posters you see here and there. Artwork for the train stations and suchlike for official notices.'

'How very talented of you,' Jane said.

'I understand that your own dear mother is also in the arts. A famous artiste. Shall we have the pleasure of seeing her this evening?' Mr Briggs looked around as if expecting Elsa to suddenly appear from under the piano.

Jane looked discomfited by his suggestion, so Arthur quickly stepped into the breach. 'Jane's mother is the singer and actress,

Elsa Macintyre,' he explained to Alicia Carstairs who was looking puzzled.

'Yes, my mother has been working in London a lot lately. She's been very busy with radio shows and some concerts for the troops,' Jane said.

Arthur knew that Jane avoided her mother whenever possible.

'Oh, it's terribly important to keep up morale. I expect you remember that, Mr Briggs, from the Great War,' Alicia said.

Mr Briggs cleared his throat and looked a little sulky. 'I was barely in my teens then, dear lady, but yes, I agree. That's why this delightful little party is such a pleasure to attend, Miss Treen.'

Arthur suspected that Mr Briggs liked to be considered younger than his age and objected to Alicia placing him firmly on a par with herself. Benson was now handing around canapés, which were being happily accepted by the guests.

'Mrs Dawes has done a splendid job with the canapés. It's so difficult these days with the shortages. Unless, of course, one can find something, well, shall we say, that's been put away in the shops,' Jane said.

Arthur had to admire the way she was fishing for information about black market goods.

'I understand perfectly, my dear. Still, if we all continue to tighten our belts and pull together then I'm sure this conflict will be over soon,' Mr Briggs declared, accepting a tiny savoury biscuit smeared with anchovy paste.

'Yes, yes, although one does like a few treats every now and again,' Alicia said as she cradled her sherry glass.

Jane excused herself to go and circulate and Arthur swiftly extricated himself to follow her, leaving Mr Briggs to be entertained by Miss Carstairs.

'How do you think it's going so far?' Jane asked once they were a little apart from the other guests. They had placed themselves near the door to the hall as if about to fetch fresh supplies of food or drink.

'Useful, I think. At least in terms of finding out more about Russo and Gambini. I suppose we also need to try and discover anything on these black market problems,' Arthur said. 'That was very nicely done just then, by the way.'

He had just finished speaking when the doorbell sounded.

'Who is that? I thought everyone was here. I hope we don't have any lights showing, I don't want a fine,' Jane said as she went to the front door, ensuring she turned off the hall light before opening it. Arthur followed a little behind her.

'Janey, honey pie, I can't tell you how relieved I am to find you at home.' The glamorous well-dressed woman on the doorstep turned her head to call to the taxi that had dropped her off. 'It's all right, you can go now. My daughter's at home.'

The motor car drove away.

'Mother? What on earth are you doing here?' Jane asked.

Arthur came up to stand with Jane in the doorway. He could tell from her posture and the tone of her voice she was shocked and upset.

'I've been bombed out of my apartment, darling. Roof damage. It will take ages to fix. Shortage of materials and manpower apparently. Stephen had mentioned you had gone to Kent so I guessed you must be here.' Elsa fluttered her eyelashes in Arthur's direction. 'Do be an angel, sweetie pie, and bring my case inside. It's frightfully heavy.'

Arthur stepped around Jane to hoist Elsa's case into the hall.

'You can't stay here. This was Father's house,' Jane said as Elsa also stepped inside the hall and closed the front door.

'Honey, it was also my house and now it's yours. I presume my old room is available. Be a doll and pop those up to my room, why don't you.' She smiled at Arthur. 'Now then, is that the sound of a party I hear? My, my, things are looking up already.'

Elsa ignored her daughter and deposited her vanity case and sable-trimmed coat in Arthur's arms, before swishing away into the drawing room.

Arthur had seen and heard the phrase about steam coming out of a person's ears before. Now, looking at Jane, whose ears were decidedly pink, he could see where the saying had come from.

Jane remained where she was for a moment, and he could see her physically attempting to calm herself.

'Um, what do you want me to do with these?' he ventured. The vanity box and coat were surprisingly heavy.

Jane fixed him with a look that made him wish he hadn't asked. 'Personally, if you chucked them all back outside, I wouldn't care. However, since it seems my mother has invited herself to stay, I suppose you should take them upstairs. The room next to Benson's.'

Arthur set down the vanity box and took Elsa's coat to the coat stand. Jane stood rubbing her temples as the noise from the drawing room increased in volume. The sound of chatter was interspersed with bursts of laughter and the volume was increased on the gramophone.

'Are you all right, Jane?' Arthur picked up Elsa's vanity box ready to carry it upstairs.

'Do I look all right?' she snapped before sucking in a breath and slowly releasing it. 'I'm sorry, Arthur, as you can tell being in proximity with my mother tends to have this effect on me.' She glanced towards the open door to the drawing room. 'I suppose I had better go in and do some damage control before she's leading them in a conga line around the vegetable garden.'

Arthur nodded awkwardly and set off up the stairs as Jane squared her shoulders and ventured into the drawing room. He had just placed the vanity case on the bed and drawn the curtains when Benson appeared bearing Elsa's suitcase. He set it down at the foot of the bed.

'You should have called me, sir,' he said as he switched on the lamp, looking reproachfully at Arthur.

'You were already busy, and Jane's mother gave me little choice in the matter,' Arthur said.

'Miss Elsa does seem to have a somewhat forceful personality,' Benson agreed.

Arthur grinned but refrained from saying that it was clear it was one thing Jane had in common with her mother. 'Is everything going well downstairs?'

'I believe so. Miss Elsa was attempting to persuade Miss Jane to accompany her on the piano when I left the room,' Benson said.

Arthur could imagine that this was not something that Jane would appreciate. 'Have you discovered anything pertinent to our cases while you were circulating the room?' Arthur asked.

'I have heard some new names mentioned. A Herbert and Annie Simms who apparently keep a hostelry in the village, the Green Dragon public house,' Benson said.

'Oh, and what was the context?' Arthur knew Benson was very good at discovering information and extremely discerning.

'Mr Briggs and Captain Prudhoe were in conversation and Miss Hargreaves appeared uncomfortable when their names were mentioned. The captain made a joke about ensuring his off-duty soldiers did not spend too much time there,' Benson said as he moved about the room checking that all was prepared for Jane's mother's unexpected stay. 'Mr Briggs looked at Miss Hargreaves and at Miss Carstairs and said that several people enjoyed visiting the hostelry.'

Arthur raised his eyebrows. 'Implying that both ladies also spent time there?'

'It is not something that I would have thought would be considered appropriate if Miss Hargreaves did so, given her role within the village. It seemed more personal than that though. It seemed he was insinuating something slightly different,' Benson said. 'Miss Carstairs said it was a respectable public house, she appeared to be familiar with it and the occupants.'

'What do you know about the pub and the people keeping it?' Arthur asked.

'Not much, sir. I shall endeavour to learn more in the village tomorrow.' Benson turned down the covers on the bed and felt the sheets to ensure there was no sign of damp.

'Yes, perhaps a pint might be in order. We know Miss Hargreaves was connected to the man on the beach,' Arthur said thoughtfully. It would be good to know if the landlord of the Green Dragon was somehow involved in the puzzle or if it was simply a red herring that could be discarded. His manservant clearly felt there was something there worth investigating, and he knew the kind of information that Arthur found important.

'Good work, Benson.'

CHAPTER TEN

Jane entered the drawing room to discover her mother was, as usual, the star attraction. Everyone was gathered around her as she regaled them all with the story of how her apartment block had been bomb damaged. Doctor Denning, an old friend of her mother's, was hanging on her every word.

Elsa, being Elsa, managed to weave humour into her story as well as managing to make herself the heroine of the hour as the plucky little woman. Jane suspected that if her mother had thought she could convince them all that she had actually clambered on the roof and disarmed the incendiary herself, she would have.

Jane walked away and poured herself a glass of sherry and took a large gulp, wishing it was some of the whisky and soda she had locked away in the sideboard.

'I say, your mother is quite a gal.' Lloyd Briggs appeared at her elbow and looked admiringly across the room at Elsa.

'Oh yes, she certainly is,' Jane agreed as she watched her mother slip her arm through the vicar's as she started on another story.

'I'm a big admirer of her music. I always try to listen to her concerts on the radio,' Mr Briggs continued with a slightly star-struck look in his eyes as he continued to gaze at her mother.

'She is very popular.' Jane's heart sank as her mother moved away from the group towards the piano. She knew all too well what was going to happen next.

'Janey, honey, come and accompany me.' Her mother patted the top of the piano stool and smiled disarmingly at her.

'Oh, yes, Miss Treen, please do.' Captain Prudhoe gave Elsa an admiring look.

Jane could see that she was not going to be able to escape so swallowed the remainder of her sherry before walking over to sit at the piano. Someone had stopped the gramophone music in anticipation.

'What did you want me to play?' she asked once she was seated.

'Well, haven't you any of my music?' Elsa demanded.

'No, Mother, you took it with you when you left, remember? I can play a few popular melodies from memory.' Jane kept her tone even.

'Oh well, I suppose that will have to do,' Elsa agreed with a frown. 'Play "Nobody's Baby".'

Jane gave herself a little shake, stretched her fingers and began. As she had expected everyone gathered around to listen and there was a spontaneous burst of applause when Elsa finished.

'How marvellous,' Alicia Carstairs said.

'Oh, you are all much too kind.' Her mother favoured the assembled group with another of her dazzling smiles.

Jane noticed that Arthur had slipped back into the room and was watching her from the door. He gave her a small smile and she felt some of the tension ease from her shoulders. Elsa, having milked the applause, gave her the next request.

Elsa continued to entertain for the next hour with Jane accompanying her.

Eventually, Jane managed to excuse herself from playing any more since it was getting late.

'Miss Treen, I must confess, I've not had an evening I've enjoyed more for a long time,' Captain Prudhoe informed her as he and his date prepared to leave.

'I'm so pleased you enjoyed it, Captain Prudhoe,' Jane said as Benson assisted her guests to find their coats and hats.

'It was quite super,' Miss Carstairs agreed happily as she accepted Mr Briggs's offer of a lift to her cottage.

Doctor Denning said farewell to her mother and offered to walk Katie Hargreaves home.

After Benson had closed the front door behind the last of their departing guests, Jane went back into the drawing room to rejoin Arthur and to confront her mother.

Elsa had kicked off her patent-leather shoes and was seated at the end of the sofa, her feet tucked up underneath her with a cigarette in her hand. Arthur was seated in his now customary chair beside the fire trying not to look as if the smoke from her mother's cigarette was bothering him.

'Janey, honey, come and sit down, tell me all your news. Your friend here was saying you weren't sure how long you would be staying in Kent, is that right?' Elsa gave Arthur a calculating glance through slightly narrowed eyes as she tapped some ash from her cigarette into an ashtray.

Jane took the vacant chair opposite Arthur. 'That's correct. Why exactly are you here, Mother?'

Elsa waved her free hand in a careless fashion. 'Honey pie, I told you. I was bombed out and Stephen had happened to mention that you were working in Kent.'

'I rather think Stephen should be more careful with the information he gives out,' Jane said.

Elsa sat herself more upright. 'Oh pish, darling. He assumed that you would have already told me. You being my daughter and all, so don't go getting that boy in trouble. You know I'm good friends with his mother.'

'Then if you are such good friends maybe they could have put you up there instead of you trekking all the way here,' Jane snapped.

Benson tapped at the door and entered bearing a tray loaded with china and a plate of daintily cut sandwiches.

'Forgive me, Miss Elsa, but I thought you might be hungry after your journey,' he said as he deposited the tray on the coffee table.

'How very thoughtful.' Elsa swung her stocking-clad feet off the sofa and back down to the floor before picking up the plate.

'Cocoa?' Benson asked, looking at Arthur.

'Thank you.' Arthur accepted his manservant's offer.

'Miss Jane?'

'Thank you.' Jane decided that perhaps a milky drink might be a good idea after all to go to bed on. The speed with which she had drunk her last glass of sherry had given her a touch of heartburn.

As she accepted her drink from Benson, she spotted Marmaduke sidling into the room. He had clearly spotted sandwiches being prepared and come to investigate. Elsa noticed him before Arthur.

'Janey, honey pie, you surely aren't still harbouring that flea-ridden cat?'

'His name is Marmaduke, and I assure you he does not have fleas.' Jane leant forward and called her pet towards her.

Her mother had much the same expression as Arthur as they looked at her cat.

'Your room is ready, Miss Elsa. I have placed a hot water bottle to ensure the bed is properly aired,' Benson informed her mother as he prepared to leave the room.

'My, that is so kind of you.' Elsa bestowed one of her

dazzling smiles on him and Jane could have sworn she saw a tinge of pink creep into his narrow cheeks.

With Benson gone, Marmaduke jumped up onto Jane's lap and allowed her to stroke him. Arthur continued to watch him warily as if he were an unexploded bomb and her mother ate her sandwiches in silence.

Jane knew her mother was sulking and ignored her pointed sighs and disapproving glances every time she looked at Marmaduke.

'Well, I think I shall turn in. It's been a long and tiring day,' Elsa finally announced once the last crumb of her supper had been devoured. She picked up her own cup of cocoa. 'Good-night, Janey, goodnight, erm...'

'Arthur,' he obliged.

'... Arthur, of course. Do forgive me.' She gave Jane another sharp look and swished out of the room, closing the door behind her.

The instant she was gone, Jane closed her eyes for a moment and leaned her head back against the armchair.

'I, erm, expect she'll be here for a few days?' Arthur asked.

Jane opened her eyes. 'Unfortunately, yes. Unless of course she gets bored.'

'I see.'

Jane looked at him. 'Are you concerned it may compromise our work having her stay here?' That would give her a good reason to ask her mother to leave.

Arthur shook his head. 'Not if we are careful. It may even prove beneficial. It makes it appear that we are not unduly concerned about the death of the prisoner or the black market business.'

Jane could see what he meant. 'I suppose so. Mother is awfully good at distracting people,' she agreed. 'She is even working her magic on Benson.'

Arthur blinked at her uncomprehendingly. His hair had

already started to escape from the confines of whatever potion he had used to tame his curls, and he looked like a rumpled baby owl.

'I don't follow,' he said.

'Never mind.' Jane stifled a yawn. 'We had better turn in ourselves since we are visiting Mr Briggs's farm tomorrow.'

Arthur swallowed the rest of his cocoa as Jane persuaded her beloved cat to jump down from her lap without clawing her skirt.

'You come along to the kitchen, Marmaduke, darling,' she soothed as she picked up the tray ready to take it out of the room.

Arthur eyed the cat suspiciously. 'It doesn't really have fleas, does it?'

Jane glared at him. 'No. That was just my mother being objectionable. Come on, Marmaduke, Uncle Arthur doesn't mean it.'

Her cat gave Arthur a baleful glance out of his good eye and stalked off in her wake, tail held high in the air.

* * *

The sunshine had returned the next morning, and Arthur was in a surprisingly good mood as he dressed ready to go downstairs for breakfast. The scent of toast greeted him as he descended the stairs, and he could hear the sound of music from the wireless as he entered the dining room.

Jane, as he had expected, was already seated at the table cracking open the top of her boiled egg.

'Your mother not up yet?' he asked as he took his seat opposite her.

'Don't be ridiculous. She's an artiste. They rarely rise much before lunch. No doubt she'll expect breakfast in bed and cause as much trouble as possible while she's here.' Jane rolled her eyes as she looked suspiciously at the pale-yellow butter substitute in the dish on the table.

'I see.' He didn't really but didn't wish to annoy Jane before she had drunk her coffee.

'Benson has filled me in on these people at the Green Dragon. He said that Miss Carstairs also reacted to the mention of their names. He's going back into the village today and he plans to have a drink at lunchtime at the pub.' Jane plunged her toast into her egg, making the yellow yolk splurge out stickily down the sides of the blue and white striped china eggcup.

Arthur managed to suppress a tut of disapproval as Benson appeared bearing a small teapot and another egg. He placed them in front of Arthur.

'Thank you, Benson. We need to find out who this Annie and Herbert Simms are, and if they have any connection to either our dead man or any of the black market stuff,' Arthur said.

'I shall endeavour to find out more in the village today,' Benson said.

'We have the joy of visiting Mr Briggs's farm this morning to talk to him and the land girls. I do hope the rain hasn't made everything too muddy,' Jane said.

Arthur sincerely hoped that was the case too. He had no desire to go wading across a muddy farmyard. There was a reason he was more suited to desk work. He set about carefully excising the top from his egg as Jane set aside her spoon and helped herself to more coffee from the pot in front of her.

'As well as looking around the farm I'm interested in discovering what kind of cases are coming before Mr Briggs in his role as a magistrate,' she said.

'Any black market cases, you mean?' Arthur carefully cut his toast into neat little triangles.

'Yes, he must have his ear to the ground I would have thought,' Jane mused.

'He may be more helpful than Inspector Topping,' Arthur agreed once he had finished arranging his breakfast to his satisfaction.

'Marmaduke is probably more helpful than Inspector Topping,' Jane remarked drily as she eyed his breakfast arrangements.

Benson tried unsuccessfully to hide a small smile as he made his way back out of the dining room.

Jane sipped her coffee with a thoughtful air. 'Do you think there might be a link between Russo's death and this upsurge in black market activity?' she asked.

Arthur wiped his fingers on the white linen napkin. 'There is nothing to connect them at present. Still, someone wanted Russo dead for a reason, and I don't think it was because he was a prisoner of war.'

'Do you think his friend was behind the murder? If Gambini is a part of this same criminal gang?' Jane asked.

Arthur frowned and went back to carefully scooping his egg from its shell. 'It's hard to say. It is a possibility but why remove Russo's clothes and where are they? Why would he kill him? The timeline too makes it difficult, not impossible, but difficult. There could not have been much time between Russo dying and his body being found.'

'Perhaps that may become clearer when we see how the land lies at the farm. There may be paths and bridleways that we are not aware of that Russo or Gambini may have used.' Jane set her empty cup back on its saucer.

'To move around without being noticed, you mean?' Arthur was quick to pick up on the inference of Jane's words.

'Yes. Perhaps for clandestine meetings or it may be that Russo saw something or heard something that he was not supposed to know about.' Jane's forehead creased into a frown and Arthur could see she was thinking.

'Russo was killed away from the camp, and we know that

both he and Gambini did not really have much freedom of movement, merely the illusion of it. The work on the farm and the journey to and from the camp was strictly timed so there was not much leeway. Hence anyone targeting him must be someone with local connections,' Arthur agreed before starting on his last triangle of toast.

'Well, while you finish mincing at that piece of toast I shall go and get Cilla from the garage and then we can set off,' Jane said, placing her cup down and rising from her seat.

Arthur sighed and decided to forgo the remainder of his breakfast. He had forgotten that going to the farm would involve being driven there by Jane.

CHAPTER ELEVEN

Jane noticed that Arthur looked quite pale under his many layers of wool as she pulled to a halt near the white wooden gates of Lloyd Briggs's farm. She hoped he wasn't one of those people who suffered from motion sickness. He always appeared to look quite ill whenever he travelled with her.

'Right, let's go and see who is around. Mr Briggs should be expecting us at least.' Jane climbed out of the car and waited for Arthur to join her beside the gate.

Chafford House Farm was a large building built originally, Jane guessed, as a country gentleman's residence. It definitely appeared far too grand to be a mere farm with its porticoed entrance and range of outbuildings. In the warm sunshine set against the green grass and surrounded by autumn flowers it looked a very pleasant place to live and work.

'Very nice,' Arthur observed. 'Not quite what I was expecting. It would seem that the actual working part of the farm is a little way behind the house.' He nodded towards a large barn lying beyond the building in front of them.

Jane lifted the latch on the gate and together they crunched their way up the driveway to the house.

'It would appear that Mr Briggs is quite a wealthy man,' Arthur said. 'Have you ever been here before, Jane?'

She shook her head. 'No. I vaguely remember this place as a child being quite run-down. It certainly seems to have had a change in fortune since then.'

They paused on the front step and Arthur tugged on the black cast-iron bell pull. Deep inside the house they heard a bell ring announcing their arrival.

After a moment the door opened and Mr Briggs himself greeted them. 'Miss Treen, Mr Cilento, welcome to Chafford House Farm. Do come in.' He ushered them into a large square hall laid with black and white floor tiles. Oil paintings of prize-winning cattle and horses in ornate gold frames lined the walls.

'Now, may I offer you both some refreshments or would you prefer to look around the farm first?' Mr Briggs asked genially.

He was dressed this morning like a country squire with tweed jacket and smart trousers. Jane suspected that he was keen to impress his respectability upon them.

'Perhaps we could take a tour of the farm first? It all looks most interesting,' Jane suggested.

She had no desire to be sidetracked by Mr Briggs into sitting around taking tea while there was work to be done. Besides which she was very keen to see how the farm operated and where the land girls and other farm staff were housed. She would bet her last shilling that they would not be staying in the main house.

'Aha, no mucking about I see, straight to business, eh? A lady after my own heart, Miss Treen. Very good, come with me, I'm sure you'll find that everything has been done properly and is in perfect order,' Mr Briggs said in a hearty manner as he took them through the house and out through the back door.

The rear of the house opened onto a small stone paved patio with a logia that marked the entrance of a substantial walled vegetable garden. Jane and Arthur followed their host as he led them round a path outside the walls and on to the farm itself.

There was the large barn they had seen from the bottom of the drive. Then further along the track there was a milking parlour and a large hen house with a fenced area where the chickens were kept. In the distance Jane noticed an oast house.

'We have orchards, hops, arable farming and cattle,' Mr Briggs explained as they took a grassy path out of the mud. 'We also have pigs at the other side of the farm near the woods.'

'And where are your farm staff housed?' Jane asked.

'Just along here, I have two workers' cottages which I had fixed up for them. There are four land girls here in one cottage and my chief farmhand, Jeb, in the other cottage. He's been here for years and knows the place like the back of his hand. He organises the work,' Mr Briggs said as they paused in front of two small red-brick semi-detached cottages with pocket-hand-kerchief sized gardens in front of them.

'Do you supply them with food?' Jane asked.

'They get their own breakfast. Lunch is delivered to the barn where there's a table and chairs set up each day unless it's very cold or wet, then they eat in the farm kitchen. Dinner at night is in the farm kitchen at seven on the dot. My housekeeper sees to all of that.' Mr Briggs tucked his thumbs into the pockets of his waistcoat and looked very pleased with himself.

'What time do the girls start work in the mornings?' Arthur asked.

Jane noticed he sounded a little breathless and wondered if they had walked too quickly for him. Mr Briggs, like herself, moved quite speedily whereas Arthur moved at a snail's pace.

'Six o'clock sharp,' Mr Briggs said.

'And the prisoners would arrive when?' Jane asked.

'They would be here for eight and leave at four. I supply them with lunch and refreshments with the others while they work.' Mr Briggs looked as if he was ready to move on.

'What is the routine when they arrive?' Arthur asked.

'Well, the girls have done the early work, seeing to the cows, feeding the chickens and the pigs. Jeb meets the men at the gate and takes them up and puts each of them with a couple of the girls and then they start the manual work. Picking, ploughing, woodland management, all that kind of thing. The jobs vary from day to day. They all meet up for lunch and then go off again. When they finish, they check out with Jeb and go back to camp.' Mr Briggs started off once more along the track.

'So, on the day Russo was killed he would have told Jeb he was leaving before Gambini also said he was setting back?' Arthur trotted along behind the other man.

Mr Briggs stopped so suddenly that Arthur nearly bumped into his back. The farmer turned to face him. 'Well, yes, I suppose he must have, mustn't he? You can ask him yourself in a minute.'

'Gambini said that he told the land girls he was leaving and waited at the gate for Russo before worrying he was going to be late back himself. He assumed his colleague had left without him and they had missed each other.' Jane looked at Mr Briggs.

Mr Briggs's complexion had turned slightly puce. 'I'm sure Jeb will be able to satisfy your questions. I'm not really hands on here much myself at the moment. My magistrate's work at the court keeps me very busy.'

He commenced walking again and they followed behind. They had gone past the end of the walled garden area now and spread out before them were several open fields growing a variety of crops. The ground fell gradually away towards some distant woodlands, an orchard and the piggery.

Jane wrinkled her nose as a very faint waft of pig reached her on the breeze. The farm was more extensive than she had imagined so she could see why Mr Briggs had been eager to recruit more labour from the camp. It would have been impossible to maintain production on such a large scale otherwise.

She recalled someone mentioning that Mr Briggs had lost a land girl so must have been short-staffed.

She could see some figures in one of the fields, accompanied by a horse-drawn cart. It looked as if they were cutting cabbages.

'There's Jeb now.' Mr Briggs quickened his pace even further as he avoided the puddles on the rutted road to reach the field.

Now they were closer, Jane saw there were two young women in muddy coveralls, their hair tied up under brightly coloured headscarves. They were working with an elderly man. The man looked to be in his mid-to-late sixties, his skin darkened with either dirt or from the sun. A red-spotted neckerchief was at his throat and his jacket and moleskin trousers were grimy and tattered.

'Jeb!' Mr Briggs called and waved his hand in the air as he approached.

The unexpected noise caused the horse to snort and whinny in disapproval.

Jeb left the two girls to continue cutting and tossing the cabbages onto the cart while he came to see what his master wanted.

'Now then, Jeb, this is Miss Treen and her colleague, Mr Cilento. They've been sent from the war office about Russo, the man who drowned on the beach,' Mr Briggs said.

Jeb inclined his head in acknowledgement and thankfully didn't offer to shake hands. 'Oh yes, you're from Lunnon then,' he said slowly.

'That's right. Mr Briggs was just explaining your routine here at the farm when the prisoners arrive and how they fill their day and what happens when they leave,' Jane explained.

'Oh yes.' Jeb avoided meeting his employer's gaze, preferring to fiddle with the large, curved knife he held in his hand from where he had been cutting the cabbage stalks.

'Perhaps you could tell me what usually happens when the prisoners arrive.' Jane waited for Jeb to respond as he thought about her question.

'They gets here for eight. The girls have done the early jobs and are having their breakfast then. I meets them at the gate and we walks up while I tell them what jobs need doing.' Jeb licked his lips and glanced swiftly at Mr Briggs who stood beaming avuncularly at his employee.

'You assign them to work under supervision with the land girls?' Arthur asked.

'That's right, sir, yes. We meets up for lunch and I checks up on what they've been doing. Then they does the afternoon jobs.' Jeb shifted his weight from one foot to the other and looked over at the girls who had continued to cut cabbages for the cart.

'And what time do the prisoners leave?' Jane asked.

'Four o'clock. They have to be back at camp for five or they are marked as missing or late. There's a bit of time built in for if a job takes longer.' Jeb edged a little further away towards the cabbages as if eager to get back to his work.

'If the men were late or failed to arrive, I presume you inform the camp immediately?' Arthur asked.

'That's the procedure, sir, yes. I haven't had cause though to do that with the two men the captain sent. Good workers, both of them,' Jeb replied.

'On the day Russo died, did you see both men leave and give them permission to go?' Jane asked.

'Well...' Jeb looked again at his employer and Jane noticed Mr Briggs give a barely perceptible nod of his head.

'The girls with Gambini finished about ten past four and he went to the gate to wait for the other one. The two girls who had been with Russo come from out the barn and were walking back to the cottage. I heard Gambini call over to them to see where his mate was.'

'You hadn't seen him or dismissed him for the day yourself?' Jane asked, her tone taking a frosty tinge.

'Well not exactly, no. I had checked on him an hour or so before like when they was working hauling some logs out of the woodland down yonder.' Jeb appeared very uncomfortable.

'But you didn't dismiss him? Or know for certain that he had left the farm?' Jane persisted.

Mr Briggs opened his mouth as if to answer while Jeb merely looked uncomfortable. She held up her hand to prevent Mr Briggs from answering her question. 'Well? Did you see him leave? Or give him permission to finish that day?' she asked.

'Really, Miss Treen, I think...' Mr Briggs tried again.

'Thank you, Mr Briggs, but my question is to Jeb,' Jane replied firmly, forcing the farmer to subside.

'No, miss. I seen the girls and they said as he had finished a bit ago. It was his time to leave so I didn't see no harm in it. Then the other one, Gambini, like I said, he came down a bit afterwards. I didn't know as Russo had left the farm. I thought he was still about seeing as Gambini was waiting for him.' Jeb appeared relieved now that he had finally confessed what had happened.

'You thought Russo was still on the farm even though the land girls had said he had finished for the day. Was it usual for him to hang around?' Arthur asked.

'He'd sometimes pick some flowers out the hedgerow like afore he went. Since his mate was waiting for him, I thought that might be where he was. I had no reason to think as something could have happened. They always left together and come together.' Jeb squared his shoulders apparently eager that no blame should be attached to him in the matter.

'And you have told this to Inspector Topping?' Arthur asked.

Jeb exchanged another fleeting glance with Mr Briggs. 'I answered all of the inspector's questions, sir, yes.'

Jane thought his reply was somewhat evasive.

'Which of the girls were working with Russo on the day he died?' she asked.

'That was Carol and Eileen there.' Jeb inclined his head towards the two women working in the field.

'Then I need to speak to them,' Jane said.

Jeb exchanged another cryptic look with Mr Briggs and went back to the cabbage field to speak to the women. The women who were both bent over scything cabbage stalks paused in their activity to look at Jane, before straightening up and coming over.

'Jeb said you were from London wanting to ask about Antonio,' the shorter of the two said.

Jane introduced herself and Arthur and explained why they were there. 'I'm Carol,' the shorter girl said, 'and this here is Eileen. We were with Antonio all day that day.'

Eileen nodded her head in agreement. 'We worked in the field in the morning and then after lunch we started on the wood. We had a break in the afternoon for a drink as it was so hot, then went back to it.'

'You were cutting and clearing in the woods near the piggery?' Arthur asked.

'Yes, we wanted to get some logs cut and shifted while it was dry. Antonio knew a lot about timber cutting and he was strong, so he was a big help. We finished a bit early as we got it done faster than we thought,' Carol said.

'We hauled the logs up to the woodshed at the back of the barn and got them unloaded. It was really hot, and we were all quite sweaty,' Eileen chipped in.

'You got on well with the prisoners?' Arthur asked.

Eileen looked at Carol. 'Yes, they're all right. Antonio was the nicer of the two. He was always up for a laugh and a chat. Matteo can be a bit grumpy and grumbles a lot.'

'How was Antonio Russo that day? Happy? Quiet? Anything at all that seemed out of the ordinary?' Jane asked.

Mr Briggs seemed to have lost interest at this point and had wandered further down the track and had his head together with Jeb. Jane wondered what he was saying to him.

'He seemed a bit distracted, I suppose. He wasn't quite as talkative as usual,' Carol said.

'After our afternoon break especially. I asked if he was all right with the heat and he laughed and said Italy was hotter, so it didn't bother him, but he did seem as if something was on his mind,' Eileen agreed.

'When you finished with the logs why did no one find Jeb to let him know that Antonio had finished the task for the day? I understand that the prisoners had to, in effect, clock in and clock out with your farm foreman?' Jane asked.

The two girls looked embarrassed. 'Most of the time they did ask Jeb if they could go but, well, we knew that Antonio was sweet on someone in the village, and he used to meet her for a few minutes on his way back to the camp,' Eileen said.

'So, we thought there was no harm in his occasionally going a bit early. We knew he had to be back at the camp on time or Captain Prudhoe would send out soldiers to find him,' Carol explained.

'What time did you last see him?' Jane looked at the girls.

'About three thirty?' Carol ventured. 'He was walking back up past the walled garden.'

Jane blew out a sigh. She was beginning to understand what had happened the day Russo had been killed.

CHAPTER TWELVE

Arthur wondered what Mr Briggs was saying to his farm foreman. There had definitely been something odd going on while Jane had been trying to extract answers about the farm's routine.

'Are we in trouble?' Carol asked. She seemed to be the younger of the two girls.

Jane shook her head. 'You and Eileen are not responsible for the supervision of the prisoners. By that, I mean you are not their guards, and you are not the people who oversee their arrival and departure. That responsibility falls on Jeb and on Mr Briggs. It seems, however, that some laxity has been allowed to creep into your routines.'

Carol looked relieved at Jane's reassurance. She rubbed her cheek with the back of her hand, leaving a smudge of dirt behind.

'However,' Jane continued, 'I would advise both of you to remember that these men are prisoners for a reason. Charming and pleasant they may be, but they are still the enemy. You must retain your guard and remember this.'

The girls nodded their heads dutifully.

'Did you wonder why Matteo Gambini was at the gate waiting when you knew Antonio Russo had already left?' Arthur asked.

Eileen shrugged. 'I think we assumed they had an arrangement to leave together so we thought Antonio must be still around the farm somewhere.'

'How was Gambini when he realised Russo wasn't coming?' Jane asked.

'He was cross. He was muttering something in Italian and he rushed away. I assume because he didn't want to get in trouble for being late back to camp.' Carol looked at Eileen for confirmation and the other girl nodded vigorously.

'You don't know of anyone who may have wanted to harm Antonio at all? Anyone here at the farm or in the village?' Jane asked.

Both girls shook their heads. 'I don't think so. They walked through the back lanes mostly as some of the people weren't very nice to them when they first started here,' Carol said.

'They'd spit at them or throw stones. You know, catcall after them. That seemed to have stopped though really and I don't think anyone would have wanted to seriously hurt them. It would have caused too much trouble. People did know that they were trying to make amends by helping at the farm,' Eileen said.

'We know Antonio had a local girl he was sweet on. Was this lady Katie Hargreaves, the school teacher?' Jane asked.

'Yes, he would take her wildflower posies. She had helped him with his English and loaned him some books.' Eileen looked nervous. 'That is all right, isn't it?'

'Yes, I'm sure that Captain Prudhoe was aware that she had given him materials as part of the English language tutoring she provides to the prisoners in her free time,' Arthur said.

Carol and Eileen appeared relieved.

'Miss Hargreaves didn't have a former boyfriend at all in the village who may have been jealous of Antonio's attentions?' Jane asked.

Carol shook her head. 'I don't know Katie too well. We've met her a few times when there has been a dance at the village hall, but I don't think she has a particular boyfriend.'

'No, her friend seems to be Annie Simms from the Green Dragon, but Annie doesn't get out much,' Eileen said.

'Is there anything at all that either of you can think of, however small, that may be relevant to Antonio's death?' Arthur asked.

'Only, well, we were surprised when we heard he'd drowned. He told us that he used to spend the summers when he was a boy on his father's fishing boat. He said he could swim like a fish,' Carol said.

'I see. Thank you.' Jane let the girls return to their work. Arthur thought it was interesting that Annie Simms's name had cropped up again. Perhaps that was why Katie Hargreaves called at the Green Dragon.

Mr Briggs bustled over to rejoin them.

'Now, I presume you have the information you require?' he asked, looking first at Jane and then at Arthur.

'It's been most helpful.' Jane favoured him with a smile. 'Perhaps we could see the rest of the farm now?'

Mr Briggs looked slightly taken aback by her request. 'Well, of course, it may be rather muddier further on.' He glanced down at her nicely polished shoes.

'Well, let's see how far we get. I should like to see the woodland where Russo was working on the day he died.' Jane smiled at the farmer once more.

Arthur suppressed a groan. He knew why Jane wanted to see the woods. He knew it would be good to understand the landscape and lie of the farm. He just wished that this activity didn't require him to march for half a mile down a muddy track.

Jane and Mr Briggs walked on in front with Mr Briggs

explaining which crops were in which fields. The smell from the piggery was becoming more noticeable now they were closer. The track wasn't as bad as the farmer had suggested, probably as the sun was drying up the puddles in the ruts.

Arthur even risked loosening one of his scarves as they walked since the heat was stronger than when they had set off. Ahead of them the woods lay green and cool with dappled shade just beyond the piggery. A seagull shrieked overhead, and he realised that they could not be far from the coast. The woods must run down towards the cliffs.

They walked past the piggery which consisted of several small shelters and a fenced enclosure. Several sows and their piglets were snuffling around in the mud. Jane paused briefly to coo over the piglets before continuing on with Mr Briggs.

Arthur couldn't see the attraction given the smell emanating from the enclosure. At least inside the wood the trees provided some respite from the sun. Evidence that woodland management was being carried out was obvious from the cleared areas and signs of recently cut trees. A large space had been cleared leaving just a few shrubs and some bracken.

The path continued on through the trees and Arthur wondered if it led to the sea. He had looked on a map before breakfast and had seen that the farm was located on high ground. The woods must be the ones that had been visible from the dunes on the opposite side of the small bay from where Russo had been found.

Jane and Mr Briggs had halted on the path and Arthur caught them up.

'This path, where does it lead?' Arthur asked.

'It goes right the way to the edge of the cliffs,' Mr Briggs said. 'At least that's what I believe.'

'Is there a route from there down towards the beach?' Jane looked around at the path and Arthur guessed she was assessing how well used it might be.

'I've never taken it myself but there may be a rabbit path of some kind. It's not terribly safe as the cliff edge can be unstable. There have been rockfalls and people don't go to that end of the sands usually,' the farmer said.

'Are there any barriers? Any fencing on the other side of the woods?' Arthur peered through the trees trying to see how much further it was to the cliffs. He thought he could see the sea in the distance. His feet ached, however, and he wasn't eager to walk much further.

'There was a fence years ago but when I acquired the farm it had fallen into disrepair. With the war and shortages, it's not been a priority to repair it especially as access to the beach is restricted,' Mr Briggs explained.

Jane exchanged a glance with Arthur. 'I'm just going to take a look. Please don't feel you need to accompany me, I shan't be long.'

Jane quickly walked off along the track leaving Arthur with Lloyd Briggs.

'She's a very determined lady, your assistant,' Mr Briggs observed as he looked at Jane's retreating back.

'Oh, Jane is my senior, actually. I'm her assistant,' Arthur explained. 'And yes, she is very efficient.'

Mr Briggs appeared slightly discomfited that the positions were reversed. Arthur guessed he was of the school that assumed the man must be in charge.

'It was a most delightful evening yesterday. Thoroughly enjoyable. Will Miss Treen's mother be staying long in the village, do you know?' Mr Briggs asked.

Arthur gave a slight shrug. 'I'm really not certain what Elsa's plans might be.'

'I presume that you and Miss Treen will be returning to London yourselves as soon as you have completed your report on the death of the Italian?'

Jane had now vanished from view.

'Again, it all depends. We came originally for a brief holiday. There are a few issues, however, which the war office has requested we look into during our stay. Speaking of which, Mr Briggs, I understood you to say you were the local magistrate for this area?' Arthur said.

Mr Briggs visibly puffed up with pride. 'I am indeed, it's a most responsible position. It takes up a great deal of my time.'

'Oh, I don't doubt it,' Arthur assured him. 'What kind of cases are you seeing now? I presume the kinds of offences may have changed since the start of the war.'

Mr Briggs placed his hands behind his back, reminding Arthur of a rather plump, prosperous pigeon about to commence strutting. 'Yes, you're quite right, with the younger men away fighting there are fewer cases of affray, drunkenness, that kind of thing. Vagrancy has decreased. Obviously, one still gets theft and poaching especially with the food shortages and rationing becoming more of an issue.'

'I suppose, too, black marketeering must also be a concern. Mr Wood, the inspector for the war office, seemed to feel this was on the rise. He mentioned gangs operating out of London,' Arthur said in a mild tone.

'Is that what he said, eh? Well, I suppose the man has to try and justify his job. I can't say I've had too many cases brought before the bench.' Mr Briggs continued to look along the track where Jane had gone.

'We have been informed that there had been quite an upsurge in thefts from shops and the goods being offered locally under the counter.' Arthur was not convinced that Mr Briggs would be unaware of this considering his position.

Mr Briggs stroked his gingery moustache with a thoughtful finger. 'There are incidents reported in the papers, of course. Downplayed, one doesn't wish to cause a panic or spread unpatriotic feeling, but I wouldn't have thought this area any worse than anywhere else in Britain.'

'Have you tried any such cases?' Arthur asked.

'Oh, nothing major. Anything more serious would go to a higher court than myself. We have had a few petty things. A chappie offering bacon from a stolen pig. Good thing ours are at this end of the farm, eh?' He nudged Arthur in the ribs and chortled at his own forethought. 'That sort of thing really. Stolen chocolate. And lots of fines for showing lights in the blackout, the usual really.'

'Do you feel then that Mr Wood may be exaggerating these incidents?' Arthur could see Jane making her way back towards them along the narrow path.

'Well, I don't know. I mean he gets notified I suppose of these things, but Inspector Topping doesn't seem to feel it's an issue more than any other. And, like I said, I've not seen or heard of many cases coming before my bench or indeed, the court.' Mr Briggs too had sighted Jane and smiled genially at Arthur.

* * *

Jane was slightly breathless from the upward incline on her walk back from the cliff edge to where she had left Arthur and Mr Briggs. She had guessed that Arthur was not really up for a rapid trot through the woods to scope out the access to the beach and the dunes. Hopefully, he would have used his time to discreetly interview the farmer about the black market issues.

The path she had just taken had led to the edge of the cliffs on the opposite side of the bay to where Russo's body had been found. There had been the remains of a decaying wooden fence with a dilapidated TRESPASSERS KEEP OUT sign when she had exited the woods. The path looked, however, as if it was still in use since it had led along the cliff edge and down towards the beach.

From her viewpoint at the top, she could see where she and

Arthur had stood at the bench near where Russo's body had been found. Miss Carstairs's cottage too was clearly visible nestled in behind the dunes, slightly apart from the village. Below, as she had looked across the cliff face, she had seen openings which she presumed must be to various caves. The area had been riddled with old smugglers' tunnels years ago.

Mr Briggs greeted her with a smile. 'Everything to your satisfaction, Miss Treen?'

'It was most instructive,' Jane responded politely.

'Then shall we return to the farmhouse? I am certain you must be ready for some refreshments by now?' Mr Briggs suggested, raising his arm to indicate that Jane should go in front of him.

'Thank you, that would be most kind,' Arthur said as he fell into step behind the other two to walk back to the farmhouse.

Mr Briggs took them a slightly different route back, insisting he wished to show them the orchard before leading them along a path towards a gate in the wall surrounding the kitchen garden. Jane only half listened to his conversation, much as she had on the way to the woods. Mr Briggs was a man who seemed to enjoy the sound of his own voice. She had already endured a monologue on crop rotation so a follow-up on soft fruits and apple farming was not something which interested her.

'Forgive me, Mr Briggs, but what are the buildings over there?' she interrupted his discourse on his intentions to plant more raspberries by indicating a range of dilapidated outbuildings. The buildings were of the same brick as the main house and set in a grove of trees. Daisies and wild verbena showed in the long grass in front of a dovecote which was seemingly occupied by pigeons.

'Oh, those are old storage sheds. Not in use now as the roof has lost a great many tiles and there is woodworm in the joists. They used to be the dairy and smokehouse and were built at the same time as the original farm that used to be here. The current farmhouse is about a hundred and fifty years younger. We just keep odds and ends there now,' Mr Briggs explained.

'I see you keep it locked,' Arthur remarked.

Jane too had noticed a large, new-looking padlock on the door.

'It's not terribly safe and I don't want anyone getting hurt. Not a place anyone goes but better safe than sorry, eh?' Mr Briggs continued walking and soon they reached the green-painted door set in an arch-topped stone frame that led into the walled garden.

The kitchen garden was clearly Mr Briggs's pride and joy and it certainly appeared a most productive area. Eventually they reached the back door of the farmhouse after a pause to inspect the leeks. Mr Briggs then led them through the scullery and boot room where they cleaned any trace of dirt from their feet, before being escorted along the hallway to a large and comfortably furnished sitting room. Mr Briggs left them there and went to organise a tray of tea.

Arthur had divested himself of his hat, coat and scarves in the hall. He now sat in one of the overstuffed chintz-covered armchairs, pink-cheeked and crumpled.

'Well?' Jane asked as she perched on the edge of the sofa. 'What did you find out?' She kept her voice low, not wishing Mr Briggs or anyone else who might be in the house to overhear her.

Arthur told her what the farmer had said about his cases in the magistrates' court.

'Hmm, a slightly different story again from that of Mr Wood and indeed, Inspector Topping,' Jane said and lit one of her cigarettes, availing herself of a nearby ceramic ashtray.

She told him what she had seen when she had followed the path through the wood.

Arthur listened attentively. 'You believe that path is still being used?' He wrinkled his nose as some of her smoke drifted his way.

Jane nodded. 'It's well worn, and although obviously steep leading uphill it is a good shortcut to the beach and the far end of the village high street. It's also a good vantage point.'

She finished her cigarette and stubbed it out.

'Then, I wonder who is using it and for what purpose?' Arthur said.

CHAPTER THIRTEEN

Mr Briggs returned bearing a laden tea tray which he set down on a small rosewood occasional table.

'My apologies for the delay. My housekeeper is busy preparing lunch for the land girls and Jeb.'

'I do hope we have not inconvenienced her?' Jane said as Mr Briggs took a seat opposite Arthur. 'It is so difficult to get any household help these days. Everyone is busy with war work.'

'Yes, and rightly so, my dear,' Mr Briggs agreed. 'Perhaps you could be mother?' He indicated the silver teapot.

Jane bowed her head and accepted the task of pouring and serving the tea. She would have preferred coffee, but it was becoming more difficult to obtain of late. The tea too was somewhat indifferent, seeming to take an age to steep before gaining any kind of strength to crawl out of the pot. She was pleased to see that a plate of jam tarts had been added to the tray. The fresh air and exercise had made her quite hungry.

Mr Briggs thanked her once again for the previous evening's entertainment. 'Your mother is a most talented woman. It was

such a delight to meet her, having admired her music from afar
for so long.'

Jane responded with a tight smile. She was used to men like
Mr Briggs fawning over her mother. They were the ones
waiting at the stage door after a concert or show. They left
flowers and invitations to dine. It was all rather tiresome really.
She had often wondered how her father had put up with it for
so many years.

'I trust you found everything to your satisfaction this morning?' Mr Briggs asked as he accepted his cup from Jane.

'I believe we are gathering a great deal of information for
our report, thank you,' Jane responded.

'Mr Cilento said you were uncertain about how long you
would be remaining in the village?' Mr Briggs asked.

'That is correct. We need to see more people and we are
awaiting the coroner's report on the cause of Russo's death.' Jane
waited to see what Mr Briggs's response would be to this. It
seemed to have been presumed that the prisoner had drowned but
the position of his body had deemed this to be far from certain.

'A coroner's report? The man drowned, didn't he? I didn't
think the inspector was requesting an autopsy?' Mr Briggs
looked surprised.

'There were some anomalies which need to be investigated.
Whitehall has asked us to be very thorough,' Arthur remarked
mildly, before taking a sip of his tea.

Jane sensed that he too was curious about what Mr Briggs's
reaction might be. The prisoner had last been seen alive at the
farm. It seemed too that the proper procedures had not been
followed the day Russo had died. If the man had last been seen
at three thirty and the boys had discovered him at around four
thirty, then he had perished very soon after leaving the farm.

'Oh quite, quite, I'm sure your superiors would expect
nothing less. I would have thought though that the facts speak

for themselves. It was an exceptionally hot day, the man decided to steal some time before returning to camp, removed his clothes to bathe and got into difficulties. No doubt the cold of the sea at this time of year would be more than he had anticipated.' Mr Briggs gave a small, dismissive shrug of his shoulders.

'Perhaps,' Arthur said in a mild tone.

'Mr Briggs, as a magistrate you obviously work closely with the police and have a great deal of experience in such things. May I ask your opinion of Inspector Topping?' Jane was interested to hear his thoughts. Mr Briggs was clearly a man who thought well of himself, and she calculated he would probably be flattered by her seeking his opinion.

'Well, Inspector Topping is well thought of, I believe. I know the police have been struggling with a shortage of manpower obviously since the start of the war.'

'You would consider him to be thorough in his work?' Arthur asked.

Mr Briggs stared at him. 'I suppose so. He has always seemed a very sound fellow.'

'Interesting.' Arthur resumed drinking his tea while Mr Briggs eyed him curiously.

'An interesting morning,' Jane remarked once they were back inside the car, after bidding farewell to Mr Briggs.

'Very informative,' Arthur agreed.

Jane started the engine and crunched the car into gear. She ignored Arthur's pained expression as she coaxed Cilla into turning around in the tight space, avoiding the hedge and the gatepost.

'It's almost lunchtime. I wonder how Benson is faring at the Green Dragon,' Arthur mused as Jane sped along the narrow lane back towards the village.

'Yes, that was rather curious, wasn't it? I think once we've made all these connections between everyone the picture might become clearer,' Jane agreed as she braked sharply to avoid the butcher's lorry. Arthur winced and hung on to the edge of his seat.

Elsa was in the drawing room when they returned. The gramophone was playing, and the strains of a well-known dance band met them at the door. Jane's mother was reclining on the sofa, a pile of old magazines at her side and a box of chocolates on the table.

The scene immediately took Jane back to before the war, before shortages and rationing had become part of everyday life.

'There you are!' her mother exclaimed, sitting herself up on the sofa with a swirl of pink chiffon. 'Mr Benson said you had gone out and I was wondering when you'd be back.'

'We are working, Mother,' Jane said.

Arthur had taken his usual place beside the fire. He looked quite tired.

'Mr Benson was kind enough to bring me my morning tea and some toast before he left but I've been twiddling my thumbs since then. Luckily, I found these old magazines in your father's study, or I should have been bored witless. I suppose it was sheer dumb luck that they hadn't been burnt or taken for a paper collection by now,' her mother pouted.

Jane forced herself to count to five in her head before answering. 'Like I said, Arthur and I were working. We went to visit Mr Briggs at his farm.'

'Mr Briggs, he was the charming gentleman I met last night? Oh, he seemed so pleasant. I could have gone with you. I don't believe he was living in the village when I was here before,' Elsa said.

'No, I don't believe he was.' Jane kept her own reply short and avoided reminding her mother that she had still been in bed when she and Arthur had left.

'Such a pity. I heard at your party that he's quite a wealthy man.' Elsa had a speculative expression on her well-made-up face that Jane knew all too well.

'Yes, his farm is very large, and he has a nice house,' Jane agreed.

'Mr Benson said he was a magistrate.' Elsa produced a nail file and began to examine her nails.

Jane wondered what else her mother had managed to worm out of 'Mr Benson'. 'Yes, he is.'

'And no Mrs Briggs?' her mother continued after removing an imaginary snag from her nail with her file.

'Not that we are aware of.' Jane was all too familiar with her mother's behaviours. She had no doubt that Elsa would find a way to be taking tea at Mr Briggs's house before they had time to blink.

'By the by, some policeman called and left a message for you,' Elsa said.

'A policeman? Do you mean Inspector Topping?' Jane asked.

'I didn't take his name, honey. I'm not a secretary. He wanted you to telephone him back.' Elsa held out a hand and admired her nails.

Jane wondered if other people's mothers were as exasperating as her own or if she had been singularly unlucky in that regard.

'I'll go and telephone. I think Benson put his number on the blotter.' Arthur got up from his chair and headed to the study. Jane suspected he was glad to escape.

'Janey, where did you find him from?' her mother asked almost before Arthur was out of the room. 'Is he the man you were with back in January when I saw you at the station? The one you were with when that man got arrested at Lady Piper's party in May?'

'His name is Arthur, we work together and there is no need

for you to be so rude.' Jane tried to keep an even tone to her voice.

'I suppose it was too much to hope for that you had snagged a man at last. I swear, Janey pie, you couldn't catch one even if I gave you a net. Why you turned down Stephen I'll never know.' Her mother shook her head reproachfully.

'Stephen is an ass, Mother,' Jane replied succinctly.

Her mother merely tutted and rolled her eyes at this but thankfully refrained from saying any more on the subject.

Arthur returned to the room a minute later. 'The message was from Inspector Topping. He's had the results of the autopsy on Russo.'

'Goodness, that was surprisingly speedy,' Jane said. 'What did it show?'

'Well, he didn't drown. No water in his lungs. The results of the blood tests aren't back yet but he has a puncture mark below his left ear consistent with a hypodermic needle and a contusion on the back of his head,' Arthur said.

Elsa looked appalled at their conversation. 'Really, Janey, this is enough to put anyone off their lunch.'

Jane ignored her mother. 'So he was hit on the head and then killed by an injection. Nothing to say he was ever in the sea at all.'

'It's looking as if that might be the case. His hair was dry when they found him. I asked just while I was on the telephone. It was simply an assumption given his position on the sands that he must have drowned,' Arthur said.

'If whoever killed him went so far as to remove his clothes and leave him on the beach, then why not go the extra mile and place him in the sea?' Jane asked.

'Perhaps they were disturbed?' Arthur suggested.

'Maybe. It was a nice day and the place he was left is a popular spot,' Jane agreed.

'I think we may need to talk more to Alicia Carstairs,' Arthur sounded thoughtful.

'That dreary artist woman? Rather you than me.' Elsa sniffed and placed the lid back on her box of chocolates.

Jane wondered which of her mother's admirers had gifted them to her. She could see they seemed to be an American brand.

'Perhaps we could call on her after lunch,' she suggested, ignoring her mother's comment.

'Good idea,' Arthur agreed. Elsa crinkled her nose dismissively.

Lunch was a quiet affair. Mrs Dawes had concocted some sort of pie with scrag-end of mutton, potatoes and ingenuity. At least there were some fresh vegetables from the garden to accompany it. Dessert of tinned peaches and some evaporated milk was most welcome.

Elsa poked at the contents of her plate with her fork and ate very little. Jane was keen to finish and get going again. Hopefully by the time they returned Benson would be back with a report about what he had discovered at the pub.

Arthur as usual was taking his time, dissecting his peaches while Jane waited for him to finish.

'What am I supposed to do with myself if you two are going to see that artist woman?' Elsa asked in a plaintive voice.

'Whatever you like, Mother. We're here to work. I presume you'll need to try to find out what's happening at your apartment?' Jane suggested.

'I don't suppose I could borrow the car while you're gone? Take myself off shopping or for a tea?' Elsa suggested after giving her abandoned peaches a distasteful glance.

'You know petrol is in short supply. You can take the bus if you want to go out of the village,' Jane suggested.

'The bus?' Elsa looked at Jane as if her daughter had lost her mind. 'Certainly not. Someone of my standing on a bus. Can you imagine what that would do to my reputation?'

'Well, I'm sorry, Mother, but you can't take Cilla.' Jane saw Arthur had finally finished his dessert. 'Come on, Arthur, we've work to do.'

* * *

Arthur rose from his seat and followed Jane out of the dining room. Elsa remained at the table still pouting at her pudding. He went to collect his outdoor things, having resigned himself to another long walk through the village.

Jane and Mrs Dawes were talking together in low voices behind him at the end of the hall.

'Don't you go apologising for her, Miss Jane. I know what she can be like.' He guessed Mrs Dawes had to mean Jane's mother.

'I know, but she's bound to make more work, and you have quite enough to do already,' Jane said.

'I can handle your mother, don't you fret. Besides, that Mr Benson is a good help. Now, take no notice of her shenanigans. I daresay as she'll be back to London when she's bored of us country mice,' Mrs Dawes advised.

The rest of the conversation was lost as the two women moved off into the kitchen. Arthur put on his hat and pondered the advisability of leaving off his scarf given that the sun was still shining brightly.

Jane hurried back into the hall to pull on a lightweight jacket and placed a neat periwinkle-blue beret on top of her dark hair. He thought the colour suited her and enhanced the beauty of her eyes.

Thinking about the colour of a woman's eyes was a some-what alien experience for Arthur and he decided the heat from the morning had obviously affected him more than he thought. With that in mind he left his scarf behind and followed Jane out of the front door.

CHAPTER FOURTEEN

Jane set off at her usual brisk pace along the village high street with Arthur trailing behind her. The sun was quite high in the sky now and the gentle breeze from earlier in the day had vanished. Jane slowed her pace near the greengrocers and Arthur caught her up.

'Let's hope that Miss Carstairs is at home this afternoon.' Arthur's feet ached from the walk around the farm this morning. The heat was also making him perspire around his collar. He hoped Miss Carstairs would not only be home but would offer them some refreshments when they got there.

'I would like to look around the cottage to see what the view of the dunes is like from Miss Carstairs's home,' Jane said as they continued on towards the beach.

'Miss Carstairs claimed she was at the hospital the day Russo ended up on the sands,' Arthur panted as he tried to match Jane's renewed walking pace.

'That was unfortunate, but she did tell you she had seen other people using that breach in the wire to gain access to the beach? Whoever left his body there would have known how to get him onto the sands.'

They had reached the end of the village now and instead of heading for the rabbit path to the dunes, Jane took another broader pathway. The path passed through a small grove of scrubby trees bent and twisted by the coastal winds to lean towards the village.

As they emerged on the other side the path broadened and straightened, and Miss Carstairs's cottage came into sight. Arthur felt 'cottage' was rather too generous a term for the artist's home. The house was single storey, with thick cob walls hunkered down behind a hedge of wild dog roses full of bright red berries.

The slates on the roof were chipped and the blue paint of the windows and door was flaking away revealing layers of older paint underneath. A vine scrambled up the front of the house obscuring the diamond-leaded panes of the windows. Sand which had blown from the dunes lay on the cobbled path and against the corners of the house.

Jane opened the small wooden gate that led into the tiny garden, and they went to the front door. A black cat surveyed them suspiciously through the front window. It's yellowy-green eyes peering at them through the vine tendrils. The sound of the sea was audible in the distance on the other side of the cottage as it splashed onto the sands.

There was no sign of a bell, so Arthur raised the tarnished brass horseshoe-shaped door knocker and rapped it a couple of times. The cat jumped down from the windowsill inside the cottage and vanished from view.

'Do you think she is at home?' Jane asked. She stepped sideways to try to peer inside the cottage, holding her hand above her eyes to look through the glass.

'I'll try again.' Arthur lifted the door knocker again, rapping it a number of times against the door.

The front door was suddenly flung open, and Jane stepped back smartly from the window. Alicia Carstairs stood blinking at them from behind a pair of thick-lensed spectacles before she shoved her glasses up onto the top of her head.

'Miss Treen, Mr Cilento, how lovely to see you both. Do forgive me for not recognising you straight away. These are my work glasses when I'm working on close details. I'm as blind as a bat if I forget and leave them on. I almost broke my neck on the cat coming to the door. Come in, come in.' Alicia Carstairs ushered them both inside the cottage.

The front door opened directly into a cosy but cluttered sitting room. Alicia led them out through a small kitchen into a glass-walled lean-to at the rear of the cottage, which was obviously being used as her studio.

Canvases were stacked against a wall. A battered wooden table covered with an oilskin tablecloth held paints and pencils. Alicia swiftly moved some things to clear the space and urged them to be seated on the rather rickety paint-splattered wooden chairs.

'I do hope we're not disturbing you at your work, Miss Carstairs,' Arthur said as he perched gingerly on the nearest chair.

'Not at all, and do please call me Alicia. I was just about to have a break and make some tea.' Alicia beamed at them and absent-mindedly rubbed her cheek leaving a small smear of blue paint behind on her face.

'And you must call us Jane and Arthur,' Jane said.

Alicia stepped back into the kitchen and put the kettle on to boil. 'It's so nice to have visitors. I rarely see anyone here,' she called from inside the cottage.

'We were on our way to look at the dunes again where the body was discovered,' Jane said. 'And thought we would stop in.'

Alicia popped back out into the studio bearing a tea tray laid with mismatched cups and saucers. 'Just waiting for the kettle,' she remarked cheerily as she set it down on the table.

'Yes, you can see down to the dunes from here if you look through over there.' She waved her hand towards a French door at the other end of the studio.

Jane immediately stirred in her seat.

'Go and take a look, my dear,' Alicia urged with a smile. 'The rest of the view is somewhat obscured by the bushes in the garden but I've been reluctant to cut them back when the birds were nesting.'

Jane took their hostess up on her offer and went to look through the doors. Alicia bobbed back into the kitchen as the kettle started to whistle.

'You can see right down to the sea. There's a little path that leads out,' Jane said as she retook her seat at the table.

Arthur nodded. If Alicia had been at home when Russo had been put on the beach, then she would have definitely seen whoever had killed him.

'There we are now, tea is ready.' Alicia came to join them carefully carrying a floral-patterned china teapot with a chipped spout. She set it down on the tray.

'Did you ever see Russo here at the beach before?' Jane asked as Alicia lifted the teapot lid to poke the tea inside with a spoon.

'The man who was killed? No, I don't recall ever seeing him. I think I may have seen the other one once, very briefly. I remember because it struck me as odd, and I did think at the time that perhaps I should have alerted Captain Prudhoe.' Alicia replaced the lid on the pot and set a metal tea strainer across the top of one of the cups.

'When was this?' Jane asked as Alicia started to pour the tea.

'Oh, only a week or so ago,' the artist said as she moved the strainer to the next cup.

'What was he doing there?' Arthur asked.

Alicia shrugged as she poured the third cup of tea. 'Nothing really. He was only there for a few minutes. He sat on that bench and smoked a cigarette while he looked at the sea. I did wonder if perhaps he was waiting for someone, but no one came to join him and then he left.'

Jane picked up the milk jug. 'Why didn't you alert the captain?' she asked.

Alicia shrugged again as she set the strainer aside. 'It seemed so harmless. I wondered if perhaps he was homesick. I suppose I felt sorry for him. I know they are the enemy but one should still have humanity, don't you think?' She looked at Jane and Arthur as if expecting them to agree with her.

Jane's lips had pursed, and Arthur quickly intervened. 'It was a kind thought but perhaps now in hindsight, it may have been better to inform the camp.' He tried to be diplomatic.

'Yes, perhaps you're right. I am a silly, sentimental old biddy. The last war was so awful, so many suffered and died and I, well, I thought it would do no harm.' Alicia looked crestfallen.

'Of course,' Arthur said. He had some sympathy for the older woman's thought process. No one could have foreseen Gambini's comrade being found dead in the same spot only a week later.

It did, however, raise new questions. Had Gambini gone there to meet someone? And if so, who? It seemed there had been a lot more laxity in the arrangements permitting the prisoners to go to and from the farm unescorted than they had been led to believe. This did not bode well for increasing the use of prisoners as labourers if not corrected.

Jane had picked up her cup and was gazing around the studio. There were some landscapes hanging on the back wall of the cottage that Arthur assumed Alicia had painted. They were all of rural or coastal scenes. There was also a portrait of a very pretty young woman with dark hair wearing a green dress.

'Oh, that's a commission piece,' Alicia said, noticing Jane's interest in the picture. 'Annie Simms from the Green Dragon, her husband requested a portrait. I don't do many these days, but he was keen, and Annie is a very pretty girl.'

'It's very good,' Arthur said.

'I need to drop it in to them. I only finished it yesterday.' Alicia had her head tilted on one side looking at the picture as if deciding if she was satisfied with it.

'Do you know Mr and Mrs Simms well?' Jane asked.

'Only to talk to in passing. I've called in there a couple of times when there has been an event on in the village. I feel a touch uncomfortable going in there as a woman alone. Old-fashioned I know, in these times,' Alicia said.

'I suppose the pub is pretty popular,' Jane said. 'I thought someone mentioned at the party that Miss Hargreaves went there.'

'Oh, I wouldn't know about that.' Alicia gave a small nervous laugh. 'I don't socialise much in the village. I expect she is the same as me, calling in when an event is on. Unless she and Annie are friends. They must be about the same age.'

'I suppose your work keeps you busy,' Arthur said, looking at a sketch for a poster about carrying identity cards.

'Yes, it does and of course the villagers seem to feel I'm rather odd living here alone with a cat. The children think I'm a witch.' Alicia chuckled.

Arthur could see that a silver-haired elderly woman living alone with a black cat in a run-down cottage could appear that way to children. The children had said as much when they had met them at their den.

'This cottage is so old. I didn't realise anyone was living here until we came to the dunes the other day,' Jane said.

'It is a little run-down but it suits me very well. It's one of the oldest houses in the village, I believe.' Alicia glanced around her with an air of satisfaction.

'It has good light for a studio,' Arthur agreed.

'I must say, I so enjoyed your party yesterday evening. It was so pleasant to be doing something normal again. Your mother has a most delightful singing voice. I can see why she is so popular,' Alicia said, looking at Jane.

'Thank you. I'm pleased the evening was successful.' Jane placed her now empty teacup back on its saucer and returned it to the tray.

'I hope you manage to get all the information for your report. I expect you will be going back to London soon,' Alicia said.

Arthur wondered why everyone seemed to want them to leave the village. Almost everyone that they had spoken to so far had asked how long they were staying and when they planned to go.

'We came here originally for a short break so being asked to do this has somewhat derailed our holiday. We have a few more people to see and some things which need to be followed up and then we shall see. We shall be making some recommendations about increasing security around escorting the prisoners,' Jane said.

'Yes, quite, I suppose so.' Alicia looked a little flustered and Arthur guessed she was thinking about Gambini's excursion to the bench at the end of her garden.

The sound of youthful voices carried in the air and Alicia rose to glance through the French doors. 'The children are out of school.'

Arthur realised that even if Alicia was engrossed in her work, she would hear people outside near the dunes even if she didn't look to see who they were.

'Are there any villagers that come here regularly to the dunes, apart from the children?' he asked.

'One or two, courting couples on an evening. People walking their dogs,' Alicia said.

'Anyone we would know?' Jane asked.

Alicia smiled gently. 'Probably not.'

It was clear that she was not prepared to elaborate. Arthur suspected that, with most of the young men having enlisted, the couples who stopped by the dunes at dusk were older, or perhaps conducting illicit relationships. He finished his tea.

'I fear we have interrupted your work for long enough.' Jane smiled at their hostess. 'We really should get going.'

'Not at all, my dear, please stop by anytime. I enjoy a little company to break up my day,' Alicia assured her as they rose from their seats ready to leave.

They thanked her for their tea and Jane extended an invitation to her to call at Ashbourne House if she was in the village. Social niceties completed, they waved goodbye and set off back down the path towards the village once more.

'Gambini never mentioned visiting the beach,' Jane said as they walked back through the trees. 'Really, Captain Prudhoe needs to return to picking up and dropping off the prisoners. This laxity is far too much. I cannot think what his commanding officer was thinking in granting permission.'

'I suppose Gambini was unlikely to say anything about it given the circumstances. And, yes, you're right about the camp tightening up.' Arthur was thinking hard about everything they had learned so far.

It was odd how the Simms's names kept cropping up and each time there was a frisson of something about them. He would be very interested to learn what Benson had discovered when they got back to the house.

* * *

Jane slowed her pace as they walked home. She could see that Arthur struggled to keep up with her when she walked at her usual speed. The heat of the day and the unaccustomed amount of exercise meant that even after walking slowly he was audibly wheezing when she opened the front door.

Benson immediately rushed forward to assist Arthur with removing his coat and hat. The manservant then disappeared, before returning promptly with Arthur's medical bag. Jane watched from by the piano as Benson expertly set up Arthur's equipment and soon had him breathing in his medication.

Her mother was no longer reclining on the sofa and Jane wondered where she had gone. She had taken the precaution of taking the keys to the car with her when they had set off for the dunes. The word 'no' never meant much to Elsa and Jane was certain she would have just driven off to town if she had found them.

Once Arthur was breathing more easily, Benson started to tidy away some of the equipment into the bag.

'Miss Elsa said that she will not be home until later, Miss Jane. She has gone to call on Doctor Denning,' Benson informed her.

'Thank you, Benson.' Jane wondered if her mother would try to persuade the doctor to take her into town.

Arthur's colour had improved and his breathing was steadier as he finished his medication. Once Jane was satisfied that he was recovering well she turned to Benson.

'How did things go at the Green Dragon? Did you learn much about the landlord and his wife?' she asked, seating herself on the end of the piano bench and lighting her cigarette.

She was keen to learn more about the mysterious couple. Were they mixed up in Russo's death? Or was it just a red herring?

CHAPTER FIFTEEN

Benson cleared his throat and straightened his back in preparation for delivering his report.

'I went into the village first and performed a few small errands for Mrs Dawes. People were very keen to discuss Miss Elsa's return to the village. It seems the vicar's wife had mentioned it in the post office.'

Jane blew out a thin stream of smoke, taking care to ensure that none of it went in Arthur's direction. 'This village loves to gossip,' she said.

She had no doubt that tongues would be wagging. Her parents' separation had caused a frenzy of speculation some years ago. It had been no secret in the village that the parting had not been amicable. Her mother's fame had made the situation even more gossip-worthy.

'It made it easier to raise the subject of the Green Dragon during conversations, since people were more amenable to chat. The feeling I got was that the landlord was not very well liked. He is considered to be rather abrupt and quick tempered. However, it is the only public house, so people are wary about what they say,' Benson said.

'And the landlady, Annie Simms, what did people say about her? Alicia Carstairs has painted her portrait, and she is a very pretty woman,' Jane said.

Benson gave a gentle sheep-like cough. 'The consensus amongst the villagers was that the marriage is not a happy one. Mr Simms is reported to be very controlling where his wife is concerned. She rarely mixes in the village, although she seems to have a friendship with Miss Hargreaves. Mr Simms is some years older than his wife.'

'Her husband commissioned the portrait,' Arthur said, after having set his mask aside. He coughed gently and cleared his throat.

Benson switched off the machine. 'I went to the Green Dragon for lunch as we had discussed. They have a simple menu of sandwiches or pie.'

Jane looked at him. She had no desire to listen to a culinary review.

Benson continued to talk as he cleaned Arthur's equipment and carefully replaced it in the bag.

'Mr Simms was behind the bar. He is a heavyset man of about fifty years of age. I ordered my lunch and a pint of beer and took a seat nearby. There were already two elderly gentlemen in the pub when I arrived. I gathered from their conversation they were there most days.'

Jane nodded. It sounded as if Mrs Simms was indeed some years younger than her husband if Alicia's portrait was not being overly flattering.

'Mrs Simms brought my pie out to me when it was ready. She is a very pretty young woman, in her early twenties from her appearance. She did seem intimidated by her husband, barely staying long enough to set my lunch down before going back to the kitchen,' Benson said.

Jane sensed from Benson's demeanour that he disapproved of what he had observed. 'What happened then?' she asked.

'A man came in and started to converse with Mr Simms at the bar. They spoke in low tones and clearly didn't wish to be overheard. I feigned interest in my pie and tried to listen to the conversation. I heard them talking about a delivery and a storage problem. I had the impression that it was not beer that was being discussed.'

'The cellars of a public house would be ideal for concealing contraband,' Arthur said.

'True, and it could easily form part of a network. Good work, Benson.' Jane extinguished her cigarette.

'We need to keep an eye on the Green Dragon. There is no sense in rushing these things if we are to link the pub to whatever is happening with these black market gangs. It's a good lead but by no means a certainty that this is what was being discussed,' Arthur cautioned.

'I hope the information we requested from the brigadier about Mr Wood's reports might arrive tomorrow. He also promised us a list of premises that had been targeted, didn't he?' Jane said.

'He did. It would be useful to see if there was any kind of pattern that I could discern. Obviously, one assumes the gangs are opportunists in the sense that they cannot act until there is a raid.' Arthur looked thoughtful and Jane guessed he was already thinking about the implications.

'Quite so, but we have to assume that they are lying in wait and are organised ready to act immediately on any opportunity that may arise.' Jane rose from the piano bench and paced across the carpet towards the front window.

'Once I have the information from Whitehall and Mr Wood, it may be possible to triangulate the activities on a map to search for a possible base and routes to where the goods are being taken before distribution.' Arthur shifted in his chair, the movement making him cough more harshly.

Benson slipped silently from the room and returned quickly with a glass of water, which he placed next to Arthur.

Arthur accepted gratefully and took a sip.

'I suppose the next question is, does any of this have something to do with Russo's murder? Or is that an entirely separate issue which we should leave to Inspector Topping?' Jane had no particular faith in the inspector's ability to solve the Italian prisoner's murder, but rules were rules.

'There is nothing substantial to link the two cases at present, but Russo's death is problematic.' Arthur set down his glass.

'Well, we know that Gambini isn't telling us all that he knows.' Jane walked back to the chair opposite Arthur's and sat down.

'I would also suggest, Miss Jane, that the schoolteacher, Miss Hargreaves, may also have useful information,' Benson suggested mildly as he finished with Arthur's equipment and snapped the fastener on the bag shut.

'Yes, we still don't know why her name was linked to the Green Dragon, apart from this alleged friendship with Annie Simms. From what you described it sounds like a very traditional public house. Alicia Carstairs said she had only visited when there had been an event on in the village. I presume that's when more of the villagers would go. I know they used to go in the past when we had harvest events and things.' Jane drummed her fingers lightly on the arm of the chair.

'Alicia Carstairs said she thought Miss Hargreaves and Mrs Simms were friends, so that supports what Benson has learned. We need to speak to Gambini again too, I suppose.' Arthur's breathing sounded much easier now. 'Jane, did I see some local maps in your father's study?'

'Besides the one you found already?' Jane asked. 'Yes, Father loved old maps so he has quite a few. He also has walking guides and county maps. I presume you wish to look at access to nearby towns and villages?'

Arthur nodded. 'I may as well make a start on looking at the routes this gang or gangs may be taking. Mr Wood felt they were London based but that would take too long so there must be another base at some point between here and the capital if they are to mobilise when the raids start.'

'Yes, London would be an end point unless the enemy were going for the harbours and dockyards as a target,' Jane suggested.

'Or an airfield,' Benson added. He picked up the medical bag. 'Would you like me to find the documents you require, sir?' He looked at Arthur.

'It's all right, Benson. I'll get them. I know where Father kept them.' Jane jumped up from her chair, eager to be useful.

'Very good, Miss Jane. I shall return to assisting Mrs Dawes in the kitchen.' Benson exited the room, taking the medical supplies with him.

Jane gave Arthur a wry smile. 'Have I offended him? I didn't mean to.'

Arthur smiled back. 'No, it's fine. He's simply used to being the person that finds all my papers.'

Jane was not convinced, but decided she could always apologise to Benson later if she had stepped on his toes by offering to retrieve the maps. She went into her father's study and looked along the shelf where he had stored his papers and documents on the local area and the county. There was a large selection combined with his books of folktales and smuggling legends.

She pulled a bundle from the shelf and placed them on her father's desktop to sort through them all. The faint scent of his cigar smoke still lingered on the paper, and it took her back to when she had been younger, spending time in this very room discussing books and plays.

A wave of nostalgia swept through her, and she found

herself blinking away a couple of tears that had crept unheeded into her eyes at the memory. She gave a determined sniff and dashed them away with the back of her hand before returning to her quest.

Once she was satisfied that she had extracted the most useful documents, she returned the others to the shelf. She gathered up the remaining papers and added a notebook and a pencil to the pile, before carrying it into the drawing room.

'I think these are probably the best ones for what we need.' Jane deposited the bundle of papers onto the side table next to Arthur.

'Thank you.'

'Are you feeling all right now?' Jane asked when Arthur made no move to look at what she had collected. He still looked pale, and she wondered if all the exercise they had done today had been too much for him.

'I'm perfectly fine. I just need to rest for a moment or two before going through all of these.' He glanced at the documents.

'Would you like some tea or something to revive you?' she suggested, feeling slightly guilty that she hadn't considered his physical limitations when walking all around the farm and then down to the beach and back. She knew he led a very sedentary lifestyle because of his asthma.

'Thank you, Jane.' He closed his eyes, and she hurried out of the room towards the kitchen.

Mrs Dawes was rolling out pastry on a marble slab at the huge, scrubbed pine kitchen table when Jane entered the room. Benson had removed his black formal jacket and was at the sink with his sleeves rolled above his elbows peeling potatoes. Music was playing softly from the wireless her father had installed in the kitchen. Late afternoon sunshine streamed in through the windows which overlooked the vegetable patch and the Anderson shelter.

'Is everything all right, Jane?' Mrs Dawes asked. 'Your mother's not back yet, is she?'

'No, I just came to make some tea for Arthur. I think all the exertion today may have been a bit much for him,' Jane explained, guiltily casting an apologetic look at Benson.

'I shall fill the kettle, Miss Jane.' Benson set down his potato knife and collected the kettle from the top of the range. 'I'll bring a tray to the drawing room when it's ready.'

'Thank you, that's very kind of you,' Jane said as Marmaduke appeared round the slightly open door of the pantry and wound himself affectionately about her legs.

She bent to stroke her cat while he hummed with pleasure.

'I was just telling Mr Benson about the Simms. He said he went there for lunch today,' Mrs Dawes said as Jane straightened back up.

'Oh yes?' Mrs Dawes was sure to know the Simms's backgrounds. They had not been the landlords at the Green Dragon when she had lived at home with her father. That had been a rather grumpy older man who had retired to Whitstable.

'They came from London. Leastways, that's where he is from. She is a Kentish maid from Romney,' Mrs Dawes said.

'There seems to be quite an age gap between them,' Jane said as Marmaduke stalked off once more towards the scullery and the open back door.

'That's right. He's at least twenty years older than her. She worked for him I think at his last place, and they got married. They're an odd couple. She doesn't mix much, keeps herself to herself. He's one of those that's always giving it large. Boastful, he is,' Mrs Dawes said.

The kettle on the top of the range started to whistle and Benson busied himself making tea.

'I take it that you don't care for him much?' Jane asked her housekeeper.

Mrs Dawes shook her head. 'I don't know either of them that well, but my husband says he's not much liked. Too full of his own importance.'

'And Mrs Simms?' Jane asked, knowing that Mrs Dawes was more likely to know more about the landlady than the landlord.

'She often goes walking down to the sea. Has bad nerves, that's what he says anyway. It's why he's so protective of her.' By he, Jane assumed Mrs Dawes meant the landlord, Herbert Simms. 'Personally, I think she goes to get away from him. It's about the only place he lets her out of his sight.'

Benson had finished preparing the tea tray.

'I'll take it down, Benson. Thank you,' Jane offered, seeing the manservant was about to roll down his sleeves to don his coat.

'Very good, Miss Jane.'

She collected the tray and Benson returned to his potatoes.

Arthur opened his eyes when she clattered back into the drawing room bearing the tea tray. He sat up and moved the pile of papers over so Jane could set the tray down on the table.

'Mrs Dawes was telling me some more background on the people at the Green Dragon.' Jane explained what her house-keeper had said while she poured their tea.

'Annie Simms likes to walk to the sea each day? Hmm, I wonder if that was how the request from Herbert to Miss Carstairs to paint her came about.' Arthur rubbed his eyes as if to shake off his tiredness.

'I suppose it could be. Alicia is bound to have seen Annie by the dunes,' Jane said.

'I wonder if Gambini could have been hoping she might come down there that day Miss Carstairs saw him loitering by the bench,' Arthur suggested. 'A pretty woman and a younger man, their paths may have crossed somewhere.'

'Alicia was very reticent, wasn't she, about courting couples?' Jane handed him a cup of tea.

'Yes, perhaps she was protecting someone?'

Jane thought that made sense. Alicia hadn't reported seeing Gambini there because she had felt sorry for him. What else had Alicia seen that she felt wasn't worth reporting?

CHAPTER SIXTEEN

Jane wasn't sure whether she should be relieved or concerned when her mother failed to return in time for dinner. However, since Elsa had said she was going to Doctor Denning's house she decided not to worry. No doubt her mother was happily gossiping and entertaining the doctor's household and had probably been invited to stay and dine.

After their own meal of chicken pie with vegetables from the garden and a dessert of jelly and evaporated milk, they returned to the drawing room to look at the maps Jane had retrieved from the study.

Benson opened up the folding rosewood card table and they spread the county map on the green-baize top so they could look at the areas Mr Wood had mentioned when he had called the other day.

'We really need that list from Mr Wood and those reports from London,' Jane remarked as Arthur studied the map. He had the notebook open and was making cryptic squiggles inside it.

'I agree but we may as well try and see what we're working

with. Do pass me that ruler, Jane,' Arthur muttered absent-mindedly as he squinted at the map.

She passed him the ruler. 'Shall I bring the lamp closer, or do you need your glasses?' she asked.

'Glasses, hmm, yes.' He fumbled in his pocket and pulled out a small pair of wire-framed spectacles which he popped on the top of his nose.

Jane suppressed a sigh and went and moved the silk-shaded table lamp closer to cast more light on the map. 'Has that helped at all?' she asked.

'What? Hmm, you're casting a shadow, Jane.' Arthur made more squiggles in the notebook.

Jane gave up and went and helped herself to her much-depleted sherry stock. She knew what Arthur was like when he had the bit between his teeth, and she was unlikely to get much out of him until he had finished whatever he was doing.

She retook her seat and sat quietly sipping her sherry. At first, she thought she was mistaken but as she listened, she heard the very faint far away drone of aircraft. A shiver ran along her spine, and she wondered which way they were headed. Were they British fighters flying out over the sea towards France and beyond? Or incoming enemy planes?

Her answer came moments later with the wail of the warning sirens in the village.

'Come on, Arthur, we have to go to the shelter.' She jumped up and hurried to top up her glass. If she was going to be stuck in the shelter for a while she might as well enjoy her sherry.

'Arthur! Shelter, now!' she commanded, realising her companion didn't even seem to have noticed the warning.

She took hold of his arm and tugged him to his feet. He glared at her and put his glasses back in his pocket.

'Very well, I'm coming.' The sound of the planes overhead was louder now, and she could hear the distant boom of the anti-aircraft guns firing further down the coast as they grabbed their coats and stepped outside.

Mrs Dawes had gone home an hour or so earlier. Benson was already inside the shelter with a very disgruntled Marmaduke who expressed his displeasure by hissing at Arthur when they entered.

'Poor Marmaduke. He hates the sound of the sirens. I found him on a bomb site as a kitten. That was where he lost his eye.' Jane crouched to get inside and took a seat on one of the old chairs her father had used to make the shelter more comfortable. Marmaduke promptly came to hide behind her legs.

Arthur kept a safe distance from her cat and placed himself on another chair. Benson also had Arthur's medical bag and the biscuit tin from the kitchen.

'Did you seriously bring your sherry with you?' Arthur suddenly noticed the glass in Jane's hand.

'Well, I had no intention of leaving it behind,' she said. Frankly, if she was about to meet her maker then she would rather go enjoying a nice glass of sherry.

The heavy wooden door was closed, muffling the sounds from outside. The hurricane lamps cast a yellow glow around the confined space, and it felt quite cosy, all things considered. Jane was thankful her father's forethought meant staying in the shelter was much nicer than many other shelters she had been forced to take refuge in before.

Benson produced a pack of cards and they whiled away the time playing games whilst waiting for the all-clear. Jane wondered if her mother was safely inside the shelter at Doctor Dennings's house. At least she hadn't heard any loud explosions nearby.

'Listen,' Arthur said suddenly. Marmaduke stopped licking his paw and stood, his back arched.

It took Jane a moment and then she heard the drone of airplane engines overhead once more.

'I think the planes are returning,' Arthur said.

Jane knew this could be a concern. Any ammunition left was often dumped as the enemy returned across the channel. Living so close to the sea there was an increased risk of being caught by this action. The raids might not be so heavy as the ones at the start of the year, but they were still ongoing.

The anti-aircraft guns boomed again, and Marmaduke yowled a protest.

'Hush, darling,' Jane soothed. 'It's almost over.'

Once the remaining aircraft were out of range the all-clear should be given and they could discover what, if any, damage had been done to the house and the village.

Benson picked up the cards from the small folding table and put them back in the box. The noise from the anti-aircraft guns died away and a few minutes later the all-clear siren sounded.

They returned to the house and Benson volunteered to walk into the village to see if any damage had occurred. Jane offered to have cocoa ready for his return.

'Thank you, Miss Jane. I shall also call at Doctor Dennings's house and see if your mother wishes to be escorted home,' he suggested.

'Good man, Benson. I'm sure Elsa will appreciate it,' Arthur said.

Jane nodded. 'Yes, thank you.'

She appreciated his thoughtfulness. It wasn't nice being out in the dark since there were no street lights any more.

Benson left and Arthur accompanied her into the kitchen. Marmaduke stalked past them both, his nose in the air, still clearly having not forgiven them for keeping him in the shelter.

Arthur leaned against the dresser and watched as Jane busied herself with a small, enamelled saucepan and the milk.

'It will be interesting to find out if any damage has been done in Romney or one of the other towns,' he said.

Jane added some milk to a saucer and set it down for Marmaduke. 'If the looters have been out?' she asked.

Arthur nodded. 'I'm sure Mr Wood will inform us as soon as he knows something.'

'Then depending on the goods taken and any new information, we can try to track the perpetrators down.' Jane placed the pan on top of the range to heat the milk. 'How do they get there so quickly, do you think?' she asked, turning to face him.

Arthur frowned and scratched his head making his always somewhat wayward curls stick up. 'My assumption is that as soon as the planes are heard approaching the coast the gang are readied and in their vehicle or vehicles.'

'You believe they then drive to the nearest large towns and wait?' Jane shivered. It conjured up an unpleasant image. Men lurking in the shadows ready to pounce on the death and misery of others.

'In more densely populated areas such as London, they are already on the spot. It's simply a case of waiting to see which areas are hit and then capitalising on the damage. Here, I think they would have to operate slightly differently,' Arthur said.

The milk in the pan started to bubble up and Jane grabbed a cloth to wrap around the pan handle, lifting it from the heat. Arthur placed three thick china mugs ready on the pine table-top, while Jane retrieved the tin of cocoa powder from the pantry.

'Hmm.' Jane spooned the cocoa into the mugs before adding the hot milk. 'Perhaps we should make a journey into Folke-stone or somewhere tomorrow and take a look for ourselves to see if any fresh damage has occurred,' she suggested.

'We still need to talk to Katie Hargreaves about her relationship with Russo. She may be more forthcoming if there is no one else around,' Arthur said.

'True. The same could be said for Gambini but that is problematic. Captain Prudhoe's presence and that of the guard is inhibiting but we cannot see him without them.' Jane stirred the mugs of cocoa, turning the milk a rich-brown colour.

'Yes, I fear he will not say anything at all if we try and interview him again under those circumstances, at least not unless we have something more to ask him.' Arthur looked at her.

'Other than what he was doing by the dunes and who he may have been meeting?' Jane passed a mug to Arthur.

His fingers brushed hers and she withdrew her hand quickly once he had hold of the mug. The brief moment of contact in the cosy intimacy of the kitchen had been oddly disconcerting.

She turned away quickly to place the milk pan to soak in the sink, hoping the telltale blush in her cheeks had not been noticed. Thankfully she knew that for someone so clever, Arthur could be remarkably obtuse in other matters.

'I wonder if Inspector Topping has any suspects in mind yet for Russo's death,' she said as she busied herself at the sink.

'It's difficult to know who it may have been. Katie Hargreaves may be a suspect, possibly aided by Annie Simms. Russo was known to be sweet on her and he may have made unwelcome advances,' Arthur suggested.

'That would indicate some premeditation, and we have no reason to think there had been a problem. She could have just reported his behaviour to Captain Prudhoe.' Jane could see how she was a possibility, but why would she not simply have had the prisoners' freedom revoked?

'True, but perhaps the brigadier was on the right track in thinking there might be a connection between Russo's death and the black market gang. Miss Hargreaves and Mrs Simms could be part of the network.' Arthur leaned back in his chair.

'Mr Briggs is also under consideration, I suppose. He was at the farm when Russo disappeared before his death,' Jane said.

'Yes, and he has the links and influence if Russo had uncovered something incriminating, then Briggs would have to get rid of him. He also seems to have some influence over Inspector Topping.' A crease deepened on Arthur's forehead.

'We can't even rule out police corruption, can we?' Jane asked.

'No, I don't suppose we can,' Arthur agreed.

'Or we could be entirely mistaken, and Russo was killed by someone we don't know. One of this gang if he happened to stumble on something at the wrong time.' Jane shivered at the thought. The black market men would probably be quite ruthless.

There was a faint sound from the hallway.

'I think that was the front door opening,' Arthur said.

'Oh, I do hope there was no damage in the village.' Jane dried her hands on a tea towel and hung it on the Sheila Maid.

'Janey pie, I'm home!' her mother sang out as she entered the kitchen in a cloud of perfume and laden down with parcels.

'Where is Benson?' Jane asked, peering around her mother for Arthur's manservant.

'Mr Benson kindly escorted me home and has carried my hat box upstairs for me.' Her mother drew off her gloves and removed her tiny navy hat with its peekaboo veil, placing it on the table with her parcels.

'There appears to be no damage sustained in the village,' Benson said as he entered the kitchen.

'Thank heavens for that. I had to endure the most ghastly hour in Doctor Denning's Anderson shelter. I had to leave all my purchases in the house. What if it had been bombed?' Her mother produced her compact and fluffed up her curls while looking at her reflection in the small mirror.

'A tragedy,' Jane remarked drily. 'I've made cocoa, did you want some?' she asked.

Elsa gave an exaggerated shudder. 'Ugh, no thank you, honey. I think there is some vermouth in the cabinet. I shall have a spot of that to settle my nerves before bed.'

Jane handed a mug to Benson before collecting her own drink. 'Shall we go to the drawing room?' she suggested.

Elsa waltzed ahead of them with her packages, leaving her hat on the kitchen table. Jane swallowed a sigh and picked it up to transfer it to the hallstand. By the time she joined the others in the drawing room Elsa was ensconced on the sofa being served her drink by Benson.

'Honestly, Janey, I am completely exhausted.' Her mother raised her crystal glass in a cheers motion as Jane took her seat opposite Arthur.

'I take it Doctor Denning took you shopping?' Jane asked, before taking a sip of her rapidly cooling cocoa.

'It really was terribly kind of him. I managed to get one or two necessities. So difficult with the shortages and some things being rationed, but still. We had a lovely tea at the Lyons Corner House. Such a pity that there was no waitress service.' Elsa frowned at her. 'Janey pie, you really should start using face cream.'

'I take it you dined at Doctor Denning's house?' Jane ignored her mother's remark. She was quite used to her mother making unwanted suggestions about how she could improve her appearance.

'Yes, he had no surgery this evening, so he was free. I have to be honest, his housekeeper is not much of a cook. Still, he did have a rather nice bottle of wine. Such a treat these days. Then the wretched siren went off, so I had to endure the shelter with both Doctor Denning and Mrs Pyle, his housekeeper. Such a dreary woman. She knitted what looked like half a sock while we were stuck in there.' Elsa gave a delicate shiver of distaste.

'Most distressing, Miss Elsa,' Benson remarked from his seat on one of the upright mahogany occasional chairs.

Jane bit the inside of her cheek to prevent herself from saying something she might regret.

'And how was your day, Janey? Did you go to that shack and

visit that mad artist woman? Why anyone would rent that old cottage I cannot imagine. It's so old and must be rife with damp and mould.' Elsa took a sip of her drink.

'Yes, we went to see Miss Carstairs at her cottage. It was most informative.' Jane wished her mother would retire to bed so she could discuss plans for tomorrow with Arthur and Benson.

'That sounds about as exciting as watching Mrs Pyle knit a sock,' Elsa remarked.

'Which town did you visit for your shopping?' Arthur asked.

'We drove to Folkestone. It's really the only place with any decent shops anywhere near here. I should have liked to have gone to Canterbury but it's a long way for an afternoon outing. Although Folkestone is much changed from how it used to be. It's fortunate that, being a doctor, Samuel has access to petrol.' Elsa brightened at Arthur's interest in her activities.

'Has there been much damage there from the bombs?' Arthur continued.

Jane sipped her cocoa and marvelled at Arthur's skill at extracting something useful from her mother's conversation.

'The main shopping street wasn't too bad, all things considered. Quite a few places boarded up but on the whole it was not too affected, so far as I could tell. There was quite a bit of damage on the outskirts and near the sea at one point, but we kept away from there.' Elsa finished her drink and placed her empty glass on the side table. 'Well, I think I shall call it a night. A lady needs her beauty sleep.' She twinkled at Benson. 'Janey, honey, I advise you to turn in too. Your complexion really is looking rather muddy these days. I do have the most marvellous cream I can give you.'

Elsa said goodnight to Arthur and left the room. Jane blew out a huge sigh once she heard the stairs creak as her mother made her way to her bedroom.

'And that lady, gentlemen, is my mother.' She shook her head and drank some more of her cocoa, wishing she had added a nip of brandy to her mug.

Benson opened his mouth as if to speak.

Jane glared at him. 'If you say one word to defend her, Benson, then you and I may fall out.'

'I was merely going to say that you have a delightful complexion, Miss Jane.' Benson looked slightly affronted.

Arthur grinned. 'Nice save, Benson, old chum.'

Jane turned her attention to him.

'You do have nice skin, Jane. Definitely not at all muddy,' Arthur added hastily.

Jane sighed and wondered sometimes why she bothered.

CHAPTER SEVENTEEN

Jane came downstairs the next morning to discover what appeared to be a fresh, blustery autumn day. Small white-puffy clouds scudded swiftly across a clear-blue sky and the leaves on the laurel hedge rustled and crackled in the breeze.

'I take it Arthur is not yet downstairs?' Jane asked when Benson appeared bearing a pot of coffee and a full toast rack.

'I believe he is in the study, Miss Jane. He has not had breakfast, however,' Benson said as he deposited the toast in front of her.

Jane helped herself to coffee and wondered what Arthur was up to in the study. She had given him all the maps and guidebooks that she had felt would be useful. She had just started on her toast and jam when he joined her at the breakfast table.

'Morning, Jane.' He beamed happily at her across the toast rack.

'Good morning. You seem jolly pleased with yourself?'

Benson wafted in and placed a small china teapot in front of Arthur and a dish of some kind of cereal.

'I was looking up a few things, then I called the brigadier.

You know he's always in the office early. I wanted to ensure those copies of Mr Wood's reports had been sent out. They should be here today from what he said.' Arthur poured milk over the contents of his bowl and stirred everything around with a spoon.

'I see.' Jane winced as her companion started to crunch his way through his breakfast. 'Did he have anything else for us?'

'Only that he had received a precis of the coroner's report on Russo. The man was full of morphine. That must have been what was in the hypodermic that killed him.' Arthur dabbed the corners of his lips with his napkin.

'Morphine? Who would have access to that? A doctor, a vet?' Jane's mind raced.

'He said he had asked our friend Inspector Topping. Apparently, Doctor Denning reported five phials being stolen from his surgery just after Easter.' Arthur leaned back in his seat looking like the cat who had received the cream.

'That is most disturbing.' Jane put down her last triangle of toast and looked at Arthur. Surely, her father's old friend was not involved in anything untoward.

'I agree. Someone took those phials, who most probably intended keeping them for the sole purpose of murder. Topping had thought they had been stolen by an addict. There are many men who served in the last war who became dependent on such medication.' Arthur placed his spoon in his empty dish. His expression now sombre.

'This would indicate that Russo's death was not down to something personal, would you agree?' Jane asked.

Arthur nodded. 'I think he was lured to the beach and killed there. After seeing the access from the dunes, and from the cliff path on Mr Briggs's estate he couldn't have been taken there after death. It would be much too difficult and would require manpower. Someone would have seen them and there would have been traces.'

'We are assuming then, that based on what we have learned, he was lured there, hit on the head and injected with a lethal dose of morphine. That makes sense given the tight time frame. Someone, presumably his killer, then removed his uniform and left him there hoping his death would be seen as a drowning?' Jane said.

Arthur nodded. 'Yes. I don't understand why his uniform was taken, however. Unless it was to simply support the idea that he had gone to the beach to swim or to try to make some kind of bid for freedom.'

'It also made his body less noticeable I suppose to anyone walking by. It could be that the killer needed time to either get away or to establish some kind of alibi. If the body had been found later it could have helped the murderer. The children discovering Russo so soon after he had been killed was unforeseen,' Jane said.

Arthur helped himself to a slice of toast. 'I think it was too much effort to drag him down the beach and into the sea, so whoever killed him was forced to leave him above the high-water mark. This, I suggest, means he was probably killed by someone acting alone.'

'And because his clothes had been removed no one would know he had not in fact got wet.' Jane sat back in her chair. It seemed they had worked out a satisfactory hypothesis. All they needed now was to discover why he was killed and who by.

They had not long finished breakfast and were still debating on how best to obtain more information when the doorbell rang. They had moved from the dining room to the drawing room to continue their discussion.

'Mr Wood to see you, miss.' Benson ushered a flustered and harassed-looking Mr Wood into the drawing room. He had a large manila folder under his arm.

'Mr Wood, do sit down. I assume that folder contains the

information we requested from you?' Jane ushered him towards the sofa.

Benson, at a silent signal from Arthur, disappeared to the kitchen to prepare tea for their guest.

'They were at it again last night, during that raid. As soon as the bombs started dropping. They cleared out a grocer's shop and a draper's last night, they did.' The words burst from Mr Wood like water from a ruptured dam. Indignation bubbling up like a spring.

'Which area was this?' Arthur asked as he took the folder from the government official.

'Inland again, at Ashford this time. They turned up wearing ARP hats and armbands and started to load the stock into their lorry. One of Topping's men even helped them!' Mr Wood was quite pink in the face now at the impudence of the thieves.

'One of the constables?' Jane asked.

'They had the nerve to say that I had sent them when he asked them what they were doing. Using my name, brass neck that's what that is. Sheer brass neck.' Mr Wood glowered furiously at Jane as if she was somehow responsible for this affront. His Scottish burr stronger in his anger at the impudence of the thieves.

'Oh dear.' She was at a loss for a moment to know how to respond. 'Did the constable or the shopkeepers get descriptions of the men or of the vehicle?' she asked.

'They got given some made up papers to sign. Which they did, of course, as it all looked official. It gave the men permission to store their goods safely in a warehouse until their premises could reopen. The usual story. With the fires and smoke and the all-clear not having sounded, they didn't take much notice. The lorry was blue and the description of the two men much as before.' Mr Wood sank back on the sofa and buried his head between his hands. 'It has to be stopped, Miss Treen.'

'I quite agree, Mr Wood, it is deplorable. Did you go out yourself during the raid?' she asked.

'I did. I went into Folkestone, at great personal risk, I might add. The fires and the smoke were terrible. By the time I went from there and reached Ashford where the thieves had been, they had already left. There was just that fool of a constable who told me he had helped my men pack up the goods.' Mr Wood lifted his head up as he spoke.

Benson re-entered the room bearing a tray of tea.

'I thought some refreshments might be welcome,' he said as he set the tray down in front of Jane.

'Thank you, Benson. Mr Wood was telling us that the thieves struck again at Ashford during last night's raids,' Jane said as the manservant served the tea, handing a cup to Mr Wood.

'Oh dear, Miss Jane. Most deplorable,' Benson remarked.

'It's an affront to decent people, that's what it is. To steal goods during a war from innocent people, well it's treachery in my book.' Mr Wood's voice rose in his excitement.

'Quite so,' Benson agreed as he passed a cup of tea to Arthur, who had already opened the folder and was browsing the contents.

Benson's calm demeanour seemed to quell some of Mr Wood's excitability. Once everyone had been served the manservant discreetly withdrew.

'I presume the gang arrived shortly after the bombing commenced. Was this before the all-clear sounded?' Jane asked.

Mr Wood nodded vigorously. 'Yes, not long after the warning sirens and once the incendiaries started. There is an airfield along that flight path so they must have been aiming for there. The gang were obviously lying in wait for just such an opportunity. I must have missed them by just a few minutes. That idiot constable had escorted them out of the area.'

'This is the complete list of dates, times, and shops that you know to have been targeted so far, along with their locations?' Arthur asked, looking up from the papers he had been studying.

'Yes, exactly what you asked me for,' Mr Wood agreed before taking a sip of tea.

'Hmm.' Arthur returned his gaze to the documents the government inspector had provided.

'Is anything jumping out at you, Arthur?' Jane asked.

'It's hard to say. I need to plot it all on my map and triangulate the results. Mr Wood, have any of these goods turned up on resale, under the counter so to speak?' Arthur asked, his eyes still fixed on scanning the contents of the folder.

'I get wind of dribs and drabs but everybody is close mouthed. People don't like to admit they have cheated the system, you see, to get hold of something they shouldn't have done. Then if it's something like extra sugar or dried fruit or something for a wedding cake, then nobody wants to be a snitch. It's so difficult to prove that they didn't already have things in their pantry, or they hadn't been saving their ration up.' Mr Wood suddenly looked deflated. 'I try my best but I'm one man covering a large area.'

'It must be very difficult.' Jane could appreciate the enormity of the inspector's task.

'I do know that whoever is behind this must be getting very rich off it all. There'll always be people who'll pay to have a few extras, and all those shillings are lining somebody's pockets,' Mr Wood said.

'And in the meantime, the shopkeepers lose everything. Their premises and their livelihood with all their stock gone,' Jane said.

'What are you going to do?' Mr Wood asked as he finished his tea.

'We're working on the problem right now. This part always takes the longest. Gathering information and planning before we can act.' Jane glanced at Arthur who was lost in his own world again studying the documents.

'Well, I hope you can find something out. I've lost all faith in Inspector Topping and his men,' Mr Wood said.

Jane finished her own tea and set the cup aside. She smiled politely at the government inspector. 'We shall keep you informed of our progress. Thank you for bringing us all of the information. I can see already that my colleague is finding it most helpful,' Jane said as Mr Wood rose from his seat.

'Well, I hope it gets sorted soon,' Mr Wood said as Jane escorted him out of the drawing room into the hall.

He gathered his hat and coat from the hallstand. 'I'll telephone in a couple of days, if I don't hear from you,' the official said as Jane opened the front door.

'Yes, that would be good. We can update you then if there is no breakthrough beforehand,' Jane agreed and waved him off.

She breathed a sigh of relief once the door was closed, and headed back to the drawing room in search of a cigarette.

'Phew, poor Mr Wood, he seems to take all of this so personally,' she said as she subsided onto the armchair opposite Arthur. Jane plucked a cigarette from her bag and lit it. Arthur lifted his head to frown at her as some of the smoke drifted towards him.

'I need to look at my map.' He turned to the pile of books and papers Jane had procured from the study the previous evening. Benson had tidied up their papers and put the card table back in its usual place.

Jane moved the tea tray to the top of the piano out of the way in readiness. Once Arthur had found the map he wanted, he spread it out on the coffee table. He put on his spectacles and started making small crosses with a pencil, looking at the notes he had made in his notebook as he did so.

'Ruler, Jane.' He held out his hand without looking up from the map.

Jane sighed and placed the wooden ruler in his hand.

'Just pull that corner straight, can you?' He flapped the hand holding the pencil towards a bent over portion of the map.

Jane gritted her teeth, feeling like a surgeon's assistant as she followed his instructions. She watched as he began placing the ruler on the map, looking at his notes from where he had been trying to link the places before the raid of the previous evening.

Slowly a pattern began to form on the map as she watched. The raids and the looting at Ramsgate, Folkestone, Hythe, Ashford and several other towns all around the coast and just inland started to emerge. He disregarded the ones closer to Canterbury and that direction as outliers. Instead, he tracked the ones closer to their current location.

'Interesting,' he muttered once he was done.

'We are well placed here looking at that map. Not in the centre, but with good road access to all of the places that have been targeted in the aftermath of a raid,' Jane said as she looked at the results of his work. 'I agree, it is most interesting.'

'There is quite a cluster of shops that have had goods stolen, which are within twenty to thirty miles of here. Now, the gang need both to get into the town and out of it quite quickly. Plus, they need a safe storage place for the goods.' Arthur squinted at the map.

'I would have thought that would rule out most of the towns on the coast. The places would be far too risky, and they are crawling with military personnel. They need somewhere more out in the countryside, not many neighbours with a good road link to get in and out of these towns swiftly,' Jane said.

'Are you thinking of a barn or farm?' Arthur asked.

'I think that is very likely. What do you feel?' Jane asked.

'I agree. The other possibility is the one we considered yesterday, a public house such as the Green Dragon. Deep cellars would be safe from the raids, and they are used to having goods delivered and unloaded. The lorry could lie low for the night and then deliver goods as bold as brass in daylight without anyone taking too much notice if the goods were packed in boxes or barrels,' Arthur said.

'What about those outbuildings belonging to Mr Briggs?' Jane asked.

'The one with the shiny new padlock? Possible but I think it's too small and the roof appeared to be missing. I think it would need to be somewhere watertight and larger.'

Jane nodded slowly. 'I do agree with Mr Wood on one thing. There is a lot of ground to cover. Even assuming that you are correct, and we have narrowed down the area in which they are based, it is still a large area.'

Arthur leaned back slowly in his seat. He took off his glasses and returned them to their case. 'I think we may be forced to take action ourselves,' he said, pinching the bridge of his nose between his fingers and rubbing.

'What do you mean?' Jane's pulse speeded up. She had an idea of what he was about to suggest but needed to hear him say the words.

'The next time there is a raid, we need to drive to the nearest town. Follow the damage.' Arthur looked at her.

'I suppose the smoke and the glow of the fires would tell us what areas had been hit. The same method we think the black market men are using. We could drive to the top of Hartes Hill. It offers a good vantage point.' Jane swallowed.

She knew what they were considering carried huge risks. To be out and deliberately driving into an area that had been bombed with all the perils of unexploded devices, unstable buildings and out of control blazes was not something to be taken lightly.

'I know it's dangerous, but we really do need to have sight of these men to try and find where they are going. Inspector Topping seems to have neither the resources nor the will to take action,' Arthur said.

'I suppose there is no point in looking for the storage sites for the stolen goods?' Jane said.

'How many ruined cottages, disused old barns and outbuildings are there? Or public houses or old smugglers' tunnels?' Arthur asked. 'I read some of your father's books earlier, before breakfast. There are so many possibilities.'

Jane knew he was right. The villages near the coast and just inland had received stolen goods from across the channel for centuries before the present conflict. She knew that the cliffs and coastline were riddled with old tunnels and hiding places. Some of which even led into vaults below the churches.

Back then it had been tobacco, brandy and lace. A shiver ran along her spine, little seemed to have changed over the years.

CHAPTER EIGHTEEN

Elsa wafted downstairs shortly after eleven in a cloud of rose-scented perfume and pink chiffon.

'What are your plans for today, Janey pie?' she asked when she saw that Arthur and Jane were still seated in the drawing room. 'Are you going out somewhere nice?'

The post had been delivered and they had been reading the reports that Mr Wood had sent to the department. Arthur had added more information to his map.

'I'm not certain, Mother. We are working.' Jane ignored the hopeful tone in her mother's voice. She knew Elsa would think she could join them if they were going into a town.

Her mother gave a dismissive sniff at this reply.

Benson appeared and deposited a nicely set, small round silver tray of coffee at her mother's side. Jane looked at him through narrowed eyes.

'Benson, do we know if Mrs Simms has a regular time of day when she likes to go for her walks?' she asked.

'I believe it is around three to four, Miss Jane, when the pub is shut before the evening trade,' Benson said.

'That's around the time the children are let out from school too. When Russo used to meet Miss Hargreaves with his posies of flowers.' Jane looked across at Arthur.

'Do you think that would be a good time of day for us to try and talk to both of them?' Arthur asked, meeting her gaze.

'It has to be worth a try. Have you found much in these reports so far that might be useful to us?' Jane asked.

The bundle she had read had been a litany of complaints from Mr Wood interspersed with the details of which shops had been targeted. Attached to the back of each report was an inventory list supplied by the shopkeepers. These were not necessarily very accurate in some cases since they had been uncertain of what had been destroyed and what had been taken.

'There is a pattern in the types of goods,' Arthur said.

'Oh?' Jane had to admit she had been swamped by the lists of canned peaches, tinned pilchards, sugar, etc. that had been attached to the reports.

Arthur edged forward on his seat to show her his notebook. It took a second or two to decipher his untidy handwriting.

'Look, Jane,' he urged.

She realised that he had grouped the lists of goods taken rather than the types of shops. They seemed to consist of grocery products, many of which were luxury goods or rationed staples. The other grouping was of clothing, rolls of material, threads, buttons, hats and coats. The other much smaller group was of shoes and leather goods. There was also one which was wines, spirits, tobacco products and liquors.

'There are a few outliers obviously,' Arthur said, moving back once he was satisfied that Jane had understood what had been taken.

'Interesting. They seem to have been quite specific. There are no perishable items and no domestic goods,' Jane said.

Elsa waited as Benson poured her coffee and served her.

'What are you doing? If it's shopping, then that is my forte,'

Elsa asked, accepting the bone china cup and saucer with a smile which called a tiny hint of a blush to Benson's cheeks.

'These are stolen goods, Mother, taken from shops during air raids by gangs of thieves and placed on the black market,' Jane explained.

'Surely, that is a matter for the police,' Elsa said, before taking a sip of coffee.

'Normally, yes, but the police resources are stretched at present, and this racket is getting out of hand.' Jane had no intention of saying too much in front of her mother.

'Well, I must admit obtaining a few extras under the counter is hardly the crime of the century. With all these privations, one sometimes has to do what one can to make life more comfortable.' Elsa waved a careless free hand.

Arthur looked at Elsa. 'I can understand the temptation but the hardship the scale of these thefts is causing to the shopkeepers shouldn't be underestimated,' he reproved her in a mild tone.

'I do hope you aren't buying things under the counter?' Jane looked at her mother.

'Janey, honey, you know I can't help it if my admirers give me gifts,' Elsa said with a pout.

Jane thought that was not really answering her question, but it probably confirmed her thoughts on where the box of luxury chocolates had come from that her mother had been eating the previous day.

Benson had remained silent throughout the conversation, moving quietly about the room tidying up. Jane wondered what he had thought of Elsa's ideas about obtaining or receiving black market goods. She knew the manservant was somewhat spellbound by her glamorous mother.

This was nothing new. She had often puzzled over her parents' marriage. She could see why her academically brilliant father had been dazzled by Elsa, but she had never understood why her mother had married her father.

Elsa had been pursued by men her whole life. Men falling over themselves to do things for her, take her out, give her gifts. Why had she chosen to marry a rather dull professor who disliked the bright lights of London and New York? It was a mystery. Now it seemed she had added Benson to her tally of admirers.

'Do you have plans for today, Mother?' Jane asked.

'Not really, darling. I'm hoping to hear soon about some dates to return to make more recordings for the Home Service, although I shall need to book a hotel if my apartment is not repaired,' her mother said.

Jane knew this was a hint that her mother could use Jane's own small apartment while Jane was still in Kent. The last time she had let her mother borrow her flat for the weekend, however, it had not gone well. The place had been left dirty and her mother seemed to have held a party. There had been used glasses and plates left all over the place. She had still been finding fragments of crêpe paper party streamers for weeks afterwards.

'I'm sure you'd be able to book a room somewhere nice.' Jane's reply was interrupted by the sound of the telephone ringing in the study.

Benson left the room to go and answer it.

Jane went to move when Benson returned a few seconds later. She assumed the call would probably be from either Inspector Topping or from the brigadier.

'The telephone is for you, Miss Elsa,' Benson announced on his return. Jane subsided back in her chair as her mother went to take her call.

Arthur started to replace the reports that he'd read back in the envelope they had arrived in.

'Shall we try to talk to Annie Simms and Katie Hargreaves later this afternoon then?' he asked.

'I think so, don't you?' Jane handed over the papers she had been reading and he put those away with the rest.

'It seems the most logical course of action. As for the other matter, we shall have to be ready and wait to see when the next raid occurs,' Arthur said.

'I take it you intend to try to catch the thieves in action, sir, miss?' Benson asked.

'We need to see if we can follow them and discover the distribution network. The men committing the crimes may not be the ones organising it,' Arthur said.

'I shall make sure Cilla has a full tank of fuel and is ready to go should the sirens sound,' Jane assured him.

'I suggest that I also ready the gun, sir. These kinds of people can be very dangerous,' Benson said.

Arthur paled slightly at his manservant's suggestion but nodded his agreement. 'Thank you, Benson.'

Her mother came back into the room looking very pleased with herself. 'That was Mr Briggs, I am invited to tea at Chafford House Farm this afternoon. He will collect me in his motor car at three. Now, I suppose I should go and select something suitable to wear. Mr Benson, do you think you might be able to press something for me?'

'Of course, Miss Elsa. It would be my pleasure,' he said.

Her mother gave him a delighted smile and whisked away to plan her attire for her afternoon engagement. Benson slipped off, presumably to find the iron and board ready to press whatever garment Elsa produced.

* * *

Arthur had plenty of time over lunch to consider the plans for venturing out during the next air raid. It was undoubtedly a risky affair to attempt but if they should find the people they were looking for, it could ensure the arrests of the ringleaders.

Jane's expression at Benson's mention of taking the gun with them had mirrored his own feelings. It was not something he cared to do but Benson was correct to suggest it. The men running the black market operation were not the kind of people one could reason with. They were also likely to be armed.

Benson had suggested a route to the beach where they were more likely to encounter Annie Simms. Instead of taking the more direct route along the high street he had suggested a side road past some old fishermen's cottages. This was quieter with fewer people about and it seemed likely to be the reclusive Annie's preferred route.

They had set off just before Mr Briggs had arrived to collect Jane's mother for her afternoon tea. A flashy black car passed them a few moments after they had left the house. The sun was warm as they walked a little too briskly for Arthur's tastes along the high street for a short distance, before turning off down a side road.

They walked past the Green Dragon public house now closed until the evening. From the front it was a small place built of stone. Large, locked metal doors to the cellar were set in the pavement below a bay window with etched glass depicting a dragon. A small track at the side of the pub revealed it to be a long building, stretching back from the road with what appeared to be a couple of extensions to the original building.

Arthur could see some wooden fencing and a gate and guessed there was probably a small garden area at the rear. No doubt this, like most gardens, now housed an Anderson shelter and a vegetable plot. It had probably once been a pleasure garden for customers to sit in peace outdoors with their drinks.

Jane slowed her pace to allow him to catch her up as they continued on in the direction of the beach. Overhead the cries of the gulls screaming in the blustery sky grew louder and he could hear the waves as they came to the end of the road. The air smelled of ozone and he could taste salt on his lips. Through the trees, gnarled and bowed from the wind, he caught a glimpse of Alicia Carstairs's cottage.

A narrow path led from the side of the last house on the street up into the dunes. Steps had been cut out of the ground and boarded with old timbers. Now though, with the sand constantly blowing from the dunes the steps were virtually buried.

They made their way up, the breeze growing stronger the nearer they got to the sea. By the time they had climbed to the top Jane's dark-brown hair was being tugged loose and whipped about her face. Arthur wished he had brought his scarf with him.

They walked out into the trees which helped to mitigate the wind coming from the sea. Ahead of them he spotted a woman seated on the bench overlooking the spot where Russo's body had been found. Her dark-brunette hair was mostly covered with a navy-blue headscarf, and she seemed huddled down inside an ill-fitting fawn coat.

Jane looked at him, her eyes asking a silent question. Arthur gave a brief nod of confirmation. They had found Annie Simms. They walked together towards the bench. The woman sitting there seemed oblivious to their presence. Her gaze was fixed firmly on the sea in front of her.

The waves were larger today, crashing onto the sands with a rush and a roar before swishing back out again, leaving behind a trail of foam and tiny black stones and shells on the wet sand of the beach.

'Mrs Simms?' Jane spoke softly, her voice just audible above the sound of the sea. Arthur guessed that she didn't wish to startle the woman.

Annie tore her gaze away from the waves and turned her head slightly to see who was addressing her. 'Yes,' she said.

Jane perched herself gingerly on the other end of the rickety old bench. The wooden boards creaking slightly as she sat.

Arthur stood at her side as Annie returned her gaze to the sea.

'You're the landlady at the Green Dragon, is that right?' Jane asked.

Annie nodded and Arthur noticed the woman's hands clench where before they had been lying loosely on her lap.

'Do you come here a lot?' Jane asked.

The woman nodded once more. Her reddish-plum lipstick dark against the pale skin of her face.

'My colleague, Arthur, and I have been sent from London to look into the death of the man from the prisoner of war camp,' Jane said.

Annie blinked and a single tear escaped and ran down her pale cheek.

'Annie, we know now that his death was not an accident, and we are trying to speak to anyone who may have seen or heard something the day that his death took place,' Jane continued, her gaze fixed on Annie's face.

Arthur glanced up at Alicia Carstairs's cottage peeping above the dunes and wondered if she was in her studio. She would see them with Annie on the bench.

Annie remained silent and still as if she hadn't heard what Jane had said.

'Were you here on the day Antonio Russo died? Did you see or hear anyone?' Jane persisted.

Annie's grey eyes widened, and she reminded Arthur of a rabbit he had once seen as a child. Caught in a snare with no place to run.

'I... I don't know anything. Surely what happened must have been an accident.' Annie stood up suddenly as she spoke.

She swayed and almost fell back onto the bench. Arthur immediately offered his hand to steady her, she clutched at his coat sleeve as she righted herself. The wind gusting against her slim body revealed a slight curve in her abdomen that hadn't been noticeable whilst she was seated.

'Did you know Russo or his companion, Matteo Gambini?' Arthur asked. 'Russo was known to your friend, Katie Hargreaves. He used to give her flowers.'

Annie immediately let go of his arm. 'I... not really, I've seen them in the village. Katie was fond of Antonio. He used to make her laugh. I don't know the other man.' She rushed her words, and Arthur knew she was lying. Her body was trembling, and she couldn't meet his gaze.

'You were the person Gambini was waiting for the other week?' He gambled on his question. He knew she couldn't have been waiting for Russo since he was sweet on Katie Hargreaves. 'Why were you meeting?'

'No, I... I'm sorry, I have to get back to the pub, my husband.' Annie bit her lip and looked at the path where Jane now stood blocking her exit.

'What do you know of Matteo Gambini?' Arthur asked. He wondered if she knew of the meaning behind the tattoos worn by the prisoners and if the gang the men belonged to had a network locally somehow.

'He... he is a good man, really. He and Antonio, they wanted to change their lives. To stay here when the war ends,' Annie said.

'Why didn't you meet him?' Jane asked. She had obviously recognised the same signs that Arthur had detected.

'You don't understand. It's personal and complicated. My husband is a very jealous man. He... I have to go.' Annie's face was white with fear.

Before they could stop her or ask any more questions, she had gone. She slipped around Jane and scurried away back down the steps leading away from the dunes like a frightened rabbit.

CHAPTER NINETEEN

'That was quite extraordinary,' Jane said as she watched their quarry slip away.

'Very strange,' Arthur agreed. 'It seems clear that there was something between her and Gambini.'

'Perhaps that may be why he didn't say anything to us when we interviewed him. He may have been trying to protect her. The opportunities for them to meet must have been very slim,' Jane mused.

'I agree, nonetheless there was definitely something there.' Arthur turned his back to the sea.

'I suppose we should walk back along the high street now. The children will be out of school, and we may see Katie Hargreaves.' Jane started along the path that led away from the bench and towards the tail end of the village.

'Do we know where she lives?' Arthur asked.

'If we don't see her at the school? Yes, she lives in the cottage next door. It comes with the job,' Jane said as she picked her way along the narrow pathway with Arthur following behind her.

Her mind was busy picking over Annie Simms's reaction to

their questions. It was clear the girl had some kind of connection or affection for Gambini. She was also frightened of her husband. Had he learned of their clandestine meetings and lured the wrong man to his death? Had he killed Russo by mistake? Or had Annie witnessed something that day that she was too frightened to speak about?

When Jane reached the start of the road she paused and waited for Arthur to catch up to her. The high street was busy with mothers and children as they made their way home from the small red-brick village school.

Arthur fell into step beside her, and she forced herself to curb her pace a little as they headed past the straggly line of shops towards the school on the opposite side of the street. The rusty wrought-iron gate that led into the playground stood open so Jane guessed Katie must still be inside.

Jane stepped through into the small play area, a rush of nostalgia for her childhood assailing her at the sight of the compact building with its white-painted sash windows and blue double-entrance doors. Carved stonework over the door bore the legend 'infants' in neat lettering. She knew on the other side of the building a similar piece of stone said, 'juniors'.

One of the entrance doors was ajar so she and Arthur made their way up the low stone step and into the square vestibule with its red quarry-tiled floor and rows of coat hooks. A couple of scarves hung forlorn and forgotten by their small owners on random hooks.

'Hello, Miss Hargreaves,' Jane called out.

She opened the door that led into the classroom. The school was one large room with a wood and glass partition down the middle. When the school was fully staffed the infants had one part of the room and the older children the other part. Now, with the shortage of teachers, Miss Hargreaves was responsible for both groups of children.

The double doors in the partition were open and Katie

Hargreaves was seated at her desk at the far end of the room. She rose from her chair as they entered the classroom through the partition doors. The air smelt of chalk dust with a tinge of stale air. A large globe stood in the corner beside a low bookcase full of books. The blackboard had been cleaned. The desktop held a pile of books and a posy of wildflowers, now wilting in a small glass vase.

'Jane and Arthur, this is a pleasant surprise,' Miss Hargreaves greeted them politely, but Jane could see tension in the other woman's eyes.

'We were on our way home when I saw the gate was open. Being in here again brings back some memories for me.' Jane lightly touched the top of one of the small sloping wooden desks which were neatly lined up in rows.

Arthur had wandered over to look at what appeared to be a nature table containing a battered bird's nest, some shells, a mouse's skull and an ammonite fossil.

'Did you attend this school?' Katie asked.

'Yes, for a couple of years before I went to a day boarding school,' Jane said, gazing around at the pupils' artwork on the walls.

'I don't suppose it has changed much,' Katie said with a smile.

'No, not really. It must be difficult though for you, teaching such a diverse age group. I know there are not too many students, but even so.' Jane gave a graceful shrug of her shoulders.

Katie sighed and stepped forward around her desk. 'It can be a challenge. I was promised some help, but it's not been forthcoming so far,' she admitted.

'Arthur and I have just come from the dunes. We heard this morning from Inspector Topping that Antonio Russo's death was not an accident,' Jane said.

Katie's knees bent and she lowered herself to sit on one of her pupil's chairs. 'I thought he had drowned?'

Her eyes were wide with shock, and it was clear she was taken aback by the news.

'I'm afraid not.' Arthur ambled back over to join them.

'Can you remember when you last saw him? Did you see him the day he was killed?' Jane chose her words deliberately. Not to be cruel but to give Katie as little time as possible to think of a way to lie to them.

Everyone so far seemed to have lied to them over something.

Katie's mouth opened and closed a few times as if she were unable to connect her thoughts to her voice. 'No, I didn't see him. Not that day. I thought that I would. He usually came by the school on his way back to the camp and would give me some flowers, or stop for a moment to practice his English. I waited by the gate, but he didn't come. I thought I'd missed him.'

'Did you see Gambini, the other prisoner that day?' Arthur asked.

Katie pressed her fingers to her temples and rubbed. 'Yes, he was hurrying along the street. He was late and looked worried. He asked me if I had seen Antonio. I told him no and he muttered something in Italian and scurried off.'

'Were you surprised by this?' Jane asked.

Katie looked up at her. 'Yes and no. I mean, Matteo wasn't always with Antonio when they were going back to camp. He sometimes caught up with him after he had been talking to me. They would have to run then to get back to the camp for the time.'

'That would be when Gambini was meeting your friend, Annie, at the beach?' Arthur said.

'I... it was just once or twice. Annie's husband is unkind to her.' Katie looked distressed by the admission.

'You were expecting to see Antonio the day he died

though?' Jane waited for Katie to reply as the girl stood once more and paced back around her desk, her arms folded.

'Well, yes, he had said he would see me the next day.' Katie paused and bit her lip. 'Then when the children raised the alarm about finding a man dead on the beach. It's been horrible, really horrible.'

'Did Antonio ever mention anything about having any enemies? Anyone who may have wished to harm him?' Arthur asked.

Katie shook her head. 'No, nothing. He was a very sweet boy. He didn't want to fight. All he ever wanted was to be home working on his father's land with his brothers. We would talk about after the war and how things could be. If he should stay here or be repatriated to Italy. He hadn't done anything that would cause someone to want to kill him.'

'You were aware of his past?' Jane asked.

Katie bowed her head and nodded. 'Yes, he told me. Both he and Matteo had belonged to some criminal fraternity. Times had been hard, and they had joined to protect their families. They both wanted to escape it all. To stay here after the war.'

'I see. Feelings can sometimes run high about having the enemy so close,' Arthur said. 'Is there any sense within the village of someone holding a grudge against the two men working on the farm?'

Katie gave another faintly despairing shake of her head. 'Not really. People might ignore them or spit at them, you know, catcalling. That was early on though. Since it's become clear how much they have helped on the farm, all of that had pretty much died down.'

'Do you know of any reason at all, however small, of why someone may have wished to harm him? No one who may have resented your friendship?' Jane asked.

Katie frowned, lines puckering her forehead. 'No one really took any notice of Antonio being nice to me. He said he was worried about Matteo but he didn't say why. Not that he thought his friend would harm him, but that Matteo might get harmed. It was just an odd phrase, but it could simply have been a mistranslation giving me the wrong impression.'

'I see, thank you.' Jane could see there was little else that Katie was likely to be able to add.

'I'm very sorry for the loss of your friend,' Arthur said as he went to follow Jane back out of the school.

'Thank you.' Katie gave a brief, slightly watery smile. 'That means a lot to me.'

They walked back outside and continued to make their way back to the house.

'Jane, my dear,' Doctor Denning greeted them before they had taken many steps. He hurried across the road to meet them. 'Inspector Topping has informed me that he believes the theft of some morphine from my surgery a few months ago may be linked to the Italian prisoner's death.' He looked at Jane.

'Unfortunately, that does seem to be the case,' she said.

'Oh dear, now I feel that I was somehow remiss when I was called to the beach to see the poor man. However, I was only asked to confirm the death and not how he had died.' Doctor Denning looked troubled. 'I should have taken more notice.'

'Finding a dead, naked man on a beach, one would have thought he had probably drowned,' Jane said.

'Yes, I thought that perhaps he had been moved, you see, above the waterline. I should have asked more questions.' Doctor Denning didn't appear to be reassured by her argument. 'Thinking back, his hair was dry, but he was covered in sand and with the warmth of the sun that day he could have lain there for a while.'

'I'm sure Inspector Topping will get to the bottom of it all,' Jane announced with far more confidence than she actually felt.

Doctor Denning's expression appeared to indicate that he shared her thoughts on the inspector. 'Let us hope so, my dear.'

'When the morphine was stolen, had there been reports of other surgeries having problems?' Arthur asked.

'Not that I recall. It was very distressing. The window had been smashed and the lock forced before the thief broke into the medicine cabinet. The lock was smashed right off and just the morphine was missing,' Doctor Denning said.

'And now it seems Antonio Russo has been murdered by an overdose of morphine.' Jane shivered as she spoke.

'Quite a puzzle.' Arthur's tone was grave.

'It is indeed. By the by, Jane, I trust your mother returned home safely with your manservant after the raid last night?' Doctor Denning asked.

'Yes, she did. I think she enjoyed her outing. You know how my mother loves to shop,' Jane said.

'Is she at home now? I could call on her before my evening surgery?' The doctor consulted his pocket watch.

'I'm afraid she is probably still out. Mr Briggs has invited her to tea,' Jane explained. She knew the doctor had always held a candle for her mother even while she had been married to her father. Doctor Denning had been her mother's longstanding, platonic admirer for many years.

Doctor Denning looked a little despondent at this news. 'Ah, I see, well give her my regards and if she is free for lunch tomorrow, I should be delighted to take her out.'

'Of course,' Jane agreed.

The doctor lifted his hat to her and nodded to Arthur before continuing on his way.

'Your mother is very popular,' Arthur observed as they walked the last few hundred yards to the house.

'With the gentlemen you mean?' she asked somewhat astringently. 'Yes, all my life,' she added as she opened the front door and stepped into the hall.

As she had expected, her mother hadn't yet returned from her outing. While Arthur took off his coat, Jane headed for the kitchen. She desperately needed a cup of coffee and a cigarette after talking to Annie and Katie.

Mrs Dawes was busy preparing a casserole for supper and out in the garden Jane was slightly surprised to see Benson digging in the vegetable garden with Mr Dawes. Marmaduke was sat at the end of the row where they were working, supervising their activities.

Mrs Dawes noticed her gaze as she dried her hands and put the kettle on to boil. 'He's a real treasure is Mr Benson. He picked all the last of the raspberries for us earlier. Mr Dawes is ever so grateful for his help. I hope that will be all right with Mr Cilento?' her housekeeper asked.

'Oh, I'm sure it will be fine,' Jane assured her.

She had assumed Benson to be a city man, more used to interiors than digging outside. She waited for the kettle and brushed aside Mrs Dawes's offer to assist her in preparing the coffee. The housekeeper had enough to do, and Jane had no intention of adding to the woman's workload.

Once the coffee was ready, she carried the tray along the hall to the drawing room, where she deposited it in front of Arthur. He had his notebook open, and his glasses perched on his nose once more. His hair was sticking up at the front where he had removed his hat.

'What are you doing?' Jane asked, depositing the coffee tray down on the table as she spoke.

'I'm just making a few notes of what Annie and Katie said. Or in Annie's case, didn't say.' He peered up at her over the top of his glasses as she poured his coffee.

Jane poured her own drink and settled back in her chair. She reached inside her bag for her cigarettes and lit one, heaving a sigh of relief as she did so. 'Yes, she was scared, wasn't she? It sounded as if she and Matteo are, or were, conducting some kind of liaison,' she said.

'You noticed she was pregnant?' Arthur asked.

'Yes.' It had crossed her mind to wonder who the father of the baby might be. Although it might be too early to suspect the Italian of being the father. It was also plain that there had been far too much leeway in the supervision of the prisoners' work party.

CHAPTER TWENTY

Jane was upstairs when her mother returned home, leaving Arthur to greet her when she entered the drawing room.

'Oh, is Janey not around?' Elsa asked, glancing around the room as if half suspecting Jane might be hiding behind the curtains to avoid her.

'No, she's gone upstairs to change for dinner. I daresay she won't be long,' Arthur said.

'I see.' Elsa wandered over to the small cocktail cabinet and poured herself a whisky and soda. 'Can I get you a drink, erm, Arthur?'

'No, thank you,' Arthur refused politely. If they were to end up trying to track down the black market gangs in the dark, should the siren sound, he would rather be sober.

Then again, if Jane was driving, he might decide to rethink that.

Elsa strolled over to the piano and touched a couple of the keys lightly with her fingers. She cut an elegant figure in her pretty pale-green floral dress.

'Are you musical at all, Arthur?' Elsa asked.

Arthur hated these kinds of social situations. He was not

good at small talk. 'Um, no, not really. I like listening to music, but I don't play an instrument.'

Elsa looked disappointed and Arthur suspected that if he had said he was musical he would have been invited to play.

'And have you known my daughter long?' Elsa asked in a curious tone.

'Um, I've been working for her department since the start of the war.' Arthur fidgeted in his chair.

'Janey can be a sweet girl really, you know. She lost someone right at the start of the conflict. She doesn't talk about it.' Elsa grimaced and took a sip of her drink before continuing. 'It's made her, well, somewhat hard.'

'Oh, um, I see.' Arthur had no wish to discuss Jane's private life. He knew she would be mortified if she thought her mother had breached her confidence in such a way. 'Did you have a nice afternoon with Mr Briggs?' he asked, in an effort to redirect the topic of conversation.

'Honey, he has the most gorgeous house, doesn't he? Such a gentleman, he treated me to the most delicious tea, scones, fruit cake, oh it was divine. Just like before all this dreadful rationing.' Elsa drifted back to sit on the sofa. 'I shall be so glad when this war is over.'

Jane walked into the room in time to catch the end of her mother's sentence. She had changed from her usual daytime tweed suit and silk blouse into a dark-blue dress with pearl buttons. 'I think everyone will be glad when that happens, Mother.'

'I was telling your friend about the delicious tea I had with Mr Briggs. Such an interesting man.' Elsa took another sip of her whisky and soda.

Arthur relaxed a little, glad that Jane hadn't heard the earlier part of her mother's conversation.

'Doctor Denning was intending to call on you this afternoon, but I told him you were out.' Jane too went to the cocktail

cabinet and poured herself a very small sherry, ignoring
Arthur's disapproving frown.

'Dear Samuel, such a sweet man,' Elsa mused.

'He wanted to know if you would like to dine with him
tomorrow,' Jane said as she took her usual seat opposite Arthur.

Elsa immediately beamed with delight. 'What a darling. I
shall telephone him later when he's finished his surgery. Thank
you, Janey pie.'

Benson was his usual urbane and immaculate self as he
served a dinner of casserole of mutton, followed by rhubarb
crumble and custard. Arthur found the rhubarb rather tart
despite the generous helping of custard. He suspected that the
lack of sugar was to blame with honey failing to work well in its
place.

They had just returned to the drawing room where Benson
had drawn the curtains and lit the lamps when the air-raid
sirens started.

'Right, let's get going. I'll fetch the car around.' Jane jumped
to her feet.

'I'll get the other things, Miss Jane.' Benson glanced towards
Elsa who was looking confused.

'What car? Where do you think you're going? Janey, there is
an air raid starting,' Elsa said.

'Go to the shelter, Mother.' Jane bustled past her. 'And take
Marmaduke.' She disappeared out of the house into the darkness of the front garden.

Arthur had put on his hat and coat as Benson came downstairs carrying a small leather bag.

'What's happening?' Elsa demanded. 'What are you all
doing?'

'Please don't be alarmed, Miss Elsa. Go to the shelter.
There is a lantern by the back door for you to take with you,'
Benson said as he and Arthur prepared to leave the house.

The drone of the airplane engines was already audible,

mixing with the sound of the anti-aircraft guns booming from further along the coast.

'If you think I am going to sit in that tin shed on my own while you three are gallivanting around the countryside in Cilla then you can think again.' Elsa grabbed her fur coat from the hallstand. 'I'm coming with you.'

'Please, Miss Macintyre, go to the shelter. The mission we are undertaking is incredibly dangerous.' Arthur heard a beep of the car horn, indicating Jane was ready to go.

'Not on your nelly, I'm coming along,' Elsa declared.

Arthur blinked at her use of the slang.

'Miss Jane will not be happy,' Benson warned.

'Honey, nothing I do ever makes my daughter happy. I'm used to it. Let's go.' Elsa followed Arthur out of the door and into the waiting car.

'Mother, what on earth are you doing?' Jane glared at her mother with a horrified expression. Benson had taken the front seat beside Jane, while Arthur had opted to sit in the back next to Elsa.

'Miss Elsa would not be dissuaded, Miss Jane,' Benson explained as Jane released the car's handbrake and they pulled away into the street.

The headlamps of the car had been fitted with special covers which gave only a limited view of the road ahead. Arthur started to regret his decision to sit in the back as Jane swung the car around the narrow lanes heading for a local viewpoint. The crumble he had eaten earlier was not sitting comfortably in his stomach.

All around them they could hear the planes and see flashes and flares of light from the guns and from incendiaries dropped further ahead, which gave the sky an eerie orange-yellow tinge.

Soon the car was steadily climbing, trees bowed over either side of the lane, the branches casting eerie shadows as the clouds raced over the moon. A minute or two later they were at the viewpoint. Benson produced a small pair of binoculars from his overcoat pocket.

'What are we doing up here?' Elsa asked as Benson scanned the landscape focusing on where the glow from the fires seemed the most intense.

'We are working. You are here for the ride,' Jane snapped as Benson adjusted the viewfinder.

'I think Ashford has been hit, Miss Jane.' He handed the field glasses to her and she took a look for herself.

'I think you're right. It's not too far away so we may get there in time.' She tossed the glasses back to the manservant and crunched the car into first gear. The car roared away throwing up a hail of gravel from the back wheels, which made Elsa squeak in protest.

'There's no guarantee that we are going to find them or that they will be there,' Arthur said as the car lurched at speed around a corner.

'I know, but we have to try something, and this is as good a way as any to catch them in the act,' Jane said as the car bounced over a pothole, making Arthur clutch at the car door to keep from sliding on the seats.

'Catch who?' Elsa asked as they drew closer to the outskirts of the town.

No one answered her as they looked out of the car windows seeing sparks and plumes of black smoke against the unnatural brightness caused by the fires.

The orange glow up ahead was more intense and Arthur could smell smoke and burning wood. He drew his scarf up to cover his nose and mouth. Jane slowed the pace of the car down as they headed for the heart of the conflagration.

'How are we going to get through, Miss Jane? The wardens will be stopping everyone,' Benson asked.

'The men we are after have a lorry. They will be looking for businesses that fit the list of those which Arthur identified earlier. Grocers, drapery, tobacconists. I'll get us as close as I can to the high street, then we may need to go on foot to see if they are here,' Jane said. 'I don't want to risk Cilla's safety.' She patted the car's steering wheel affectionately.

'Or your mother's,' Elsa muttered crossly.

Jane halted in a side street. They could hear the roar of the fire now combined with sirens and shouting.

'I'll park here, and we can get to the high street through a passageway just down there if it's not blocked. Something on the high street has been damaged so our quarry may be here already.' Jane went to get out of the car.

'Jane, I think you should stay here while Benson and I check things out. If the men are here, we may need to follow them in a hurry,' Arthur said, before securing his scarf more firmly over his face.

'We'll be back to report as soon as we can, Miss Jane.' Benson slipped the gun from the bag and stowed it discreetly under his coat.

Arthur heard Elsa gasp as she glimpsed the weapon.

'We will also have a better chance of passing unnoticed in the melee.' Arthur opened the car door and got out, giving Jane no further opportunity to protest. Benson followed suit and the two men set off towards the heart of the conflagration.

* * *

'Why did Mr Benson have a gun?' Elsa demanded as soon as the men had gone. 'Janey pie, what is going on?'

'Mother, this is not your concern. You should have stayed at the house with Marmaduke and gone to the shelter.' Jane sat upright behind the steering wheel. Her gaze fixed on the entrance to the alleyway where Arthur and Benson had vanished.

She was in no mood to answer her mother's questions.

There was a loud crash up ahead and she saw a shower of sparks fly up into the night sky, followed by more shouting. She hoped Arthur and Benson would be safe. What they were doing was extremely risky.

'Fine, have it your way, as usual.' Elsa had folded her arms. Jane could see the stubborn set of her mother's jaw in the rear-view mirror. 'You drag your own mother out during an air raid without saying where we were going. There's a man carrying a gun going into a conflagration and I'm supposed to not ask questions?'

'No one dragged you anywhere, Mother. You were told to stay at the house. This is none of your business, and if you breathe one word of anything that you might see or hear tonight, then I swear I shall never speak to you ever again. I'll also tell the press your real age.' Jane reverted to staring through the windscreen, desperately looking for Benson and Arthur's return.

'You wouldn't!'

'Try me,' Jane said.

'I'm just saying I have been very ill-used, Janey,' Elsa retorted.

Jane was about to reach for a much-needed cigarette when she saw the figure of a man emerge from the alley half running, half stumbling towards the car.

'That's Arthur.' She started the engine, expecting to see Benson following behind.

Arthur reached the motor car and flung open the passenger door to fall, gasping into the seat.

'Get ready, the lorry will be going past any minute. It has to come this way. The wardens have blocked the other exit where a chimney has fallen,' Arthur panted, taking gulps of air between each piece of information.

'Where is Benson? Has something happened?' Jane started to turn the car around so she would be facing the right way ready to track the lorry. Her heart raced and she prayed nothing bad had happened to Arthur's manservant.

'He's fine, he's in the back of the lorry,' Arthur said.

'He's where?' Jane almost stalled the car. She gave Arthur a horrified look.

'He spied an opportunity to sneak in and hide behind the stuff the gang had stashed in there. Bales of cloth and boxes of all kinds of things. They were almost finished loading when we found them.' Arthur had regained more of his breath now.

Before he could tell her much more a lorry emerged from behind them, having clearly come from the stricken high street.

'This is them, Jane, get ready.' Arthur leaned forward, his hands gripping the sides of his seat. The lorry drove past, and Jane waited until the rear lights were just visible before setting off in pursuit.

'What did Benson think he was doing getting in the back of that lorry?' Jane asked through gritted teeth as her quarry picked up speed once they were clear of the town. 'Did you instruct him to do that?'

'Of course not. He saw his chance and went for it. I came back to warn you to be ready,' Arthur said.

The tail lights on the lorry were barely visible now. The sound of the sirens had faded, but in the distance Jane could still hear the thud of the guns defending the coastline and the drone of aircraft. She could only assume that any enemy planes that had survived the raid were now on their return flight path.

She prayed that the lights of the lorry and the car would not be seen from the air, faint though they were. Otherwise, if an enemy pilot had any ammunition left, he might try to take them out as he flew overhead.

'Do you have any idea where we may be headed, Jane?' Arthur asked as they lurched around another corner in the pitch-dark.

'It's tricky with the darkness and the lack of signposts. I

think we are heading somewhere in the direction of the village though.' Jane frowned as she forced herself to concentrate on the road.

Could the location of the black marketeers' base be closer than they had realised?

'Jane, they are slowing ready to turn off or stop.' Arthur clutched at her arm, and she slowed the car to a crawl, crunching her way down the gearbox.

The lorry had indeed slowed right down then stopped at a gate. A male figure jumped out of the passenger side of the cab and opened the gate allowing access. Jane turned off the car engine as they watched, hidden by the hedgerow to see what was happening.

'It looks like a barn of some kind,' Arthur said.

'There's a car parked next to it. I can just make out the shape.' Jane watched as the man ran around to unlock the barn doors, opening them up so his companion could drive the lorry right inside the building.

'Are they intending to unload?' Jane's heart was thumping so loudly now she thought Arthur must surely be able to hear it. If the men started to get things from the lorry, then Benson would be in grave danger of discovery.

'I don't know. If they do, we may have to cause a diversion.' Arthur's jaw was set.

The lorry was inside the barn now and the engine had been turned off with only the light of flashlights showing in the interior.

'They're coming out,' she said. She breathed a sigh of relief that they hadn't gone to the back of the lorry.

The men left the lorry inside the barn and closed the doors. It looked as if they were securing them with a padlock.

'Benson is trapped inside the lorry, inside the barn.' Jane looked at Arthur. They heard the sound of the car which had been parked at the side of the barn starting up.

'Get down, in case they come this way,' Jane urged. 'Mother, get out of sight.' She could only hope that the men would drive off in a different direction.

She peeked through the steering wheel to see the car paused for the men to close the farm gate, before driving away.

'I got the registration of the car,' Arthur said as they cautiously emerged once the car was out of sight.

'Good work, we'll get Inspector Topping on that tomorrow. Now, we need to go and rescue Benson.' Jane hoped that Arthur had his lock-picking kit in his pocket.

'Let's hope we can get him out quickly. I could use a drink,' Elsa said as Arthur and Jane prepared to get out of the car to approach the barn.

CHAPTER TWENTY-ONE

'There's a flashlight in the bag.' Arthur fumbled inside the brown-leather bag that had previously held the gun. He extracted the rubber-cased torch and he and Jane got out of the car together.

'Hey, wait for me.' Elsa opened the rear door of the car and picked her way cautiously over to the farm gate in the darkness.

'Mother, go back to the car,' Jane said as Arthur lifted the latch to push the gate ajar.

'What, and be there on my own like a sitting duck? What if those gangsters or whoever they are come back?' Elsa huddled into her coat, pulling the sable fur collar closer to her face.

Arthur realised the guns they had been hearing in the distance had fallen silent. The sound of the planes had gone, and all was quiet once more and still.

'I think the raid has finished. We need to go and free Benson.' He hoped his manservant was unharmed. Arthur led the way down the muddy, rutted track leading to the barn. He played the flashlight over the sturdy padlock on the rusty corrugated metal doors.

'Hmm.' It was a type he hadn't opened for a while.

'Can you unlock it?' Jane asked, an anxious note in her voice.

'Hold the flashlight still while I get out my kit.' Arthur handed the torch to Jane so she could keep a steady light on the lock. He delved into his coat pocket for the tool kit that Benson had thoughtfully placed there before dinner.

'I can't hear Mr Benson. He won't suffocate in there, will he?' Jane's mother asked.

'I doubt the back of the lorry is airtight, Mother,' Jane assured her as Arthur took out his kit and unrolled the leather pouch that held a small selection of metal picks.

'Well, I don't know, do I? It's a shame he has the gun. We could have shot the lock off,' Elsa said.

'I rather think that is something that only happens in the movies, Miss Macintyre,' Arthur said politely as he crouched down with his chosen pick to work on the padlock.

'The guns have stopped. I guess like you said, the all-clear must have sounded,' Elsa said.

'I expect so,' Jane replied in a distracted voice.

'Jane, just shine the light there a bit more, please,' Arthur asked, indicating the area where he was working. It was a fiddly business crouching down and trying to keep a steady hand.

'Is that better?' she asked, adjusting the angle of the torch.

'Perfect.' He gave the pick a final twist and felt the lock spring open. 'That's done it. We're in.' He straightened up and lifted off the open lock so they could push open the barn doors to get inside.

Jane shone the flashlight into the barn as they went in. The barn was empty apart from a couple of ancient boxes at one end and the dark-blue lorry. Elsa clung onto Jane's arm.

'Benson, can you hear us? We're coming to get you out,' Arthur called when they reached the rear of the lorry.

'Yes, sir, the door appears to be locked and there is no

handle on this side.' Benson's voice was muffled but he sounded perfectly well.

'Are you safe in there, Mr Benson?' Elsa called.

'Perfectly, Miss Elsa,' he assured her.

Arthur breathed a silent sigh of relief. He had played down his fears to Jane when he had gone back to the car, but he had been gravely concerned for his friend. It had been a moment of madness when Benson had leapt into the back of the lorry when the men's backs had been turned. He had been too late to dissuade him from taking such a risky decision.

'I'll work on the lock,' Arthur assured him. 'Jane, I need your help with the light again.'

Once more, Jane trained the torch on the back of the lorry. This time keeping it focused on the lock holding the door handle. Arthur selected a different metal tool from his kit, longer and slimmer, and set to work.

The lock on the lorry was trickier than the padlock so it took a few minutes before he felt it click. Elsa paced about behind Jane until he finally turned the handle and opened the lorry door.

He extended his hand and assisted Benson down from the lorry.

'Thank you, sir, I'm much obliged.' The manservant brushed down his dark-grey overcoat and straightened his hat, looking remarkably unperturbed by his ordeal.

'Are you hurt, Mr Benson?' Elsa asked, looking worried.

'Not at all, Miss Elsa. A little shaken as the suspension on the rear of the lorry is not designed for passengers,' Benson said as he reclosed the doors of the lorry. The back of which seemed to be crammed full of stolen goods.

'Did you overhear anything useful while you were in there?' Arthur asked as he tucked his tools away in his coat pocket.

'I'm afraid I was being tossed around rather and everything

was quite muffled. However, I believe the one man is called Charlie,' Benson said.

'Come, we need to get out of here,' Jane suggested. 'You can tell us everything once we are back at the house. Poor Marmaduke will be terrified by the raid.'

Arthur made sure the padlock was refastened on the barn door as they left. He had no wish to alert anyone that someone else may have been present in the barn. They hurried back up the track to the car. He reached out to steady Jane when she tripped on a clump of grass.

'Thank you.' She kept her hand on his arm until they reached the car.

Benson had given his support to Elsa who was now complaining bitterly about getting dirt on her patent evening shoes. The manservant closed the gate before assisting Elsa into the car. This time he rode in the rear seat beside Jane's mother and Arthur decided to sit in the front passenger seat.

Much to his relief Jane drove at a more sedate speed back to the house despite her concern for her cat. She pulled up at the gate and Benson, Elsa and Arthur alighted. They went inside the house while Jane drove Cilla back inside the garage.

Elsa hung up her fur coat, while Arthur unwrapped himself from his precautionary layers of wool.

'What time is it?' she demanded in a fractious tone. 'It feels as if we have been careering about the countryside forever.'

'It's one a.m., Miss Elsa,' Benson replied soothingly. 'Might I suggest a small nightcap? And if you would like me to clean your shoes for you, please leave them in the hall later.'

Elsa immediately softened. 'Dear Mr Benson, you are so very thoughtful, and after your own dreadful ordeal this evening too.'

Arthur heard noises from the kitchen and guessed that Jane had re-entered the house via the back door. He excused himself and went to see what she was doing.

He discovered her fussing over her abominable cat, murmuring endearments and treating it to a few scraps of sardines from a tin.

'Poor Marmaduke must have been horribly frightened with no one in the house and all the noise from the raid.' Jane straightened up as Arthur entered the kitchen. 'He really does get scared by the noise of the sirens.'

'I have to say that Marmaduke doesn't strike me as the kind of animal who would be scared of anything,' Arthur said dubiously. The cat glared at him balefully from his one good eye.

Jane gave him an equally reproachful look. 'I'm going to make cocoa. Do you want some?'

'Yes, that would be nice, thank you.' Arthur took a seat at the pine table in the centre of the kitchen, while Jane bustled about getting the milk and putting it in a pan on the hob.

'Do you think Benson will want any?' she asked, holding the milk jug above the saucepan.

'I don't know, he was getting your mother a drink, I believe.' Arthur glanced towards the green-baize-covered door that divided the service part of the house from the living areas.

'It may be a while before he joins us then.' Jane set the milk aside and reached down two mugs from the dresser. 'Mother will no doubt need some attention.'

Arthur suspected she was probably right. Benson certainly appeared to have fallen under Elsa's spell. Something that both confused and bewildered him in equal measure.

Jane finished making the cocoa and joined Arthur at the kitchen table, taking the seat on the opposite corner. Now the adrenaline from earlier had left her system she suddenly felt quite exhausted.

Arthur stood and fetched the biscuit tin from the pantry.

He placed a biscuit in front of her and one in front of his cup, before putting the tin back. 'I suppose we'd better go easy on these. I'm not certain how easy they are to obtain.' He retook his seat.

Marmaduke was now stretched in front of the range, curled up on the old blanket he liked to sleep on in a nice cosy spot. Jane picked up her biscuit and nibbled at the edge of it. She was relieved to see her pet seemed to have recovered from being alone during the raid.

'Thank you for this.' She smiled at Arthur.

'I think we need the energy after tonight's escapade,' he said.

'What happened when you reached the high street? You only had time to give me a brief outline of what you and Benson saw before we had to follow the lorry,' Jane asked.

Arthur sighed and ran his hand distractedly through his already untidy hair. 'It was chaos as you might expect. There were fires in several buildings, which the brigade and the ARP wardens were attempting to extinguish. A building which had been hit previously had been damaged again and was about to come down so that posed quite a risk.' He paused and took a sip of his cocoa before continuing. 'We saw a blue lorry parked near a draper's shop. The shop windows had been blown out by the explosions and there was a fire nearby. Two men were taking the stock from the shop into the back of the lorry aided by the shopkeeper. She was an older lady and looked absolutely distraught, as you can imagine.'

Jane had no difficulties in picturing the scene. 'Did you get a good look at the men?' she asked.

'It was dark and smoky but they fit the men Mr Wood described. We could see the gang had almost finished their task. The taller of the men gave the shopkeeper a form to sign. He then gave her another sheet of paper, I assume one of those bogus forms that Mr Wood refers to in his reports.' He paused again to drink more of his cocoa.

'I assume that is when Benson decided to climb into the lorry?' Jane asked.

Arthur gave a brief nod of affirmation. 'The men were distracted. The wardens wanted them to move as the building nearby was about to fall and they needed to clear the area. Benson got into the lorry, and I ran back to ask you to stand by. The top end of the high street had been blocked off, so we knew they had to drive past where you were parked.'

Jane leaned back in her seat and surveyed him levelly over the rim of her cocoa mug. 'It was extraordinarily risky. We were fortunate that we managed to follow the lorry and keep up. It was equally lucky that Benson was not discovered.'

Arthur looked a little shamefaced at her reprimand. 'We knew it was dangerous, but it was also our best chance to catch these men. I suppose the big question is what do we do next?'

'That is quite problematic. If we alert Inspector Topping and seize the lorry, we can recover the goods, but the gang will still be free to continue to operate.' Jane frowned and drank her drink as she puzzled over the problem.

'We have the car registration and model,' Arthur said.

'That is a start, I suppose. We can certainly find out who the registered keeper is, although I suspect they may be stolen or have false plates.' Jane looked at her companion.

'I think you are right, but we have to try. My thoughts are that since they didn't unload the lorry they obviously intend to return and move it on to where they will unload and store the goods. I suspect the barn is used merely to lie low for a short period when the shopkeeper realises their goods have been taken.' Arthur returned her gaze.

Jane drained the rest of her cocoa before replying. 'In other words, we need to stake out the barn and see if we can discover where the storage facility for the goods might be and then we can hopefully catch more of this gang to shut down their operation.'

Arthur finished his own drink and set his mug down on the table. 'I don't see how else we can do it. I think we need to talk to Mr Wood first thing. We should hopefully have a few hours grace as I don't think they will risk returning to the lorry until later. They need time for the attention to die away before they risk moving it again.'

Jane watched as he picked up his biscuit and snapped it in two before carefully eating the one half. 'What are your thoughts on when we should let the inspector know about this and get him involved? We shall need the police to make any arrests.'

Arthur chewed and swallowed, his expression thoughtful as he considered her question. 'It's very difficult. I think this is why we need to speak to Mr Wood first. He will have a better idea about the manpower the inspector may have available and how best to get the police to deploy it.'

'There needs to be a watch set on the lorry, and a watch also set for that car and its occupants,' Jane said.

Arthur finished the second half of his biscuit, carefully removing any crumbs from the tabletop. 'I agree.'

The clock on the kitchen wall struck the hour, startling them both with its silvery notes.

'Two o'clock. We need to get some sleep.' Jane gathered up the mugs and placed them in the sink alongside the milk pan she had put in to soak earlier.

Arthur waited for her at the kitchen door while she locked the rear door to the house and turned off the light. It was an old-world gentlemanly courtesy that after the excitement earlier, Jane found herself appreciating.

The drawing room was in darkness as they walked past the door. Her mother and Benson had clearly already retired for the evening. Arthur waited again as Jane checked the front door was locked.

It was strangely intimate, being in a dark house with Arthur, and Jane forced herself to give a mental shake of her head. She was clearly overtired if she was starting to develop feelings for Arthur Cilento. The idea was absurd.

They walked quietly up the stairs.

'Goodnight, Jane.' Arthur's voice was soft in her ear as she switched off the landing light and opened her bedroom door.

'Yes, goodnight.' She scuttled inside and checked her curtains were securely closed before turning on her bedside lamp. Really, she was being quite ridiculous. Anyone would think there had been brandy instead of cocoa in her bedtime drink she thought crossly.

Benson was setting the dining table for breakfast when Jane arrived downstairs a few hours later. She had taken the precaution of setting her alarm clock so she wouldn't oversleep. There was no time to waste if they were to ensure they were ready for when the men came back for the lorry.

'Good morning, Benson. I trust you're no worse for wear after last night?' Jane asked as he set a pot of coffee in front of her.

'I am quite recovered, thank you, Miss Jane,' he replied, adding a chrome jug of steamed milk to the table.

'I don't wish you to think that I am unappreciative of your bravery and dedication in hiding in that lorry, but please don't do anything like that again.' She softened her words with a smile, hoping he understood that she had been concerned for his safety.

'I sincerely hope that it will not be necessary, Miss Jane.' He returned her smile and disappeared back towards the kitchen to fetch some toast.

Arthur joined her a few minutes later. His cheeks freshly shaved and shining pink from soap. His wayward curls carefully flattened down and his tie for once lying straight. She was relieved to find that the strange tenderness she had felt towards him in the early hours had somewhat dissipated.

'As soon as I have eaten breakfast, I shall telephone Mr Wood. I'll explain what we discovered last night and get him to come here.' Jane helped herself to toast.

Benson placed a teapot in front of Arthur. 'I assume a watch will need to be set on the lorry,' he said.

'Yes, Benson, although how the operation will work still needs to be sorted out.' Arthur explained the thoughts that he and Jane had shared a few hours earlier in the kitchen.

'I see. Very good, sir. You may count on my assistance, of course,' Benson said. 'Now, I shall just see if your boiled egg is ready.'

He went off once more to the kitchen and Jane wondered afresh where Arthur had first encountered his manservant and if she could possibly ever entice him away to work solely for her department.

CHAPTER TWENTY-TWO

Jane telephoned Mr Wood before nine o'clock. She was anxious that they get plans in place before the black market men could move the stolen goods from the barn. To say Mr Wood was delighted at the news that they had traced the lorry to its hiding place would be an understatement. Jane had to cut him off in his profusive joy and request he join them at the house as soon as possible.

Her next telephone call was to Inspector Topping requesting that he trace the owner of the car they had seen leaving the barn. This call was met with a very different reception.

'My dear Miss Treen, I really don't have the time or resources to spare on such a wild goose chase...'

Jane cut him off, mid bluster. 'Neither I nor my department will brook your excuses, Inspector, please find out if this car has been reported stolen and if not, who the registered keeper is and their address. I also expect you to attend at my house as soon as possible as we have made a significant breakthrough in the black marketeering gang. There is no time to be lost.'

The inspector started to protest that he was not prepared to be ordered about by a civilian.

'I shall expect you within the hour,' Jane said firmly and replaced the receiver in the cradle.

Arthur had finished his breakfast and was in the drawing room. Benson had once more pressed the folding card table into service and Arthur had his map spread out on top of it. He was now marking the location of the barn.

'How does the site of the barn tie in with the areas you had marked already?' Jane asked, peering at the web of lines he had produced in faint pencil strokes.

'I think I may have the possible areas for storage and ongoing distribution of the goods narrowed down to two main possibilities.' He scratched the top of his head absent-mindedly with the end of his pencil. His dark-blue tie was already drifting to settle closer to his left ear.

'Which are?' Jane asked.

'Look here.' He indicated a point on the coast. 'If they unload in one of the coastal towns or near them, then they have a market all along the coast to split the goods into smaller parcels for resale.'

Jane could see what he meant. They were also towns which were often hit hard by the bombing raids so depravation and access to goods was impacted. A ready market for the stolen goods to sell to people desperate for a few items they couldn't obtain via rationing or over the counter.

'And the other area?' she asked.

'Going out in the other direction. I don't think they would take it inland since it would make no sense to do so. The risk of being seen or having goods traced back to them would be much greater.' He pointed out the area he meant on the other side of the county's coastline.

'That's more towards Canterbury. Which do you think is

the most likely direction they would choose out of those two?' Jane asked.

Arthur tapped the end of the pencil against his teeth as he considered. 'I would have thought anywhere from here along the coast to Folkestone and beyond would be the strongest possibility. The chances of a distribution network are far more likely because of the road links and possibilities available for storing goods.'

The front doorbell rang, and she heard Benson going to answer it.

'That will probably be Mr Wood. I have asked him and Inspector Topping to join us as soon as possible. We need a watch on that barn as quickly as we can,' Jane said.

A moment later, Mr Wood scurried into the room, his cheeks pink and glowing, with Benson following on his heels as the black market inspector was still removing his coat as he entered.

'What a breakthrough. My dear Mr Cilento, Miss Treen, at last. Now what happened last night? And where is this lorry?' he asked as Benson finally managed to take the man's coat to hang it on the hallstand.

Jane gave him a brief explanation of what they had done and how they had tracked the gang.

'The lorry we followed from Ashford was left in a barn here.' Arthur showed the excitable government inspector the map and explained his thoughts on the possibilities for where the goods were most likely to be moved to.

'I have asked Inspector Topping to attend as soon as possible this morning too. I have also requested he discover who the registered keeper of the car might be that we witnessed the men drive away in,' Jane said.

'The people involved seemed to fit the description you provided. Benson thought he heard the name Charlie mentioned,' Arthur said.

As he was speaking, the doorbell rang again, and Benson returned to the room accompanied by a very indignant-looking Inspector Topping.

'This had better not be a fool's errand, Miss Treen. I have a lot to do today. The damage from the air raids the last two nights are taking up a great deal of my time.' Inspector Topping glared at her.

'Inspector, so good of you to join us. As my colleague will explain, time is of the essence this morning. I assure you that your presence is extremely necessary. Now do you have information on the vehicle that we requested?' Jane asked.

The inspector puffed out his chest and glowered at her. 'The car you described and with that registration was reported stolen from Folkestone three months ago. I have to say that I really do object to the high-handed demand—'

Arthur cut him off. 'Thank you, Inspector. Folkestone, then it looks as if that is the most likely route they will take.'

'Perhaps, Inspector, if you take a seat we can explain the events of last night.' Jane indicated a spot on the sofa beside Mr Wood. 'Arthur, could you run us through events and your thoughts on where this gang may try to store the stolen property.'

Jane fixed Inspector Topping with a steely glare and he was forced to sit. Benson stood quietly to one side, his hands clasped loosely behind his back as if awaiting instruction.

Arthur took both men through everything that had happened, giving a brief and succinct outline of the previous evening's events. Mr Wood looked admiringly at Benson when he heard about the manservant stowing himself away in the lorry.

'Oh, I say, what pluck!' he interjected.

Inspector Topping merely scowled as Arthur continued.

'Now you are both caught up to date so to speak we need to

act quickly if we are to catch this gang in action and break up the network,' Jane said.

'Yes, we need a watch set on the lorry.' Mr Wood was almost bouncing in his seat with excitement.

'And how do you propose we do that? And go on from there? I keep trying to tell you that I have no resources to spare. My men already have their hands full with the aftermath of these bombing raids. I can't spare a constable to sit in a field watching a barn. Even if I did, how is he to alert anyone? Hmm, answer me that?' Inspector Topping glowered ferociously at Arthur and at Mr Wood.

'I take it you do not have access to radio?' Arthur asked.

Inspector Topping's complexion turned even redder. 'No, we do not. Newfangled gadgetry such as radio has not been extended to our force as yet. They haven't even sorted out all the problems with it in London. Radio, indeed.'

Jane knew that some police forces were more advanced with the use of radio than others, despite the issues over frequencies. It was clear the Kent force was not one of the more advanced forces in adopting the technology.

'Ahem, if I may perhaps make a suggestion? Mr Wood, I believe you have a vehicle? And, of course, Miss Treen has a motor car too. Perhaps we may be able to use these in some way,' Benson said in a calm, almost apologetic tone.

'Good thinking, Benson. If Mr Wood watched the barn today and, Jane, you could perhaps lie in wait at this point here.' Arthur indicated a road junction on the map. 'I am certain they will move the goods during daylight so the lorry can be left in readiness for the next raid. Inspector Topping, you could have a car on standby, I suggest here.' He indicated another point. 'Then when they return for the lorry, we can pick them up and follow them to where the next vehicle takes over.'

'So Mr Wood follows them to where I am waiting, then I

take up the pursuit?' Jane asked trying to understand what he meant.

'Exactly, I can't see that they wouldn't pass you at that point. If they go in the other direction, then Mr Wood would simply have to follow and see where they go and we shall have to deal with that should it happen,' Arthur said.

'And the police side of things?' Jane asked.

'Yes, what is wasting my constable's time in a patrol car to do with this nonsense,' Inspector Topping demanded.

'Once Jane has taken up following them, Mr Wood can drive to where your man is waiting and give him the directions they took. If I'm correct we know they need a store and distribution centre near a built-up area,' Arthur explained. 'It has to be around Ashbourne itself or in this area here.' He indicated another point on the map.

'Then the police would follow the route looking out for the lorry and my car. We can then make the arrests.' Jane looked at the inspector.

'How long is this all going to take? We can't all be hanging about in cars forever.' Inspector Topping had lowered his voice and was rubbing his chin as he looked at the map. This gave Jane hope that he was actually considering their plan.

'While the lorry is still loaded, then they can't use it to collect more goods if there is another raid. I think they will try and empty it today,' Arthur said. 'This is a very slick operation.'

'Exactly, which is why there is no time to be wasted,' Jane said. 'Inspector Topping, are you able to support this plan?' She looked at the policeman.

'I expect so,' he said somewhat grudgingly. 'I can put a car and constable on watch at that point until six o'clock tonight. After that though my men are too stretched.'

'Very well. Mr Wood can you assist us?' Jane turned to the government official.

'I am at yours and Mr Cilento's disposal, Miss Treen,' he assured her.

'Shall I accompany Mr Wood, Miss Jane?' Benson suggested. 'It may be helpful to have two of us in each vehicle.'

'An excellent idea, Benson, thank you. Arthur can come with me and Inspector Topping can go and alert his men. I suggest you also inform the officers in the towns Arthur has indicated to be on the alert for both sightings of the lorry and the car. Thank you, gentlemen, let's go.' Jane jumped to her feet and the others followed suit.

Inspector Topping departed, while Benson hurried upstairs to prepare. Mr Wood put on his coat and Jane went to the kitchen. She picked up some apples and some biscuits and took them back with her to the hall. She offered some to Mr Wood.

'I already have a packed lunch, thank you, Miss Treen. My wife likes to make sure I eat properly while I'm at work,' Mr Wood assured her.

Benson returned and passed Arthur the leather bag from the previous night.

'Perhaps you should have this with you, sir. You and Miss Treen have the riskier leg of the operation,' he remarked.

'Thank you, Benson.' Arthur took it from him.

Jane dropped some biscuits in Benson's coat pocket.

'Thank you, Miss Jane.' He favoured her with one of his rare smiles.

Benson and Mr Wood hurried out to Mr Wood's discreet black car. Jane went around to the garage to get Cilla. Luckily, there was still plenty of petrol in the tank when she checked the gauge.

'Goodness me, the inspector is hard work, isn't he?' Jane remarked as Arthur slid onto the passenger seat beside her. He had the map with him with the markings he had made earlier.

'I expect he is under a great deal of pressure, and he is not used to being told what to do,' Arthur remarked with a grin as they set off on the narrow lane out of the village.

Mr Wood's car was already out of sight and the inspector had taken a different road back to the police station.

'Especially not by a woman, I suppose. We just have to hope this plan will work,' Jane mused. 'Do you think the Green Dragon will be involved?'

'It's possible if what Benson overheard was correct. This is the best we can do given that we don't have much manpower, and we are being forced to try and predict what the gang will do next and where they might go.' Arthur winced as Jane misjudged a pothole.

'If we don't catch them today, Inspector Topping will never let us hear the end of it.' Jane slowed temporarily to pass a farmer with a horse and cart.

'Well, he has not exactly covered himself with glory so far, has he? Either in the matter of these thieves or in the murder of Antonio Russo.' Arthur gripped on tight to the edges of the leather seat as she swung the elderly car around another corner. He really was a terribly nervous passenger, she decided.

They were soon at the place that Arthur had marked on the map and Jane parked the car neatly in a spot at the side of the road, tucking the car in against the hedgerow.

'Now we wait,' she said, settling back in her seat, her gaze fixed on the unmarked crossroads in front of them.

Arthur peered at her from under the brim of his dark-grey trilby hat. 'Have you ever done this kind of thing before?' he asked curiously.

'Oh yes, not for a while though. I did some fieldwork when this business all kicked off.' Jane tried not to think too much about that. She had lost too many friends and good people in the conflict since then. Including someone who had been especially dear to her. 'What about you?'

'Um, a little bit. I've always had more of a desk-based role as you know,' Arthur said. 'I think it may have been Cairo, just before the war, when Benson and I were last doing something of this sort.'

'How long has Benson been with you?' Jane asked. She was curious about how the two of them had met.

Arthur frowned. 'For most of my life. I think I was eight when my asthma first became a serious problem. Benson worked for my uncle and when my parents were killed, and I went to live at Half Moon Manor, he looked after me.'

It was Jane's turn to frown. 'Why Benson? Didn't you have a nanny or a nurse?'

Arthur shrugged, the crease on his forehead deepening. 'No, it was always just the staff you met when you visited the manor in January, my uncle and Benson. I had a home tutor who would visit when I was unwell, and I went to a day preparatory school. I was a day boarder at senior school too.'

Jane longed to ask more questions, but she sensed that Arthur was becoming uncomfortable. Since they were likely to be spending quite some time in the car waiting, she had no wish to cloud the atmosphere between them.

'I'm sorry you lost your parents so young. That must have been dreadful. I miss my own father so much.' She glanced at him.

'Thank you, yes, it was difficult. My uncle was very good to me, however. Your father sounds as if he were a splendid chap. He has an excellent selection of books in his study.' Arthur's gaze met hers and she smiled.

'Yes, he was. He was an academic, and books were very important to him. I have a lot of happy memories of time spent with him in his study.'

'It sounds as if your mother is quite different from your father.' Arthur returned his gaze to continue staring out through the car windscreen.

'Yes, she is. I honestly never understood how they ever came to marry. That's probably why we don't get along. I'm not at all the daughter she wanted.' Jane's lips twisted in a wry smile as she spoke. If the maternity nurse had taken refunds, she suspected Elsa would have traded her in years ago.

'I'm sure that's not really the case,' Arthur said. 'Well, maybe just a little bit.' A smile crept onto his face.

Jane nudged him in his ribs. 'Oh, do shut up and have a toffee.' She produced a tiny bag of the scarce treats from the depths of her handbag, and they chewed for a minute in contented silence.

Her sweet finished, Jane was about to have a cigarette when in the distance she thought she heard the sound of a vehicle.

'Arthur, is that someone coming along the lane?' She sat upright and placed her hand over the keys to the ignition just in case.

'Yes, it sounds heavy too, like a tractor or a lorry.' He too sat bolt upright, and they waited as the sound came closer.

'That's them,' she said as a familiar navy-blue lorry without any writing on the sides rumbled past where they were waiting.

She turned the key in the ignition. 'Hold on to your hat, Arthur. Let's go.'

CHAPTER TWENTY-THREE

Arthur thought Jane had never spoken a truer word as they set off in pursuit of the lorry. Fortunately, the morning sunshine had dried the mud coating the lanes and the lorry was easy to follow as it threw up clouds of dust as it moved along.

'Do take it steady, Jane.' Arthur's teeth chattered together as a particular bump in the road lifted him up clean out of his seat before dropping him back again. It was fortunate the suspension on the Rolls Royce was so good, otherwise he suspected he would have developed a concussion.

'I don't want to lose them, not now we've come this far. I do hope Mr Wood is not far behind us. He will have to go this way to drive into the village to alert Inspector Topping's man.' Jane kept her attention fixed firmly on the road ahead and the blue lorry which was also moving at quite a pace.

'Where are we? Are we headed towards the coast road turn?' Arthur asked. He wasn't as familiar as Jane with the countryside locally and it was hard to track where they were while following the thieves. A task made more difficult by the absence of signposts.

'At the moment, yes,' Jane said.

As she spoke the lorry reached a crossroads. Jane slowed right down so the occupants of the vehicle wouldn't see her behind them.

'They've turned the other way.' She looked at Arthur. 'That's going to complicate things. Mr Wood and the constable are going to expect us to follow along on the main road.'

'Where does this road go, do you know?' he asked. He fumbled inside his jacket for the map he had brought with him from the house.

'It goes around the lanes and through towards the back part of the village not far from the POW camp.' Jane frowned. 'Do you think they have realised we're following them?'

'Stay as far back as you can to be on the safe side,' Arthur advised.

Jane waited at the crossroads to allow the lorry to pull further ahead down the lanes, before following after it once more. Arthur partially unfolded the map and spread it across his knees to try and identify their location. The bumping and rolling of the car through the twists and turns made it difficult to concentrate.

The lanes had become narrower, and Arthur suspected that unless the road widened out soon the lorry would soon be unable to get much further. Clumps of grass were growing in the centre of the lane, and it was obvious that it wasn't used by much traffic.

Jane was forced to slow her speed by the numerous bumps and potholes. She also had no desire to be seen by the occupants of the lorry. The constant jolting made it challenging for Arthur to work out exactly where they were. He slipped on his spectacles and tried peering more closely at the road markings on the map.

'I think we are heading down a small side road that borders the far side of Mr Briggs's estate.' He frowned at the map, trying to trace the road with the tip of his finger. 'Isn't that the oast house we saw when we visited?'

'There must be a turn off soon, surely. Otherwise we shall end up at the cliffs.' Jane looked concerned. 'I don't even know if I can turn Cilla around on this road so how on earth is a lorry going to get out?'

'Stop here, Jane,' Arthur said suddenly as they drew level with an open gate leading into a field. 'Pull into this field. The road doesn't continue much further, and we don't want to drive into an ambush or find ourselves trapped and unable to get out.'

Jane nodded and carefully reversed Cilla into the field opening so the nose of the car was pointing outwards. Arthur was glad the soil was firm, and the car wasn't sinking down into the bare earth. Jane switched off the ignition and released a shaky sigh.

'Do you think we should approach on foot to find out what's happening?' she asked. 'I'm concerned that the police may not find us here since we've gone away from the route we expected to take. Where do you think they could be heading? Another barn? Those buildings belonging to Mr Briggs?'

'The road is a dead end according to the map.' Arthur slid it towards her so she could see for herself. She propped it against the steering wheel and looked at where he was indicating.

Up ahead of them he could see trees in the distance that marked the woods at the end of Mr Briggs's estate. He thought he could smell the piggery and guessed they were not far from the cliff path that led down to the beach.

'I see what you mean. Where could they be unloading the stolen goods? There aren't many buildings.' She passed the map back and he folded it carefully, replacing it in his pocket.

'There were those semi-derelict buildings we saw on Mr Briggs's farm, but the roof was badly damaged, and they seemed too small,' Arthur reminded her.

'The ones he said were unsafe.' She frowned as she looked

out to where the lorry had vanished from view. 'There is another option. All around here there are tunnels that were used by the old smugglers. They may be using some of those to either store the goods or get them into the cellars of another building in the village. When I walked to the end of the woods, I saw what looked like cave openings in the cliffs.' She took a torch from the car glovebox and handed it to Arthur to carry.

Arthur thought about what she'd said. The distance was not too great if the gang had a system to move the goods down and through a network. It would prevent anyone seeing them or their contraband. The lorry itself need never enter the village.

'That would make sense. If Russo saw them while working on the farm...' He hesitated and Jane finished his sentence.

'He would have signed his death warrant. They could have forced him down through the tunnels, killed him and left him naked on the sands and no one would have seen a thing.' Her face had paled. 'The question is, how do we stop them?'

'I don't know, but I think we need to discover what they are doing. We need to find out if an entrance to these tunnels exists and make sure our supposition is correct. They may just be using the buildings as a store after all. Perhaps a cellar. Topping's constable and Mr Wood will not find us easily here, so we'll have to be very careful not to get caught.' Arthur looked at her. He could see the fear in her eyes.

Nevertheless, she nodded. 'Do you have the gun?'

He patted his coat pocket. 'Let's pull some of these branches from the hedge over the nose of the car so she isn't so noticeable, and we'll see if we can get closer.' His own heart thumped at the idea of the task ahead but there was no backing out now.

Jane hopped out of the car and closed the door quietly, while Arthur followed her example. Luckily there were some long stems of green stuff in the hedgerow so they managed to conceal the nose of the car enough so anyone driving past wouldn't take too much notice.

'Come on, let's go.' Jane beckoned to him, and together they made their way stealthily on foot along the lane. The straggly hedge provided some cover as they headed towards the trees that marked the start of the wood.

As they drew closer to the edge of the wood Arthur crouched down beside Jane. The lorry had been pulled off the road and backed into a tight space behind what appeared to be the old buildings they had seen at the farm.

He doubted if anyone working on the farm would even know the lorry was there if they were busy in the fields on the other side or in the walled garden. Yet, if any of the land girls or the prisoners had happened to stray too close, they would have heard the sounds of the men's conversation and the bumping of the goods being unloaded.

'Nearly done, that's the last lot to go down,' he heard the one man call to his companion.

Jane crept closer and he followed behind her. She peered through the hedgerow, which was thinning as the autumnal leaves curled. He copied her example to see the lorry had the two doors open at the back. An older man in his early sixties stood beside a small wooden door at the rear of one of the semi-derelict buildings.

He realised that the farm buildings must form the boundary on the roadside of the Chafford Hill Farm estate. The building they had seen on their earlier visit had two doors. One on the side near the walled garden, and one this side.

'Hurry up will you, Bill, I'm on a promise later,' the man at the door called and cackled with laughter as he chivvied the other man along.

The man inside the building's reply was inaudible and Arthur guessed that Jane was right about there being a tunnel or a cellar concealed in the crumbling farm building. He wondered if Mr Briggs knew about any cellar or tunnel? Or if anyone was making use of his farm in this way? Or if he was the one behind it all? He had been very quick to take them away from the building.

The other man emerged, grumbling from the building. He looked younger than the first one. He took off his tweed cap and brushed what seemed to be cobwebs from the top of it.

'Never mind you being on a promise. Come on, let's get this lorry back to the barn and pick up the car. Herbert said he'd have us a pint in ready. Don't want the pub to shut before we get there.'

'Well, we can't dilly-dally at the pub, can we? Too close to home,' the older man said.

'Give over, Charlie, we deserve a pint after mauling about with all that lot. The dust has got right in my gullet.' Bill replaced his cap.

Arthur winced when Jane caught hold of his arm, squeezing it tightly in her enthusiasm for what they had just heard. He managed to stop himself from shouting out in pain and contented himself with glaring at her.

The men closed the door of the building and locked the padlock before shutting the lorry doors.

'Best make sure these are shut properly, eh? You left them unlocked last night,' Bill said as they went to get in the cab of the vehicle.

'I could have sworn those doors was locked. I always check them before we drive off,' the other man grumbled. 'You're as bad, thinking we were being followed on the way here. I said as you were imagining things.'

Jane nudged Arthur and they scurried quietly along the hedge until they found a gap where they could squeeze through. They crouched right down in a somewhat muddy ditch to conceal themselves. A moment or two later the lorry's engine started up and it came rumbling along the road past their hiding place.

Arthur's arm still ached from where Jane had pinched it, and he rubbed the sore spot as they stood up. 'I don't think you know your own strength, Jane. That pinch you gave me hurt. I nearly shouted out.'

There was mud all over his shoes and the bottom of his trousers. Benson would not be happy.

'I'm sorry, but did you hear what they said?' Jane didn't sound terribly apologetic. He could see her mind was busy going over everything they had just seen and heard. She scrambled out of the shallow ditch. Her shoes and stockings were also plastered in thick clods of mud. She wiped the worst of it off on some clumps of grass.

'It sounded as if your theory about the old smugglers' tunnels or a hidden cellar was correct.' He straightened up and looked around to check no one else was anywhere in view.

'Yes, and we need to find out where those stolen goods have gone.' Jane plucked some errant bits of twig from the sleeves of her heather-coloured tweed jacket. 'We need to get inside that building to check it out.'

* * *

Jane squeezed back through the gap in the hedge into the now deserted lane. Arthur trailed behind her looking as if he disapproved of her plan.

'We had a lucky escape there. They noticed the lorry door hadn't been locked and they thought they had seen either us or Mr Wood following them,' he grumbled as she walked towards the door of the old farm building.

She stopped and turned to face him, hands on her hips. 'I know, I must admit my heart was in my mouth a few times, but we need to discover where those goods are and if there is a secret cellar of some kind. Otherwise, if Topping's men raid the building, they may not discover the hiding place. These old-time smugglers were crafty. They were used to the excise men raiding the premises, so they hid things very well.'

Arthur seemed to be considering her words. 'I suppose we have a little time if the men have gone back to the other barn to store the lorry and collect their car before they go to the pub. It clearly sounded as if Herbert Simms is part of the gang. The Green Dragon must be part of the distribution network.'

'That may be why his wife was so nervous talking to us. Especially if they were all party to murdering Antonio Russo.' Jane looked at Arthur. 'Well, shall we just take a look and then get back to the others and get this lot shut down?'

She turned back around and walked up to the door where they had seen the men unloading the goods. Although the door itself appeared ancient and sun faded, there was a shiny new brass padlock keeping it shut. She remembered the other side of the building had been padlocked too when they had looked around with Mr Briggs. Did Mr Briggs know about this?

Arthur joined her and took out his lock-picking kit. 'At least this is easier in daylight,' he muttered as he examined the lock.

Jane refrained from answering. Instead, she waited patiently as Arthur carefully moved his selected pick around inside the keyhole until he felt the tumblers click.

'Jane, be very careful. If this turns out to be a tunnel rather than a cellar, then Herbert Simms may be at the other end of it. We know now that they probably killed Russo so they are dangerous men.' He placed a warning hand on her arm as she went to remove the lock.

'I know, I shall be as quiet as the proverbial mouse,' she assured him as she slid the lock free and carefully opened the door. She knew Arthur was right and she was quite frightened but they had to see this thing through.

A shaft of sunlight lit up a square room open to the sky

through the remains of the rafters of the roof. A pair of wood pigeons cooed loudly above their heads as they stepped inside, clearly annoyed by the intrusion.

They looked around the room. The brick walls were crumbling and green with moss and algae where the rain had got in. A few barrels stood empty and damaged on the flagstone floor. Smashed roof tiles lay shattered on the ground where they had slipped from the rafters. It looked as if no one had been there for years.

'Look under the barrels, Jane. There must be a trapdoor,' Arthur said in a low voice.

Together they carefully examined the seemingly innocent barrels before noticing the faint fresh scrape marks on the flagstones.

'Give me a hand,' Arthur instructed, and she helped him to move the one barrel in the direction of the marks. As they had expected the move exposed a small wooden trapdoor sunk into the stones of the floor.

Arthur looked at her and she gave a nod. He took hold of the rusty iron ring handle and lifted the door so they could see inside.

'Steps,' Jane whispered, afraid her voice might carry down the passage they had just exposed.

'A cellar, do you think? Or a tunnel to the Green Dragon?' Arthur asked as he pulled the torch from his coat pocket. 'A tunnel would have to run for at least half a mile to reach the pub. They can't have carried everything all that way, surely.'

'Perhaps the store is somewhere between here and the pub, but the access is through the pub cellar?' Jane suggested. 'Pass me the torch.'

'You can't go down there.' Arthur looked horrified.

'Just for a short way to see where it goes.' She held out her hand and he reluctantly passed her the heavy rubber-handled flashlight. 'We need to know what we're dealing with.'

'Be careful, for heaven's sake, or let me go,' he suggested.

She switched on the torch and shone it on the steps which seemed to be cut from stone and led down into the darkness. Handholds had been cut into the sides of the passage with rusty metal rings to assist anyone going up or down.

'There is enough dust down there to start you sneezing and wheezing. Stay here and keep watch. I won't be long.' She accepted his hand to clamber into the passage and set off carefully down the steps.

She counted as she went, twenty-five steps to the bottom. The steps ended in a small chamber carved out of rock. There was no sign of the stolen goods. She shone the torch around and discovered an open-topped small cart with wooden wheels bound in iron. Rope was attached to each end, and she guessed this must be how the gang transported the goods so efficiently and swiftly once they had them in the tunnel. There were grooves worn into the floor which spoke of long usage.

The passage leading out from the room continued on a downward slope and she assumed it must run through the cliffs and on towards the beach. In the olden days no doubt the smugglers would have landed the goods from the sea.

'Jane?' Arthur called softly down to her.

'I'm all right. It's a tunnel. I'll just take a quick look.'

She wondered if there was still access to the beach as they had surmised. If so, then that would have been how they had taken Antonio Russo down to the back of the dunes without being seen.

Jane waited and listened for any sounds that indicated someone else might be in the passageway ahead of her, then set off cautiously along the tunnel. The further down she went the walls of the tunnel grew damp under her fingers and she could hear the distant roar of the waves. Tiny chinks of light broke through the walls of the passageway, and she could smell the salt air.

She stopped at a point where the tunnel ran in two directions. One was obviously leading down to the beach. She guessed there must be an entrance hidden in one of the caves behind the rocks. The grooves in the floor from the cart led along in the other direction inland towards the village.

For a moment she considered turning back. Instead, she decided to venture a little further to see if she could find where the goods had been stowed. Then she could return to Arthur and they could alert the police.

The path levelled off now and became drier again as she went further from the beach. The passage branched again after a while and there was another narrow offshoot, barely wide enough to take a person. Conscious of the time passing, however, she decided to press on following the grooves in the floor.

Very quickly she found herself in a veritable Aladdin's cave of goods. Bales of cloth, tinned goods, sacks of sugar and jars of sweets. There were packets of tea, tins of coffee and packs of tobacco and cigarettes.

Overhead she could hear voices and footsteps and guessed she was somewhere under the Green Dragon. The smell of the sea had also given way to a slightly stale smoky smell tinged with the scent of beer.

Jane moved quickly and quietly around the storeroom using her torch to examine the walls for the door which must lead into the main cellar of the pub. Someone had gone to the trouble of lining the brick or rock walls with timber at some point so it was hard to see where a catch might be concealed.

She risked a few light taps on the woodwork listening for a hollow sound. Walking along the passages had disorientated her and she couldn't be certain how the storeroom related to the layout of the pub. She knew the Green Dragon had a narrow frontage but that it extended back a long way from the road.

The store was most likely to be under the front since that was the oldest part of the pub.

Eventually she spotted a knothole in the timber, big enough to insert her finger. She poked it and heard a click as a concealed mechanism unlatched the door. After listening in case Herbert Simms might be in the cellar, she risked opening it a touch and peeking out.

Her view was limited, seemingly obstructed by shelves and crates of bottles. Satisfied she could locate it again she pulled the door back towards her and closed it. Her heart thumped and her palms were damp with sweat at her discovery. Now, all she had to do was get back to Arthur so they could return to the car and get assistance.

CHAPTER TWENTY-FOUR

Jane made her way around the piles of contraband back to the passageway where she had entered. She walked as quickly as she dared on the rocky, uneven surface of the tunnel floor back towards the sea. The sooner she was back above ground the better.

She passed the narrow entrance of the other passage and wondered if it led anywhere or was simply an offshoot that had been abandoned over time. There was no time to investigate it now. She was conscious that Arthur would be concerned at the length of her absence.

The climb back along the passage was easier than she had anticipated, and she was soon at the bottom of the steps.

'Arthur, give me a hand, I'm coming up!' she risked calling out in a low voice, expecting his face to appear in the opening.

There was no reply and no sign of him in the square of light at the top of the steps. She hoped he hadn't become distracted by something or that something unexpected had happened. Jane made her way up the steps. She turned off the torch and tucked it into her jacket pocket as best as she could when it became light enough for her to see her footing.

'Arthur!' she called again without a response. Her pulse quickened.

'Arthur, we need to go and get...' Jane's words died on her lips as she emerged from the trapdoor to see the reason for her colleague's silence.

Arthur was standing beside the old barrels, his hands on his head. His hat lay discarded on the floor nearby.

'Ah, Jane, my dear, so nice of you to join us.' The speaker with a gun trained on her colleague was none other than Alicia Carstairs. The kindly, slightly eccentric artistic persona was gone. This was a woman who clearly meant business.

'I think you should hurry up and join your colleague, Jane. This is all most inconvenient for me.' Alicia briefly moved the gun in Jane's direction and motioned to her to join Arthur at the barrels. 'This operation had been running very smoothly until you two arrived.'

Jane climbed slowly out of the trapdoor, her legs trembling.

'Do keep your hands where I can see them,' Alicia instructed once Jane was standing on the stone flags of the derelict storeroom.

'How did you know we were here?' Jane asked as she went to join Arthur. Alicia kept the gun trained on her as she moved.

'Those two idiots Bill and Charlie. I saw them at the pub, and they told me about the lock on the lorry being open and that they thought someone had followed them.' Alicia moved the gun to indicate Jane should raise her hands to her head like Arthur.

'How did you get up here so quickly? It's a few miles from the village to here.' Jane looked around her expecting to see a car through the open door of the building but saw nothing.

Alicia snorted derisively. 'There is more than one set of tunnels, my dear. The cliffs around here are riddled with them. Surely, you must know that. Under my cottage there is a cellar with access into the network.'

'I suppose the beaches being closed to the public did you a favour? No one was likely to stumble into the tunnels or find any of the stolen goods accidentally.' Arthur sounded surprisingly calm given their predicament.

'Absolutely. I knew where the network ran. I used to explore it as a child when I lived in the village many years ago. No one recognised me or remembered me when I returned and took over the cottage.' Alicia looked quite pleased with herself.

'You encouraged the children to stay away by feeding into the tales of you being a witch. Then, you added to your eccentric artist reputation, so no one thought it odd when you went to the Green Dragon. Especially as you were painting a portrait of Annie Simms.' Jane felt sick as she put all the pieces of the puzzle together.

'Bravo, Jane,' Alicia said.

'What happened with Antonio Russo? Did he stumble on your hired hands unloading the goods? Was that why he was killed?' Arthur asked, drawing Alicia's attention back towards him.

Jane waited for Alicia's answer and glanced discreetly around to see if there was anything they might use to help them escape. There was nothing and the sick feeling in her stomach grew stronger.

'The land girls tend to avoid these buildings. The silly things believe the buildings are haunted and, of course, Lloyd Briggs knows they are unsafe, so he rarely comes here. He very kindly had new padlocks put on after the land girl who left in June was injured. It wasn't hard to get keys made without his knowledge. Russo heard the men and came around into the lane from the woods that afternoon. His finding Bill and Charlie using the trapdoor was unfortunate.' Alicia sounded thoughtful. 'I thought we could reason with him. I knew the tattoo on his arm meant he had the kind of past that might make him agree. I'd learned about that from Annie.'

'But he refused,' Jane said. Her heart was hammering in her chest, and she struggled to keep her tone calm and even.

It explained why Mr Briggs had been so cagey about the buildings if someone had been hurt and forced to leave his employ. No doubt he would have received quite a reprimand and possibly had to compensate the injured girl.

'Regretfully, Russo did. He said he wanted no part in any of it. It was most unfortunate as that left me with very few options.' Alicia's mouth hardened into a firm line.

'You had him led down the tunnels to the beach and killed him. Hitting him over the head and then giving him an overdose of morphine. I take it you were behind the burglary at Doctor Denning's surgery?' Jane said.

'I knew security at the surgery was lax. I noticed where the medications were stored earlier this year when I visited the doctor about a nasty cut on my hand. The lock on the back door was flimsy and the medicine cabinet in easy reach. It never hurts to have an additional weapon in one's armoury. It was most fortuitous, and Charlie has skills in that area.' Alicia made the planning of the morphine theft sound as if she had gone shopping for pork chops for her tea.

'And your hospital appointment gave you a very convenient alibi to ensure no one could accuse you of the murder or think you may have seen something on the beach that day.' Arthur risked a glance at Jane as if confirming his thoughts with hers. She could see a warning in his eyes and wondered if Alicia had searched him and removed his gun. She couldn't see it anywhere.

'Yes, that was a stroke of luck. It was quite simple. Charlie and Bill got him into the passageways and down to the beach exit. They had knocked him out and waited for instructions from me on what to do next. They knew they couldn't let him go. I arrived as he roused and like I said I tried to persuade him to join us. When he refused, I got them to place him on the sands and used the morphine. We had to be quick because I knew Captain Prudhoe would have a party out looking for him quite speedily once his absence was noted.' Alicia gave a slight careless shrug of her shoulders as if murdering the Italian had been no great thing.

'You had his clothes removed so that it would look as if he had gone to the beach for a swim.' Arthur gave a small nod of his head as if almost approving of Alicia's planning.

'I knew that bumbling fool Topping wouldn't bother investigating properly. The man was a POW after all. Then you and your colleague arrived and started asking awkward questions. I knew once they did an autopsy they would find the real cause of death.' She gave a regretful sigh. 'And those fools, Charlie and Bill, left him above the high-water mark. Idiots.' Her mood seemed to change as she recalled her employees' failings.

Alicia took a few paces forward towards them, her back now to the open trapdoor a few feet away behind her.

'What did you do with his clothes?' Jane desperately wanted to keep Alicia talking for as long as possible, hoping that an opportunity might arise where she and Arthur could get away unharmed.

Alicia gave another shrug as if growing bored of their conversation. 'I burnt them in my log burner at the cottage. The buttons and his tag I buried on the dunes.'

'You do seem to have had things well worked out,' Arthur said. 'Did Gambini or Annie Simms know what had happened to Antonio? I assume you knew they were meeting at the bench. Does her husband know about them?'

'Herbert keeps Annie under his watch most of the time. She knows better than to say anything about the comings and goings at the pub. Gambini, like Russo, was a gang member. He has the same tattoo. I don't know if Annie had said anything to him about our little operation. I think though that he guessed it would be wiser to keep his mouth firmly shut. I suspect he knew

Russo was dead from the minute he failed to return to the camp. Gambini has told Annie about some of the things they were involved in before the war. Those two were no choirboys even though they have turned over a new leaf since.' The self-satisfied look returned to Alicia's face.

Jane knew they were coming to the end of ways to stall Alicia from whatever she planned to do next. She had to try and keep the woman talking if only to stall her for a little longer. 'This operation, as you call it, must have been very profitable?'

'It's been very lucrative, my dear, and surprisingly simple to run. Money is very important if one is to lead a comfortable life. I have always enjoyed being comfortable. Running this little scheme has been most enjoyable, it's added quite a frisson of excitement to my life. Now though, I shall have to wind things up for a little while and change my base. Once I have dealt with you two, of course. Which is such a shame as I do quite like you both.' Alicia gave a regretful sigh as she finished speaking before her gaze hardened once more.

'Mr Wood, the government inspector, is with the police right now and they will be here at any time,' Jane said trying to keep her voice calm and her tone matter-of-fact. 'You have time to leave us here and make your getaway before they go looking for you.'

'A valid point, my dear Jane, but far better I feel that they find you both dead, then you can't tell them any tales and I can be long gone before they work anything out.' Alicia levelled the gun directly at Jane, her finger on the trigger.

Jane's pulse hitched up a notch.

'Charlie, Bill and Herbert Simms will all sing like canaries. Why add to your crimes?' Arthur spoke quickly, drawing Alicia's attention once more in his direction.

As the woman focused on Arthur, Jane suddenly realised that behind Alicia a familiar male figure was starting to silently emerge through the open trapdoor. She shuffled her feet slightly on the stone floor to provide some cover in case the older woman heard anything untoward. She had to prevent her from turning around.

'Don't fidget, Jane.' Alicia glared at her. 'Those three fools will do anything to save their own scrawny necks, you are quite right there. However, I have no intention of meeting the hangman so it's far more expedient for me to dispatch you both and escape,' Alicia replied coolly.

As she finished speaking the man emerging from the trapdoor sprang forward, tackling Alicia to the ground. At the same time Arthur pushed Jane sideways as he dived to the floor in the opposite direction.

'Get down, Jane!'

The gun Alicia was holding fired with a deafening bang. A bullet ricocheted around the crumbling brickwork of the storeroom. The birds in the rafters took flight cooing in dismay while the indignant caws of the crows in the nearby trees added to the noise.

'Oof.' The breath was knocked out of Jane as she landed hard on the stone floor, jarring her shoulder. Tiny pieces of gravel scraped her cheek as she looked to where Benson was wrestling the gun from Alicia's hand.

Arthur scrambled clumsily onto his knees and then charged forward to assist Benson. Mr Wood, accompanied by a uniformed constable, rapidly appeared from the open trapdoor. The constable rushed across to assist Arthur and Benson in the struggle for control of the gun. Alicia fought them with a surprising degree of strength for a woman her age as Jane watched in horror. There was another loud bang as the gun fired again, and Alicia crumpled into a heap.

Jane rose unsteadily to her feet and Arthur came to join her. He placed his arm around her waist, his breath coming in uneven gasps. She could hear the faint sounds of a wheeze at the end of each breath.

'Is she dead?' Jane asked, looking to where the constable and Mr Wood were both bent over Alicia's still form. Benson was removing his jacket to cover the body.

Arthur gave a brief nod of confirmation. 'She turned the gun on herself. We tried to prevent her, but she was determined.'

Jane turned her face away and pressed it against Arthur's shoulder for a moment, breathing in the comforting scent of his soap mingled with tweed. Her whole body trembled as she realised how fortunate they had been to escape unharmed. More male voices could now be heard more clearly coming from the direction of the passageway beneath their feet.

Outside the building came the roar of a car engine clearly being driven at speed. It screeched to a stop outside the open door of the old building. Mr Briggs rushed into the building, red-faced and carrying a shotgun.

He stopped in his tracks at the unexpected sight of so many people in such a small space.

'What's going on here? The land girls said they heard shots.' He looked around in bewilderment. His complexion paled when he saw Alicia's body partially concealed by Benson's coat. 'Miss Treen? Mr Cilento?'

'The black market gang have been apprehended, Mr Briggs.' Mr Wood's usual excitability appeared undiminished by Alicia's death.

'I don't understand. Is that Miss Carstairs?' Mr Briggs looked at Alicia's partially covered body in bewilderment.

'If you would excuse me for a moment. I need some air.' Jane broke free from Arthur's hold and stumbled outside. Once there she paused and took her cigarettes from her pocket with a shaking hand.

'Permit me, Miss Jane.' Benson had followed her outside and proffered her a light.

'Thank you.' Jane accepted and took a pull on her cigarette. Her nerves calming as the nicotine filled her system.

'You arrived in the nick of time, Benson,' she said, once she felt more herself again.

'It appeared so, Miss Jane,' the manservant said calmly.

'How did you know where to find us?' She was curious to discover what had happened to lead Benson and Mr Wood to the Green Dragon and the passage from the cellar.

'We followed the lorry as instructed, then turned off to alert the constable waiting in his vehicle. As time passed and neither the lorry nor yourself and Mr Cilento made an appearance we were concerned. It occurred to us that perhaps the lorry may have taken a different route. We were about to retrace our steps when I recognised the car number plate from last night. I suggested to Mr Wood that we should follow it. It stopped at the Green Dragon and the men went inside,' Benson explained.

'What happened then?' Jane asked.

'I sent Mr Wood back to alert the constable. While I waited, I saw Miss Carstairs arrive and enter the premises. She didn't come out again so I went in and could see no trace of her. The two men from last night were huddled in a corner with Mr Simms, the landlord. Mrs Simms was behind the bar, she slipped this across to me over the counter.' Benson took a small scrap of paper from his trouser pocket.

Look in the cellar

Jane read the crabbed print. 'Annie tipped you off.' She hoped Annie would be all right now that her husband was arrested. Perhaps once this was finally over, Matteo Gambini and Annie might be able to make a future for themselves and her baby.

'Indeed, I think her friend Miss Hargreaves may have told her that I was in Mr Cilento's employment. I guessed from what you and Mr Cilento had said previously about smugglers in the past that there could be another entrance and exit from the premises. It would account for Miss Carstairs not being visible on the premises.'

Jane finished her cigarette, throwing the stub onto the floor and extinguishing it with the toe of her shoe as Arthur came out to join them. She hoped Katie Hargreaves would continue to support Annie. Annie would need someone to lean on, especially with a baby coming and Katie seemed kind-hearted and level-headed.

'I understand from Mr Wood that Inspector Topping is on his way here,' Arthur said.

'The constable sent for aid before we entered the Green Dragon and managed to capture Mr Simms and the men from the lorry,' Benson said.

'How did you find the secret door in the cellar? It was very well hidden,' Jane asked, looking at Benson.

'Miss Carstairs had failed to latch it properly as she left. I can only guess the men must have said something to her that aroused her suspicions. I followed the tunnel as I assumed it must lead up to where the men unloaded the goods. Mr Wood and the constable followed as soon as the other policemen arrived to take over the arrests.'

'You saw the grooves in the floor made by the cart?' Jane guessed.

'Yes, a most ingenious way to move the goods,' Benson said.

'I presume you heard what Miss Carstairs had to say when she was holding us at gunpoint?' Arthur said, before breaking into a harsh coughing fit which caused Benson to frown in concern.

'Every word,' Benson assured him.

'Well, it was a good thing you appeared when you did,' Arthur said. 'It was looking rather dicey.'

'Yes, it was very brave of you, Benson, even though it was extremely dangerous,' Jane reproved him gently.

'I thought you might overlook that this once, Miss Jane, given the circumstances,' Benson remarked coolly.

She went to speak but subsided when she noticed the twinkle in the manservant's eyes.

'Very well, just this once,' she agreed.

CHAPTER TWENTY-FIVE

Mr Briggs emerged from the building after speaking to the constable and Mr Wood.

'Miss Treen, are you all right?' he asked, looking at her with concern.

'Your cheek is bleeding, Jane.' Arthur pulled a clean white-cotton handkerchief from the breast pocket of his dark-grey overcoat and handed it to her.

'Thank you, I think I must have grazed my face when I hit the ground.' She took the handkerchief and dabbed lightly at her face. She frowned when she saw specks of blood and dirt on the pristine surface of the cloth.

'I have suggested we all return to my house while we await Inspector Topping's arrival. Mr Wood has assured me that he and the other constables have everything in hand at present. I can telephone from the house for the coroner to collect Miss Carstairs,' Mr Briggs said.

'Thank you, Mr Briggs,' Jane agreed, and she, Arthur and Benson accompanied the farmer the short distance to his car.

Jane didn't feel ready yet to drive so decided to leave Cilla in the field just along the lane for a while longer. She could collect her once she had recovered herself a little more. Right now, she was still shaken, and her hands were trembling from what had happened.

Once they were back at Mr Briggs's home, he ushered them into his comfortable drawing room.

'May I get you all some tea, or perhaps a drop of brandy? Miss Treen, would you like to bathe the injury on your cheek?' Mr Briggs rang for his housekeeper to prepare drinks for them.

After showing Jane the beautifully appointed cloakroom, he bustled off to his study to lock up his shotgun and make the telephone call to the coroner.

Jane stared at her reflection in the gold-framed mirror above the sink.

'Goodness me, what a fright,' she muttered on seeing her reflection. Her hair was in disarray, smudges of dirt were on her nose and dried blood marked her cheek.

She washed her hands, cleaned up the graze on her face and attempted to restore order to her hair, before returning to the drawing room.

She found Mr Briggs's housekeeper had supplied them with a tray of tea and some biscuits when she arrived. To her relief Arthur appeared to have recovered and was breathing more easily as he took a sip of his tea. Although she could see Benson watching him like a hawk.

'Inspector Topping has telephoned. He is currently dealing with Herbert Simms and the other two men. He asked me to let you know that he will call on you at your house later today, Miss Treen,' Mr Briggs announced as he bustled back into the room. 'Those crooks will all be facing the inside of a prison cell for quite a long time to come.'

Jane was forced to satisfy Mr Briggs's curiosity about what had happened as they took their refreshments. The farmer was appalled at learning that Miss Carstairs had confessed to murdering Antonio Russo.

'Good heavens, I would never have believed her capable of such wickedness.' He stared at Jane and Arthur.

'I'm afraid it's quite true, sir. I heard her myself,' Benson assured him.

'And all this under my nose, using my buildings.' Mr Briggs sounded most affronted.

The tea and biscuits did much to restore Jane's equilibrium, although personally she would have preferred coffee or brandy. Once they had finished they thanked Mr Briggs for his hospitality. They managed to convince him they could walk the short distance along the lane to where they had left the car.

Jane was very aware that she needed to make a telephone call of her own to Whitehall to brief the brigadier on everything that had happened. She also would need to make a full written report.

The drive back to the house was fairly silent. Arthur sat in the passenger seat, while Benson sat in the back. For once she didn't notice him making faces or clutching at the seat as she drove.

Benson and Arthur went on into the house while she drove Cilla back around to the garage. Once she had locked the doors, she made her way up the garden path and let herself in through the scullery.

Mrs Dawes was busy in the kitchen. 'Oh, Jane, I wasn't sure if any of you would be here for lunch, so I didn't prepare anything. I just saw Mr Benson and he said as some soup and a roll would be all right to tide you over until supper?'

'That sounds delicious, thank you.' A glance at the kitchen clock told her it was almost three o'clock and well past lunchtime. 'I can see we are very late.'

'Have you hurt your cheek? Shall I get you some iodine?' Mrs Dawes clucked, peering at the graze on her face.

'No, it's quite all right, it will fade very quickly I'm sure,' Jane assured her. 'It's merely a graze.'

'I've managed to get some sausages for your supper. Oh, and by the way, your mother has taken herself back to London. She's left you a note.' Mrs Dawes dried her hands on a tea towel and passed Jane a small white envelope from her apron pocket.

'Thank you.' Jane accepted the note and wandered out of the kitchen into the hallway. She opened the note on her way to the study. Her eyebrows rose as she read the message from her mother.

Darling Janey,

After last night I rather think that even with the bombs I may actually be safer back in London than staying with you. Therefore, I've decided to go and stay with Stephen's mother instead until my building is repaired. It will be more convenient for work.

Speak to you soon.

Love Mother x

P.S Please thank dear Mr Benson for taking such good care of me.

'Well really!' Jane stuffed the note back in its envelope and went into the study. She took a seat behind the desk and mentally braced herself ready to make the telephone call to London.

'Jane, dear heart, what a surprise. How is sunny Kent?' Stephen answered the telephone.

'Is the brigadier available? I need to bring him up to date with events here.' Jane kept her voice crisp and businesslike.

'I'm sorry, dear girl, I'm afraid he's in a meeting with the top brass. I can relay a message to him later if you like?' Stephen said.

Jane pictured him lounging back in his office chair, twiddling a pencil between his fingers.

'Very well. Please tell him that the cases here are resolved and a report will follow shortly.' Jane was determined not to give too much away since she knew that ostensibly they had only been officially there to assist Mr Wood with the black market problem.

'Splendid, I'm sure the old man will be delighted. I take it we can expect you back in the office soon then?' Stephen asked.

'Once a few loose ends here are wrapped up, then yes, I shall be back,' Jane assured him.

'Jolly good. I'll pass that on. By the way, I hope Elsa is enjoying her stay with you?' Stephen said nonchalantly.

Jane gritted her teeth. It had been his fault that her mother had invited herself to Kent in the first place.

'Actually, she's returned to London. I gather your mother has invited her to stop at yours for a while. I expect you'll be able to catch up with her over dinner tonight. Tell the brigadier I'll have the reports ready soon, byeee.' She hung up before Stephen could say anything in response and chuckled to herself as she pictured the annoyed look on his face at her response.

'You seem very pleased with yourself.' Arthur entered the study and took the seat opposite hers.

'I was just letting London know that the cases were resolved, and we would have the reports ready soon,' Jane replied, her smile broadening.

'And?' Arthur said.

'I just had the pleasure of telling Stephen that my mother has invited herself to stay at his house with his mother until her repairs are completed. Mrs Dawes says she packed and left at lunchtime. According to her note she feels that London is safer than Kent after last night.'

'Ah, I'm afraid Benson may be disappointed. He did seem quite taken with your mother,' Arthur said.

'She does rather have that effect on gentlemen as you've seen.' Jane noticed that Arthur too had a slight smile and wondered if he had been a little concerned at his manservant's affection for Elsa.

She was pleased to hear that the wheeze had gone now from his voice. She wondered if Benson had set up his inhalers.

'So it would seem. And are you all right now, Jane? It was a hairy business not knowing quite what Alicia planned to do when she had that gun on us.' Arthur's expression sobered.

'Yes, I'm quite recovered now. Had she been there long when I arrived?' Jane asked.

'No, you were only a couple of minutes behind her. I was waiting near the trapdoor for you to return when I heard her coming. Naturally I thought it was you and I was ready to help you out when a gun appeared pointing at my face.' His gaze met hers.

'Thank heaven for Benson,' Jane said. 'We might both have been toast.'

'Yes, he does have an immaculate sense of timing,' Arthur agreed.

Jane dropped the note from her mother on the desk and fingered a corner of the envelope.

'Once Inspector Topping has taken our statements, I expect we can return home,' she said.

For once the thought of returning alone to her small apartment in London with Marmaduke seemed less appealing than it usually did.

Arthur's hand covered hers and he squeezed her fingers. 'I suppose so. I just wanted to say that at least if I had been going to die, I'm glad it would have been with you. You were frightfully plucky today.'

She lifted her chin and met his gaze. 'You're getting quite

sentimental, Arthur Cilento, but yes, I'm very glad you were there along with Benson. We make a good team.'

'I do hope that our next case might be slightly less risky though.'

She smiled back at him and wondered if she was growing rather soft. She gently withdrew her hand.

'I daresay the brigadier will soon have another puzzle for us,' she said.

A LETTER FROM HELENA DIXON

Dear reader,

I want to say a huge thank you for choosing to read *The Seaside Murders*. If you did enjoy it, and want to keep up to date with all my latest releases, just sign up at the following link. Your email address will never be shared and you can unsubscribe at any time. You will also receive a free short story featuring Alice, from the Miss Underhay series.

www.bookouture.com/helena-dixon

I hope you loved *The Secret Detective Agency* book 2 and if you did I would be very grateful if you could write a review. I'd love to hear what you think, and it makes such a difference helping new readers to discover one of my books for the first time.

This book was difficult to write. Much of the history of prisoners of war in the UK for this period is not well documented. Even the location of some of the camps has disappeared. I also encountered difficulties since some of the information I needed is in fact still classified as secret. Therefore, I wrote this story based on probabilities mixed with hard facts advised by some of the best advice from experts in this field. I hope I succeeded in creating a realistic fictional world for Jane and Arthur.

I love hearing from my readers – and you can get in touch through social media or my website.

Thanks,

Helena Dixon

www.nelldixon.com

 facebook.com/nelldixonauthor
x.com/NellDixon

ACKNOWLEDGEMENTS

With many thanks to Sophia Pritchard for her endless hours of research and advice. Also to my lovely local history society friends and colleagues for answering numerous questions. The staff at Churchill's War Rooms in London for my questions about Whitehall. Thanks also go to my agent, Kate Nash, for her support and faith in my ability to write these books. Also to everyone at Bookouture who works so hard to make these books succeed. Thank you.

PUBLISHING TEAM

Turning a manuscript into a book requires the efforts of many people. The publishing team at Bookouture would like to acknowledge everyone who contributed to this publication.

Audio
Alba Proko
Sinead O'Connor
Melissa Tran

Commercial
Lauren Morrissette
Hannah Richmond
Imogen Allport

Cover design
Debbie Clement

Data and analysis
Mark Alder
Mohamed Bussuri

Editorial
Cerys Hadwin-Owen
Imogen Allport

Copyeditor
Jane Eastgate

Proofreader
Shirley Khan

Marketing
Alex Crow
Melanie Price
Occy Carr
Cíara Rosney
Martyna Młynarska

Operations and distribution
Marina Valles
Stephanie Straub
Joe Morris

Production
Hannah Snetsinger
Mandy Kullar
Ria Clare
Nadia Michael

Publicity
Kim Nash
Noelle Holten
Jess Readett
Sarah Hardy

Rights and contracts
Peta Nightingale
Richard King
Saidah Graham

Made in United States
Troutdale, OR
06/25/2025

32370001R00152